# FIREPROOF

# Fireproof

## DELANCEY STEWART

BUSY BEAN CAFE

HeartEyes
Press

# MASON

## COLEBURY, VT

"So you've used one of these before, right?" My new boss, a lively, dark-haired woman named Zara, was eyeing me skeptically from behind a coffee machine that looked more convoluted than the new milkers I'd brought in for my goats.

I hadn't. But I might have suggested that I had during the short interview process where Zara and her co-owner, Audrey, gave me the impression that they were desperate enough to hire just about anyone with a heartbeat and half a brain, so long as he was willing to learn.

"Technically, no," I said. I hadn't straight-out lied about it before, and I wouldn't do it now. "But I pulled a few shifts helping out back in the service."

Zara turned to face me fully, crossing her arms over her chest and giving me a grin. "Did they have a temperamental Astra in the coffee mess when you were a Marine, Mason?" She patted the complicated-looking machine that occupied much of the front counter.

I took a quick look around the interior of the Busy Bean, the place I'd hoped to begin some secondary employment today in order to bring in a bit of the money that the farm wasn't currently making. And then I realized I really needed to show Zara why I'd be an asset here, whether I'd made fancy coffee before or not. I needed a flexible side job, one that would still let me take care of things at the farm, and the hours here worked well.

"No," I said slowly, making a point to relax my hands and shoulders—I had a tendency to clench them and I knew it added to what my sister called my "resting murder face," which apparently held fast to my expression about ninety-six percent of the time and freaked people out. I blew out a breath, forcing myself to relax. "But I'm a quick learner, Zara, and I hope you'll give me a chance."

"Relax, Mason. Having you here—even if it's just another body to run plates out front—is great. We're desperate." She grinned at me, and I did relax a bit. "When we first interviewed, you said something about improving efficiencies. Audrey and I both think we could use some of that military efficiency around here. Got anything in mind? I mean, I know it's your first day."

I nodded. It was early, and the smell of coffee and baked goods was beginning to warm the air. The sky outside the plate glass windows grew brighter, and I knew we didn't have a ton of time before the Bean opened for the day. I hoped to still be here by then.

"Let's hear it," Zara said, and she stood just a hair taller, as if she was bracing herself for an assault.

I could be intense, I knew that, and I forced my posture to remain relaxed, tried to keep my voice light.

"Just a couple. For one thing, the menu board—"

"Be careful now, that's Kieran's baby. He doesn't work here anymore but he still likes to come in and beautify the board. That one's his." She was looking at the huge sunflower that was, admittedly, beautiful but that dominated the board to the point that the menu was an afterthought.

I smiled, holding my hands up in front of me, palms facing her. "It looks great," I said. "But it's not about looks. There's a lot of stuff up there, and some really loopy writing that takes a few minutes to figure out." The menu board was a dense swirl of color, the actual offerings of the Busy Bean competing for space around the art.

Zara continued to stare over her shoulder at the board.

"If you simplified the board, customers could figure out what they want a little faster. It might not seem like a lot, but when the line is to the door, seconds count."

She raised one shoulder, as if suggesting I go on.

"You might also get a hot water tap here, next to the sink. Getting hot water from the espresso machine for non-espresso drinks forces everyone to wait for the pressure and steam to rebuild here." I indicated the spout of the machine. "And time is money for a little shop like this, right?"

Her eyes had gone a tiny bit wider. "Right," she said slowly, glancing at the machine as if it had said something in response. "So you do know a bit about this machine."

"I did some reading."

She nodded, looking wary, and I knew I had to be careful. This place was Zara's baby—and Audrey's. But I could help here, and I didn't think making coffee would be that hard to learn.

"I've got one more suggestion," I said, and she looked up at me now, a smile lifting one side of her mouth.

"Why do I get the feeling you've got a lot more than that?" she asked.

A low chuckle escaped me. She was right, but just because routine and efficiency were the things that kept me sane didn't mean everyone wanted to hear about them. "I'll just give you one for now," I said.

"Hit me."

"You have a lot of regulars. They shouldn't have to wait in line if you already know what they want."

She nodded. "We've talked about that. But part of what people come in here for is the personal attention, the banter at the counter, the atmosphere."

"No reason they can't get all that while picking up their drinks at the far end of the counter. You could have them prepay, if you wanted to, or put in a text-ordering system. Or both."

Her nose wrinkled. "It's just a lot of logistics," she said. "I'm not sure we're ready to invest in stuff like that."

I nodded. Maybe they weren't, but it didn't have to be complicated. "I get it," I said. "But it could be as simple as keeping a tablet there with the shop's quick-order email account pulled up. Folks can email before they leave the house or from their cars."

"So you're going to manage the line and check email when we're slammed?"

I'd come in lots of times before starting today, watched the way things operated behind the counter when they were busy. And when they weren't.

"When you've got two people up here anyway, one of them can be designated to check. Keep notifications on the device, and there's an audio cue that an order has come in."

Zara didn't look sold. She glanced up at the clock and then out at the door. "I like you, Mason," she said. "Even if you do look like you kind of want to kill me sometimes."

"I assure you, I don't."

She laughed. "I know. But Amelia told me to give you shit about your resting murder face."

Amelia. Of course my sister would have been in here talking about me. It was like we were two halves of one personality—she got all the bright, shiny, social genes, and I ended up with the logic, practicality, and focus. Not that she was flighty or ditzy. She wasn't. But sometimes she seemed to overlook reality in favor of maintaining an upbeat outlook. I was a little more realistic.

"Of course she did."

"Anyway, let me show you how this bad boy works, and this morning we'll just have you pulling espressos, okay? Nothing fancy. Master the shots and we'll move on."

I gave her a single nod. A plan. Good.

As Zara went through the steps of making a simple espresso, I noted them all, both in my mind and in the book I kept shoved in my pocket.

"You're not going to have time to refer to your notes," Zara said, glancing over her shoulder as I made notes.

"Won't need to. Writing them down solidifies them in my mind."

She didn't say anything else for a few minutes, and we went on. By the time she was ready to open the doors, I could make a shot perfectly and with precision.

"I'll show you how to steam the milk when the early rush ends," she said, smiling at me with a bit more confidence now that she'd seen I wasn't going to completely flub the basics.

As we served the first few customers, Zara introducing me brightly to each one as the new barista, I fell into an easy rhythm that relaxed me. Every other thing in my life might have been hanging by an uncertain thread—the farm, my uncle, my mental state—but the efficiency and routine involved in making shot after shot of espresso felt like certainty. This made sense.

At least until Zara shot me a strange smile and said, "You know, Mason, every barista we've hired so far has fallen in love and left us. You planning to do the same?"

"There's not a chance in hell, Zara."

I'd already figured out that my life worked best alone, and I had no plans to change that.

## 2

# HEATHER

**WASHINGTON D.C.**

I could tell by the way the building across from mine was turning a deep gray-orange that it was well past time to leave the office, but I felt anchored to my desk, reliant on its solidity. My desk, I knew, had very few surprises for me. And I wasn't sure I could handle one more surprise.

"Hey." Morgan stepped into my office. He was technically my boss, a tall man with red hair and broad shoulders. He was also a friend—I'd had dinner at his house, sipped wine with him and his partner, Sam, more times than I could count. "You ready to go?"

Morgan had taken to checking on me at the end of the day, making sure I had someone to walk out with. I appreciated it but wished I didn't need it.

I'd been a steady, solid career lobbyist at one point, fighting for the right to education for kids who couldn't fight for themselves. Now I required babysitting, evidently.

"Yeah," I stood, leaning down to retrieve my purse from the bottom drawer of my desk. My legs ached from sitting too long, and my body felt worn out, pulled too thin. "Let's go."

Morgan was watching me, a look on his face like the one he

got when we were reading a brief about something particularly distressing happening in the school system. His pity face.

"Stop looking at me like that," I snapped at him.

"Heather," he said, his voice kind. "It's wearing on you. I can see it."

"It's over now, so . . ." The trial. My testimony. The verdict. It was all over. So my life was supposed to be getting better now. The stress of testifying against the popular senator who'd been my biggest champion at one time should have been dissipating. Things should have been calming down.

"But it's not. You're not sleeping," Morgan said, clearly referring to the dark circles I'd tried to cover with concealer. "You've lost weight."

My clothes did seem to be hanging in a way they hadn't before.

"And you've got this look in your eyes like a koala that just fell out of its tree."

I stopped in the doorway at his side, frowning at him. "Really? Is that a look you're pretty familiar with?"

He smiled in the easy way he had, lifting one shoulder and bumping me with the other. "I can imagine it," he said. "That poor little fat bear bouncing a couple times on the hard ground and then having to look up at the branches of that towering Eucalyptus like, 'Oh shit. I have to climb that fucker again?'"

Despite the ache in my bones and my mind, I laughed. "I guess I feel that way a little bit, yeah."

"How many emails did you get today?" he asked, glancing at me sideways as we made our way to the front of the office, switching off lights as we went.

He wasn't asking about typical work-related emails. I got a lot of those. He meant the nasty, hate-filled emails I'd been receiving ever since I'd agreed to testify against the senator about what I'd seen when I'd worked late one night with a group of others at his office. Basically, him with a staffer who was definitely not his wife.

7

I would never have even mentioned the indiscretion. Men cheated. I'd learned that lesson a couple times in life—my parents, my high school and college boyfriends. But then the news hit about similar indiscretions this particular senator had made with several women, some of them underage. Because he was a supporter of education reform, the allegations against him were particularly unsettling. As he was my best ally in the senate, the case was devastating to me personally. And since I mentioned to Morgan what I'd seen, he pushed me to testify.

It had been the right thing to do, but my life was a disaster as a result.

"Seven," I said, sighing. "Only one of them mentioned dismembering me in my sleep, and there were only two that suggested I was just a jealous slut."

We chuckled humorlessly about the emails, texts, and snail mail I received regularly now. I had known the senator was popular—he had a huge base of loyal supporters who were sure he could do no wrong. And his conviction had enraged them. Their anger had been pointed at those who'd helped to secure the verdict since the trial began.

"Texts?"

"Four."

"You changed your number, right?"

"Didn't matter." I had changed my number. The people who desperately wanted to reach me, to put me in my place, to frighten and harass me, had somehow found the new one quickly.

Morgan walked me down the steps of our building and out onto the darkening street. Without me asking, he took my arm and turned me toward my apartment building.

"You live the other way," I reminded him, wondering if maybe tonight he'd get sick of babysitting and just send me home. I didn't want him to, and I hated how scared I was.

"I like a walk after work," he said lightly. "And making Sam wait for me is a good thing. I don't want him to think I'm too whipped."

"You're completely whipped." I elbowed him as we walked.

"Just don't tell him that. A man likes a challenge."

I smiled up at my friend, thankful for his constant presence and good humor. I needed both lately.

"Here we are, my lady." Morgan made a silly bow as we came to a stop in front of my building and his phone began jangling in his pocket. He glanced at it. "Oh, no."

"What?" I faced him.

"Maybe tonight was the wrong night to make Sam wait. We have reservations. Gotta run!" He kissed me on the cheek and then turned, hurrying down the street.

"Thanks, Morgan," I called, fishing my keys out of my pocket.

"Get some sleep, Heather." His voice came back to me as he turned the corner.

I nodded and turned toward the doors, where I found I was tired enough to spend a whole minute trying the wrong key.

"Shit," I whispered to myself, pulling the right one from the ring and trying again.

"You shameful little slut." A deep, gravelly voice hit me from just over my right shoulder, and I spun to find a man standing there, scowling at me, his eyes burning with hatred.

I didn't say anything back. This wasn't the first time I'd been confronted on the street. I hastened to get the key working in the lock, glancing around for Morgan, who was long gone.

"You think you can bring down a good man like Senator Andrews and get away with it?"

*Shit, shit, shit.* My hands were shaking so intensely I couldn't make the key fit. Sweat trickled down my back beneath my light shell.

"It's people like you," the man went on, his tone scathing, "who take everything this country stands for and shit all over it. Who find a good God-fearing man like the senator and do everything you can to sully his good name, to bring him down to your level."

My insides had clenched so tightly I felt like adrenaline was literally shooting out of my fingertips as I fumbled the keys and watched with horror as they fell to the concrete in front of me.

"You should be careful, you little whore," the man said, leaning in so close to me I could feel the spittle hitting my shoulder as I bent down to retrieve my keys. I cast a wild glance around the street again, but there was no help in sight. I was alone, it was almost dark, and this man was so close to me I could feel the heat of his breath on my cheek. "Someone might just get it into their head to take out the trash," he said.

I made the mistake of looking up at him, this well-dressed man who was probably someone's husband, someone's father. He looked like any other businessman you might see on the streets of DC. Only this man was clearly insane, or at least enraged. At me. Because I'd testified against someone he'd believed was above reproach.

This. This was what you got for doing the right thing.

I was shaking violently now, and the man continued speaking as I finally, finally fit the key into the lock.

"I know where you live, and I know which apartment is yours, Heather Brigham. I know what you do every second of your day, and if you're not careful, I might just make sure you never have the chance to threaten this great democracy again. It's people like you—*women* like you—who pose a threat to everything this country stands for."

The key turned and I pushed the door open, feeling like I might scream or pass out or die at any second if I didn't get away from this guy.

"Watch your back," he shouted as I forced the door shut, staring at him through the glass as I backed away. Thank God he hadn't tried to push in behind me, thank God for the insubstantial door separating him from the small lobby of my building.

I gasped for breath as I jabbed at the elevator button, but the doors didn't open, and the man was slapping the glass now, still shouting about how they were coming for me, how I'd pay.

A noise filled my head, a rushing of air and terror that almost drowned the man out, but only served to spike my panic.

I flung open the door to the stairwell and ran up, taking the steps as fast as I possibly could, passing landing after landing. As I rounded the landing for the ninth floor, nearly at my own apartment's level, my toe caught the edge of a step and I went sprawling. It didn't hurt as I crashed into the stairs ahead of me, my chin hitting one as another sharp edge caught my shoulder. I felt the pressure, the hardness of the stairs, but no pain, even as the force of the fall sent my bag shuttling down the steps beneath me, lipstick, mace, and my phone scattering.

I should have hit him with the mace. But I'd been too terrified to even reach for it.

For a moment I couldn't move, my breath coming in short gasps from the exertion and the panic coursing through me. This. This was why I couldn't sleep, couldn't eat. How could I live a normal life when every regular-looking businessman out on the street was making death threats against me? How could I go on doing the right thing, fighting for the rights of those less able to fight, when I couldn't even make it through the day without worrying I was being followed, stalked?

I rolled to sit up, and noticed then that I was crying, that my shoulder throbbed, and that there was blood on my silk shell, dribbling down from my mouth.

Slowly, I managed to gather my things back into my bag, and I practically crawled up the last set of stairs, utterly drained now. I made it to my door, dead-bolted myself inside the apartment, and went to the bathroom to see where the blood was coming from.

There was a gash on my chin. The woman in the mirror stared back at me, smeared with blood and makeup, her eyes haunted and round. I couldn't go on like this. I knew it. But what choice did I have? This was my life. I needed to find a way to take control of it again.

After a long hot shower, I was able to think a little more clearly.

I'd just need to be more careful. Vary my routine, maybe move? I was an adult. I could handle this. Eventually, the frenzy would die down and the crazy Andrews supporters would crawl back into their self-righteous holes.

Because this couldn't go on. It just couldn't.

They'd get bored, I told myself, find another target. A new scandal would pop up to distract the terrifying people who seemed so dedicated to terrifying me.

It was getting late, and my pulse was still pounding in my head, even after the pain reliever I'd taken. Only now, my stomach had begun to churn, thanks to the fact I hadn't eaten much. I went to the kitchen in my small one-bedroom apartment, pulling open the fridge to find something to eat.

I'd just settled on the couch with a yogurt when my phone began to vibrate on the coffee table in front of me. My heart rate spiked immediately as my fear from before made an encore appearance, but a quick glance at my phone had me grabbing for it, hoping I could answer before I missed the call.

"Kev?" I rarely got to speak to my brother—he'd been deployed for the last six months and had only called me once in all that time despite me making sure he had my number every time I changed it.

"Hey, you." His confident familiar voice rumbled through the phone, and my heart settled in my chest.

"How are you? It's so good to hear your voice."

"I'm good, sis. Nothing to complain about."

"Where are you?" I hesitated to even ask. Half the time he ignored the question and the other half I asked until he was forced to remind me that he couldn't tell me that. Kevin was a special operations Marine, a Raider, and the missions he served for our country weren't generally the ones I heard about on the news.

"You're waiting for me to say I can't tell you, right?"

I sighed. "I'm used to it."

"What if I said Virginia?"

"The state? The state of Virginia?" I sat up straighter. I hadn't seen Kevin in over a year. Could he really be just a few miles from DC?

"No, the planet," he laughed, and that comforting big-brother tone was there, twining itself through my worry and doubt, reminding me that I wasn't alone, not entirely. "Yeah, the state. I was at Quantico for a few days and I have some leave on the tail end. Thought I'd come say hi if you've got time."

"Yes." The word was out, breathy and almost panicked, before I'd even planned to say it.

"Okay, good," he said. "I was thinking I'd drive in tomorrow morning. That work?"

It did. That would work. Or . . . "Kev?" I ventured, my voice sounding small and timid. "Could you maybe come tonight?"

He was quiet a moment, and I knew there was no way he hadn't absorbed the change in my voice, the fear in the question. "I'm on my way," he said. "I can be there in an hour. Good?"

Relief worked through my shoulders, loosened my spine. "Yeah."

"Sit tight," he said, clearly understanding that there was something going on, something to be dealt with, that once again, his sister needed some kind of saving.

I hung up, a combination of relief and shame pressing me into the cushions of the couch. I didn't want to need my brother here, but I knew that having him with me might allow me to get a good night's sleep, and it would be the first in a while.

I didn't have to tell him everything, I told myself. But Kevin had a way of getting things out of me, and I'd never been a good actress. Kevin was too used to my needing rescuing, and he was too well-suited for the role of rescuer. Some things never changed.

---

An hour later, Kevin called. "I'm parking. I'll buzz up in five."

I was relieved he hadn't just buzzed—the sound probably

would have given me a heart attack after everything else I'd been through that day. That month.

When the knock came at the door, I flew across the living room to pull it open, and seeing my brother standing there in front of me—a hat pulled low over his dark hair, the square jaw and wide grin—made me feel like maybe everything really would be okay.

Kevin let his bag fall to the floor inside the door and swept me up into a huge bear hug. It was so familiar, so comforting . . . and it had been so long since I'd felt truly safe that the tears were running down my cheeks before I could stop them.

He set me down, his hands remaining on my shoulders as he frowned down at me, undoubtedly seeing the gash on my chin, the dark circles under my eyes. And as I often did when my hero brother was around, I felt small, weak.

"Hey," he said tenderly.

I wiped at my face and spun away from him. "I have beer. You want a beer?"

"Yeah, I do," he said, following me to the kitchen. "And then I want you to tell me what's going on."

I sighed, my mind racing as I pulled the lid from the bottle and turned to hand it to him. I wanted to edit the tale, to tell him enough to make him understand why I'd just burst into tears, but maybe not enough to make him really worry or feel like this was another problem he had to solve.

We sat on the couch, facing one another. "It's so good to see you," I told him honestly. On top of everything else I'd been worrying about, there was always Kevin in the back of my mind. I never knew what kind of danger he might be in, if this might be the mission he'd never return from. He was all I had, and I couldn't imagine him not coming back. "I missed you."

He shrugged and gave me a cocky grin. "I'm good. I'm always good." He took a long swallow of the beer and then set it down on the coffee table, fixing me in his intense, blue-eyed gaze. "Now tell me what's going on. I'm guessing I'm about to find out why the hell you've changed your phone number twice in the last three months."

So I did. I told him everything, the words rushing out without me giving too much thought to how they should be formed or molded for his consideration. I told him about the senator, about the trial, about the phone calls and emails, the text messages and the harassment outside my office. Lastly, I told him about the man who'd waited for me outside my home that night.

Kevin's face remained almost expressionless, but I knew him well enough to know that the tightening around his eyes and the tiny flare of his nostrils meant there was a fire about to ignite inside him. He said nothing when I finished talking, but I watched him clench his jaw and then blow out a long breath. He finished the rest of his beer and put the empty bottle carefully down on the coffee table. And then he did what he always did, what I'd probably known he was going to do. He told me how he was going to save me.

"Pack a bag," he said.

I shook my head. I hadn't expected that his version of saving me meant running away. I couldn't do that. "What?"

"Let work know you're taking some time. The only way to keep you safe is to get out of DC until this dies." He had his phone out, was already scrolling.

"Where would I go, Kevin? I don't want to leave." That part was mostly a lie. It was more that I had nowhere else to go and plenty of work keeping me here.

"I'll handle that. Just pack. Bring a couple sweaters. Maybe a coat."

It was mid-June—where exactly was he planning to take me, Antarctica? "Kevin." I stood and stepped in front of him, made him look up at me. "Where are we going?"

"Vermont."

# MASON

"I can't believe you're working at the Busy Bean." My sister was gleeful as she sat across from me at the Colebury Diner. Her smile was wide, and not for the first time, I envied her easy way of being in the world around her. Comfortable. Happy. "Don't you have to like, talk to people there?"

She was giving me shit, as she usually did, about being a hermit.

For the record, I was hardly a hermit. I spent less time in my house than I wanted to, especially now that I was working in three shifts a week at the coffee shop in Colebury.

"Yes, I talk to people," I snapped. "I'm not a complete misfit, you know. I can be personable."

She fixed me with a level gaze and said in a flat voice, "Right."

"Just eat," I suggested. This was our once-monthly brother-sister dinner out, and while I pretended that having my little sister bust my balls was annoying, it was actually the one thing that felt right in the world. She'd been driving me nuts since we'd been kids, and being with Amelia, even if it was just this one dinner each month, helped me remember that life wasn't just about work.

"How's the greenhouse?" she asked. "You're still going to

build one at the school, right?" Amelia had a habit of asking one question on top of another, her words spilling out like eager puppies, clambering over one another for attention.

"My greenhouse—the one on the farm—is doing well. And yes, I talked with Principal Franz last week, and we picked out a space at the side of the blacktop."

Amelia actually clapped her hands in front of her and bounced in her chair, and for a split second, I saw her as the little kid she'd been. Bouncy and happy, bright and shiny. I wondered if I'd ever been that way. Amelia taught third grade at Colebury Elementary, and it was crystal clear that she'd found her calling there, her bright personality influencing all those little people, infusing them with positivity.

"Are you still trying to do the impossible in there?" she asked, inclining her head like this was a dirty secret between us.

"I've got oranges already," I informed her, feeling my chest swell a little. "And the fig tree is looking good. I'll bring you one when they're ripe if you're nice."

She shook her head. "I'll never understand your fascination with figs. They're kind of . . . gross."

Even the word brought an image to my mind—row after row of sturdy fig trees, dark green leaves and arching branches forming low canopies over the hard-packed earth of California's Central Valley. I could still smell the farm, the groves, the kitchen where my mom made jam every summer when figs spilled off the branches of those trees, bursting with pink flesh before Dad could get them all harvested and delivered.

"I like them," I said. If my sister didn't understand, it was for the best. Every image of my childhood home was tinged with soot and ash now anyway, every memory edged with pain.

"How's Uncle Billy?" she asked, lifting a French fry to her mouth.

"Was good this morning," I told her. "He still meets me every day at four-thirty in the morning to milk."

She shook her head. "But he seems okay? I mean . . . he's okay, right?"

Uncle Billy was the only family either of us had now. Our dad's brother had taken us in when our childhoods were ripped out from under us. And when his wife, our Aunt Ivy, died, he'd gone on running the dairy farm on his own, but things had started to slip.

"You asking about him or about the farm?"

"They're kind of connected."

That was true. Billy and I both lived on the land, and if we couldn't turn the finances of the farm around—pretty quickly— we'd both be looking for another place to live. And I'd become a full-time barista, I guessed. There were worse things, I knew, but the thought of losing the farm just about killed me.

"Since we made the switch to goats, things are looking better. I just wish I'd seen what was happening earlier," I told her.

"It's not your fault."

"I was working there. I saw him every day. I should have asked more questions." I hadn't wanted to take over the business so soon, but it began to be apparent that Uncle Billy wasn't the most prudent financial manager. Aunt Ivy had handled the business side of things before, and neither of them had been planning for her sudden death. "Milk prices were tanking long before I knew what was happening," I told her.

"Hey, Mase?" Amelia said, a half smile pulling at her mouth. "You're not responsible for everything and everyone in the entire world, okay? You're allowed to live your own life too."

My life was pretty much dictated by the woman across from me and the farm I was trying to save, and that was the way I planned it. How I wanted it. I lived, I worked hard, and at night I retired to my simple, quiet, ordered life. With my dog. It was all I needed. "Right." My phone was vibrating in my pocket, and I pulled it out to glance at the screen, since my phone ringing was a pretty unusual occurrence.

When I glanced up, Amelia frowned at me. She knew as well as I did that my phone was mostly decorative.

But the name that appeared on the screen was probably one of only two or three that I'd never ignore. Kevin Brigham. Brigsy, to me.

We'd served together when I'd been on active duty, pulling some pretty insane missions off in places I hoped never to have to go to again. He'd saved my ass at least twice, and I might have managed to return the favor once. I didn't have a brother, but Brigsy probably qualified.

"Give me a sec," I said to Amelia, standing and answering the call as I moved to the doors and out to the sidewalk. "Brigsy," I said. "Good to hear from you."

"Hey, brother," he said, and his familiar voice warmed something in me I hadn't realized was cold. "You good?"

"Yeah, man. Everything's good. Where are you? Back home?"

"Visiting my sister for a minute," he said. "Heading back out in a week though."

"Shit."

"It's a living."

I laughed. "Right." It was only a living for guys like Kevin, guys who couldn't fathom a life outside the military. I'd done my time because I'd had no other idea what to with myself. But as I'd served, finding myself in places so war-torn and terrifying I would never have been able to even fathom they existed before, I realized I missed the land, the farm, the stillness of my adopted home.

"Hey, you still up there on that farm?"

"Yep."

"Any chance I could pop by for a visit?"

"You're always welcome, you know that." A part of me I hated railed against this idea, knowing a guest would disrupt my routine.

"Cool. Tomorrow okay?"

That was quick, but Kevin operated on short timelines, and it wasn't like I had a pressing social calendar to coordinate. "Yeah, of course. It'll be good to see you."

"I'm gonna bring my little sister, okay? Need to maybe leave her with you for a bit."

"What?" He'd delivered this as if he was telling me he wanted to leave a cat in my care while he went on a cruise or something. "Your sister?" He'd mentioned her while we'd served. A lot, actually, so I knew they were close. But I'd never met her. I wasn't sure how old his sister was. I was picturing a kid. I definitely didn't have time for that.

"Yeah, listen. I know it's a lot, but I need someone I can trust, someplace safe. She's been through a lot. Do you have room?"

"I mean . . ." My mind twisted over itself. Kevin wasn't a guy I said no to. That was just how it was. But still . . . What would I do with a kid here? "Yeah. Sure. I've got a guest room."

"I owe you. I'll explain more when we see you. Text me the address?"

"Yeah," I agreed, feeling a little like I'd jumped on an amusement park ride I was going to regret when I saw how steep the drop was going to be. "See you tomorrow, man."

When I retook my seat inside, Amelia squinted at me. "What was that? You look . . . weird. I mean, weirder than usual."

I shook my head. "Nothing. Buddy from the military coming to visit tomorrow." She didn't need to know the rest. She'd volunteer to babysit, and then my quiet house would turn into a full-fledged circus.

Her eyebrows shot up. "Really? A friend? You're going to be social?"

"Shut it."

"You know what's funny?" She didn't need me to invite her to continue, so I focused on eating my burger. "When you talk about the Marine Corps, you start dropping extraneous words. Like tough Marines don't have time to say them. Too mission-focused and tough for 'is' or 'and.' Ooh-rah." She laughed, amusing herself even though I didn't smile.

I watched her while I chewed another fry. "You done?"

She shook her head. "Probably not."

Even though she made me nuts, I knew I was lucky to have Amelia in my life. I knew she was the one who drove us to stay close—if it was left to me, I'd probably be exactly who she accused me of being, the hermit who never left his house. Things were just easier with fewer connections, I knew. But I was glad I still had Amelia.

We finished dinner, and I said goodbye, my mind spinning a little with Kevin's request.

It seemed I was going to have a houseguest for an indefinite amount of time.

I was pretty sure I was not going to like it.

## 4
## HEATHER

The next morning it felt like I was the one in the military. My brother looked on as I finished packing, basically force-fed me breakfast, and then stared at his watch while informing me that I had twenty minutes to take care of any last-minute business that needed attending to.

I'd awoken better rested than I had in previous weeks, and the rational part of my mind was rearing up in stubbornness at the way he was directing absolutely everything.

"I need to arrange things with work," I told him, dragging my feet about leaving the apartment on his precise schedule.

"Then take care of it." He crossed his arms and leaned a hip against the counter.

"I don't need you supervising the phone call," I huffed, turning away. There were not a lot of places to escape to in my little apartment.

"Tell them you're taking an indefinite leave," he suggested.

That turned me back around. "You're kidding, right?" I shook my head in frustration, holding my phone in one hand, my finger poised over the call button to ring Morgan. "You don't just leave work for months and expect them to be okay with it."

"They'll understand. Work doesn't usually result in people

assaulting you outside your apartment building. Honestly, you could sue them for allowing this situation to arise."

I shook my head. Kevin had always been black and white, right or wrong. "I'm sure the military would understand if you let them know you needed a few months to sort things out, right?"

He frowned at me. "Different."

Of course it was. My brother's commando attitude was starting to seriously piss me off.

"Look, Kevin." I put the phone down. "I appreciate your help, and I'm glad you're here. But the knight on a white horse thing is a little much. I have a life here, and yeah—it's a little twisted up right now—but I'm not going to totally abandon it at your command just because you think I should."

He waited, watching me through slightly narrowed eyes, assessing an opponent, maybe. He was too calm for my liking, and just like always, when my older brother adopted his cool, calm attitude, it fueled my own anger, even though I knew he was right.

"You don't get to just show up and tell me what to do!" It was immature, and even to my own ears, I sounded a lot like the little girl I'd been when Kev had dragged me off a jungle gym I'd been planning to take a flying leap from with my friends. (Layla ended that stunt with a broken arm, so he might have been right.)

"I'm not," he said in the voice he might use to soothe a frightened animal. Or a hysterical sister. "I need to know you're safe, Heather, so I can focus on my own job. And having you here, with people blowing up your phone with threats and accosting you outside your home—that's not safe. Let's give it some time, let it blow over, and reassess. Mason's place is just a landing spot where I know you'll be good while we wait. And you might even like it there."

I huffed out a sigh. I was not going to like it there. I was going to dislike it there. A lot. On principle.

"I need to call Morgan." I pushed past him and into my room, taking a seat on the edge of my bed behind a closed door, and dialed.

"Hey, Heather." Morgan's friendly voice wrapped around me, calming me slightly.

"Hey," I returned.

"Uh-oh. That's not a happy hey."

"No, it's a pissed-off hey. Sorry."

"What did I do now?" he asked, his voice full of fun that I'd miss the whole time I was away.

"Not you. My brother."

"Hot Kevin is there? Or are you angry at a distance?" Morgan had been calling my brother "Hot Kevin" since he saw a photo of him in his uniform and learned he was special operations, though he assured me that my brother would still be hot even if he wasn't a Marine.

"He's here. He's trying to rescue me."

"Oh yeah?" Morgan didn't sound surprised.

"There was a man outside my apartment building last night. He was kind of terrifying. He threatened me."

"Oh my god." He made a dramatic gasp. "And I just left you there."

"It was not your fault," I assured him.

"I'm so sorry, honey. Good thing your brother is here then. How long is he staying?" His voice changed, and he asked lightly, "Do I get to meet him?"

"Morgan, are you forgetting you're married?"

"Just window shopping, Heather. I'm happy with what I've got at home. But it's always nice to look."

"So that's the thing. I need to take some time off. Kev thinks it'd be best if I get out of town for a little bit and let things settle." My voice revealed my hesitation about this plan, but I didn't expect Morgan to object, despite the work we had piled up.

"He's not wrong." I heard keys tapping and could picture Morgan at his desk already this morning, though it was barely seven-thirty. "You have a month and three days of vacation saved up," he said.

"Well, I'm not going to be gone that long," I laughed, thinking about how my brother had blithely suggested I take a few months.

"Take a month," Morgan suggested. "Where are you going, by the way?"

"Not a month," I argued, unable to imagine being away that long. "Vermont."

Morgan inhaled and made the sound people make when they see cute puppies or hear a heartwarming tale. "Vermont! Oh, Heather. You should take the whole month. Vermont is gorgeous, and you can just breathe the fresh air and recharge. Eat some cheese."

"He's got me living on a farm or something up there. I'm going to go nuts. I don't want to eat cheese." I did love cheese, actually.

"I'm clearing your schedule. Go play farmer for a month. And eat cheese. It'll do you good."

I frowned. Morgan was really not supposed to take Kevin's side so enthusiastically. But maybe they were both right—the idea of shedding some responsibility actually had me feeling a little lighter already. "Let's keep my schedule open for the month," I suggested. "And I'll check in and let you know how things are going. I don't think I'll take the whole time."

"You take the time you need. We can rearrange things here," he said. I wondered if that were true, since there were a few key pieces of legislation on the horizon that we were intensely involved with shaping. "But I'm going to miss you."

"I'll miss you too."

"Take care of yourself. We'll be here," he said.

"Thanks." We hung up, and I felt a little better. There was a plan. One month, if that, and then I could get back to my regular life. Surely the crazies would have moved on by then.

Kevin hustled me out to the car almost as soon as I hung up, and before my mind had a chance to catch up with my surroundings, we were heading out of Washington, the familiar landscape of my life turning into a blur out the windows of his Range Rover.

"Did you buy a car?" I asked him, taking a moment to admire the vehicle.

"Rental," he said.

"Nice."

"All set with your work then?" he asked.

I glared at him. I still didn't like the way he'd muscled me around. "I told them I'd possibly be gone a whole month, but that we'd play it by ear."

Kevin shot me a look, eyes narrowed, mouth tight.

"I can't just leave for an undetermined amount of time, Kevin. I have actual work to do. And I like my job!"

"Your job is what caused all this in the first place, isn't it?"

"No, one poorly behaved senator is what caused all this. Him and his crazy constituents."

Kevin shook his head. "Why you wanted to get involved in politics, I'll never understand."

"Someone has to, Kevin. There are issues under consideration that could cripple our education system, make it impossible for underserved kids to get the services and resources they need. Someone has to fight for them." This was my passion. I'd left classroom teaching a few years earlier, dismayed at the state of the urban school where I'd taught. Kids were suffering, families needed help, and I knew I could do more for them in Congress than I could in the classroom. It was exhausting—and lately, terrifying—but I knew I made a difference.

He didn't say anything else as the landscape outside shifted slowly from gray to green, wide bustling highways to smaller winding roads. Eventually, I slept, turning my face away from my domineering brother and working hard to hold on to my anger at him. But what I was finding was that the farther we got from Washington and my normal life, the calmer I began to feel.

After eight hours that felt like years in the car punctuated only by a couple quick dashes through convenience stores for gas and bathroom breaks, Kevin pulled to a stop in front of a small house on the edge of miles of verdant green fields on one side and dense trees on the other.

"This is it," he said, bringing his car to a stop behind an old pickup truck already in the driveway.

I pushed the door open and got out, my legs stiff and tight after such a long drive. The place was tidy and well-kept, though certainly not any kind of luxury home. There were planters out front, spilling over with flowers and greenery, and that surprised me a bit. Didn't Kevin say this guy was a former Marine who lived alone? He took time to grow flowers?

As we gathered my bags from the car, I peered at an odd structure off to one side of the little house. It was glassed in at an angle, low to the ground, and my mind worked to figure out what it was. A sunroom? It wasn't attached to the main house, though, and the ceiling didn't look high enough to stand up in. It was like someone had dug a deep hole and then covered it with a clear ceiling.

My ruminations were interrupted by my brother's friendly greeting.

"Mase!" I turned to see him step close to another man and wrap him in a full-out hug—not a bro-hug like the men in the city tended to use. This was a long full embrace, and it lasted a few seconds. Like brothers seeing each other again after a long time apart. I guessed that was kind of what these guys were. Something about the gesture put me more at ease. A chocolate-colored dog had come out at the man's side, and it sat now, watching the men patiently, its amber eyes happy and relaxed.

"Good to see you," the other man's deep voice returned, and he shifted his dark-eyed gaze to where I stood on the other side of the car. "Hello," he said politely. "You must be Heather."

I was. As far as I knew.

But for a split second, not a solid thought was in my mind. They'd all dropped into a dead faint when I'd gotten a good look at my host for the next month. He was broad and tall—standard Marine issue if my brother was anything to judge by—but his face was what struck me speechless. Almost black eyes that could have been lined with kohl, surrounded by dark lashes, and placed in a face so perfect he might have been a model in another life. But there was nothing soft about his perfection. The angles of his jaw were stubbled with dark hair, and the little lines around his eyes spoke of long days outside. His hair was cropped short, close to his head in a practical shear that I imagined would feel like velvet under my hand. And something in that gaze made me feel like I'd been hit by a laser, seen through, and struck dumb.

"That's Heather," my brother agreed, picking up the bags he'd dropped on the ground to hug his old friend.

Mason was still looking at me intensely, and I felt my cheeks heat under his stare. "You're older than I thought you would be."

"Um." I had no idea how to respond to that. I hadn't really put a lot of effort into my looks today, but had these last few months really made me look old?

"You still have this guy?" Kevin asked, breaking the strange tension and leaning down to pat the dog with his free hand.

"Yep, Rascal's still here," Mason said. Then he turned back to me. "I'm Mason. Sorry about the age thing. I just,"—a big hand swept over his jaw—"I don't know why I thought you'd be a kid."

"Oh," I managed, then felt immediately stupid. There was something so startling about his gaze. "I really appreciate you having me here. I know it's an imposition."

Mason didn't argue. He just nodded once, stepped close to take my laptop bag from my shoulder, and then led us both through the front door of the house.

I followed the men inside, feeling awkward and a little stunned by Mason's sheer force of presence. I wasn't sure I'd met anyone before who struck me in such a physical way, who seemed to dominate so much space. It was interesting, and if I didn't know he was one of my brother's best friends, it might have been just a little bit terrifying.

"You'll be in here," Mason said, gesturing to a doorway that branched off a little hall to the side of the front room. I stepped past him into a simply furnished bedroom. The space was clean and tidy, holding a double bed, a rustic wooden dresser, and an empty closet. A low nightstand and a lamp sat next to the bed. The linens were white, as were the walls, and not an ounce of color showed anywhere in the space, save for the dark worn wood of the furniture.

"This is nice," I told him, turning to face him in the small space and feeling surprised again at his sheer presence. "Thank you."

"There's just the one bathroom here," he said, pointing to a door we'd passed as we'd stepped into the bedroom. "But I don't need much time in there, and I'll be gone most days before you're up, I expect." Mason didn't wait for any response, his duty clearly done, and he turned and left me in the little blank room.

I took a deep breath and followed him back out to the living room, where my brother stood smiling. "Nice little place, Mason."

"It works," Mason said, moving into the kitchen, which was separated from the main living space by a low counter. "I've done a little renovating," he explained, nodding at the granite countertop and then bending to pull open the fridge. He pulled out a growler and poured three glasses of beer. "This was a vacant outbuilding originally, but they put plumbing in here when I was a kid because they had a couple full-time farmhands for a while when the dairy operation was really pumping."

Kevin accepted the glass Mason handed him and sat on the couch, looking as comfortable as ever. I took the glass Mason offered and sat next to my brother, glancing around as Kevin and Mason talked about dairy farms, the dropping price of milk, and Mason's decision to shift to goats instead of cows.

This life could really not be more different from my own, I realized. And it would be very strange to stay here more than a day or two. What in the world would I do on a goat farm?

"This is fantastic," Kevin said, holding up his glass.

"Local brewery makes the stuff. It's called Goldenpour. People come from all over to try it."

Kevin looked at me, and I realized I was supposed to weigh in on the local beer. "Good," I said, feeling like an unneeded accessory to this entire situation.

The men discussed their old unit, talked about guys they'd served with and what they were doing now, and I let my eyes wander the sparse walls and cluttered surfaces of Mason Rye's little house. It was clean, strictly speaking. But every available surface seemed to be used to hold books. There were history books, tomes on farming and goats, and not a few mystery novels scattered everywhere. And while Mason had a television, it wasn't exactly bachelor pad standard issue. It was an old tube TV, sitting on a table in one corner, and it looked like the kind of thing you might have to smack on the side to get going.

The beer, as my brother had pointed out, was very good. And as I neared the bottom of the glass, a warm glow spread out in my belly.

"I made dinner," Mason said suddenly, rising. "Just need to grill the steaks." He disappeared into the kitchen, and it sounded like he went out a back door, and soon we could smell the distinctive scent of meat cooking.

Kevin turned to me. "You'll be safe here."

I raised an eyebrow at him. Safe, sure, but bored out of my mind. "What am I supposed to do up here, Kevin?" I whispered.

"Rest," he suggested. "Pet the dog. Read a book." He inclined his head at the messy pile of books on the table at the end of the couch and grinned.

I sighed, leaning back into the couch. I would not be here a month—I was pretty sure of that already. I'd be surprised if I lasted a week.

## 5

## MASON

I stood outside longer than I really needed to, letting the steaks rest a bit out there while my mind ticked relentlessly on and on, trying to figure out how to undo whatever had been done to my life in the last hour.

Rascal was staring at me, giving me that knowing look he seemed to put on whenever I was trying to figure something out. "What am I doing, Rascal?"

He cocked his head to one side, and I had a feeling he was reminding me that I'd said yes to this.

I'd said yes, that was true. But I'd almost had no choice. It was Brigsy asking. And I'd thought I was going to be babysitting a teenager or something. Not that that would have been better. But now this? Having this woman, this . . . really pretty, quiet woman staying in my house? What was I supposed to do to host her? I spent more time out of the house than in it, especially now that I was working at the Busy Bean. And when I came home, I sat out on the back deck when it was warm, read a book, drank a beer, and petted Rascal. With a houseguest, I'd have to actually talk. Cook dinner. Play host.

It might be a bridge too far. I was used to my own space, to having things a certain way. And I wasn't sure I could change. Or that I wanted to.

And her face . . . there'd been something haunted in her eyes when we'd first said hello, and in the nervous way her fingers twisted in her lap while Brigsy and I caught up. It was like she'd only been half here, while half of her was somewhere else, someplace where there was something big to worry about.

I guessed that must have something to do with why they'd come, but I thought I deserved to know the whole story.

"Medium rare okay for you?" I asked them, pushing back in through the kitchen door with the platter in my hand.

"Perfect," they said in unison, and then they grinned at each other, and I could see the resemblance between them. When Brigsy wasn't busy being a total badass, he was a pretty funny guy to be around—light in all the ways I felt dark. And from the grin his sister had just given him, I suspected she might have some of that in her too.

I brought out the roasted vegetables and tomato salad—all things I'd grown myself.

"This smells amazing," Heather said, sitting down across from her brother at the little table in my eat-in kitchen.

"All grown just outside." It was stupid, but I couldn't help the pride in my voice when I talked about my vegetables.

"I didn't know you could ripen peppers so early up here," Heather said, scooping squash and red peppers onto her plate. "And the tomatoes?"

I wasn't a chatty guy by nature, but this? She'd opened a door she'd probably wish she could shut in a few minutes. "Normally you can't," I told them. "But I have a special greenhouse outside."

"That's what that was!" she exclaimed. "I wondered."

"It's called a walipini," I told her, encouraged by the wide smile on her face, the glimmer of interest I saw in her eyes. "I read about them once, about how they dig deep into the ground in South America, covering the of the ditch with glass or plastic angled to catch the bulk of the sun's rays. The depth of the hole allows the space to remain at a more constant temperature than a traditional greenhouse, because it's stabilized by the earth's geothermal energy." I stopped, realizing I'd just spoken more words in a row than I had probably strung together in years. Amelia would be so proud.

Kevin put his knife down and grinned at me over a bite of steak. "Did you grow the steak too? Because it's awesome."

Heather ignored him and turned back to me. "So you can grow things in there you wouldn't normally be able to grow in this climate? That's so cool. What inspired you to do that?"

For a moment, I was distracted from the question as I watched the way Heather's wavy blond hair slid over her smooth shoulder as she turned her head. She wasn't dressed provocatively—just wearing jeans and a light tank top that was totally appropriate for the warm weather we'd been having. But there was something about the way she moved that seemed so easy, so natural. It was a little bit mesmerizing.

"Mason's always liked dirt better than people," Brigsy observed, glancing my way to see if he'd succeeded in getting a rise out of me.

Since he wasn't totally wrong, I didn't bother responding to him. But I decided to answer Heather's question honestly. "I grew up in California. On a farm. I guess I miss the kinds of things I took for granted out there. Stone fruit and citrus, tomatoes and figs." I shrugged and turned my focus to my food.

"I've never had a fig," she said. "They look kind of scary. I wouldn't know how to eat one."

"Mouth," Kevin suggested. "Always a good place to start."

"Shut up," she said.

"Well, if you're here long enough, you might get a chance. That's the thing I'm most excited about out there. My trees are doing pretty well, and I'm hoping to get at least a few figs by August."

"Oh, I won't be here that long," she said quickly. "I'm thinking a week or two at most."

"A month, minimum," Kevin said, his voice having lost all trace of humor.

Heather didn't say anything in response but took a bite and chewed it slowly as Kevin waited for her to argue. I sensed some kind of power struggle going on but definitely didn't want to get in the middle of it.

"Well, however long you need to is fine," I told her, hoping she'd find a reason to head back soon.

"I'll pay rent, of course," she said. "And you can put me to work."

"You need to rest," Kevin said in a steely tone.

Heather sighed. "I'm not a child, Kevin. You've done your job, okay? I'm here. I'll stay. For a while. But you can't just railroad my life and tell me it's for my own good. I have a job, a purpose."

"What do you do?" I asked, hoping to defuse the tension at least until I could leave the room.

"I'm a lobbyist for education reform," she said, a clear note of pride in her voice. "I used to be a teacher, but I wanted to find a place where I could enact change at the heart of the system, instead of out on the periphery."

I nodded, thinking about that. "My sister's a teacher too. I'm actually about to start building a walipini greenhouse at her school to help teach some of the kids about growing their own food. Maybe send some of what we grow home with them too. My sister says there are a few who come to school hungry."

Heather nodded. "I saw it every day. It breaks your heart." She smiled brightly then. "That's amazing, by the way. I love that idea."

"See?" Kevin said. "You won't be bored. You can help Mason build a waffle house."

"Walipini greenhouse," Heather and I said in unison. And then we turned to look at one another, and she burst out laughing as a strange sense of satisfaction bloomed in me. I couldn't remember the last time I'd made a woman laugh.

I cleared dishes with their help and brought out some of the

Dark Horse Mochaccino cupcakes I'd brought home from the Busy Bean that morning.

Not long after that, Heather announced that she was exhausted and slipped away to the guest room.

"Mind if I crash on the couch?" Kevin asked. I'd already assumed he was planning to stay. I wondered if he might tell me why they'd come now that Heather was in bed.

"Sure," I said. "I'll grab some blankets for you. Rascal will probably keep you company. That okay?"

"As long as he doesn't mind if I snore," Kevin said.

"He'll give you a run for your money there."

Kevin laughed, and I went to get some blankets as Rascal nosed around.

Soon, the house was still around me, and I lay in my bed contemplating the strange and sudden shift that had just upended my very quiet world. The cottage felt like it always did, except there was something else in the atmosphere now, something soft and comfortable and calm. For the first time in a long time, I wasn't alone. It was an interesting sensation.

# 6

## MASON

For anyone who doesn't usually get up at four o'clock in the morning, the hour probably feels oppressive—cold, dark, unwelcoming. But for me, those pre-dawn moments were often the clearest I got all day.

And that next morning, as Brigsy and Heather slept in my house on the edge of the farm, I really needed some clarity.

I hadn't slept well, and as I greeted Uncle Billy inside the glowing, early morning warmth of the barn, I was glad for the routine of pre-dawn milking. Uncle Billy pulled up his stool in the milking parlor, and I brought the goats in by twos and ushered them up onto the milking platform, securing them there so they could eat while he milked. We'd been doing this for a few years now—the operation was different than when we'd had cattle—but we had it down to a finely tuned process, one that required little discussion between us beyond the kind of subdued hello you offer someone when the sun hasn't yet risen.

Uncle Billy was moving slower these days, and the milking took longer. I could have done it myself and had offered lots of times when I'd noticed the way he lowered himself to the stool slowly, as if his joints ached, or the way he had to sit up every few minutes and stretch his back. He was nearing seventy-five, and though he was still healthy and pretty spry, he couldn't do as much as he'd once done. And between that and our income taking a huge hit as we'd transitioned from dairy cattle to goats, we couldn't afford any extra help.

While I moved goats from the barn to the parlor and out to pasture, I thought about how inconvenient having a houseguest for an indefinite amount of time was going to be. It wasn't that I had anything against Heather—almost the opposite. There was something inside me that I could feel leaning in when she spoke, that wanted to stand just a little closer, that pushed me to speak to her when I would normally have remained silent. But giving in to those kinds of longings would end badly for everyone involved.

I moved from one place to another, the dark, cool morning wrapping its wet fingers around my limbs as I worked and my mind gearing up for a long day—one that would be complicated by the woman living at my house. The woman with the vulnerable expression in her eyes. The one who reminded me of a wounded animal—one that needed help and protection.

I'd always had a soft spot for vulnerable things, something Kevin certainly figured out while we'd served together. That was where Rascal had come from, actually. We'd found him as a puppy in an abandoned building when we'd cleared a village in Syria during a mission the government would never acknowledge we'd been on. He'd been dehydrated and hurt, one of his back legs broken and twisted at a terrible angle. I'd scooped him up and tucked him into my vest without a second thought, and he'd been with me since.

I returned to the cottage just before six-thirty, and Kevin was in the kitchen, the smell of bacon and coffee wafting through the air.

"Honey, you're home," he quipped as I came through the door. Rascal said hello, and I made a quick visual sweep. No sign of Heather. I wondered if she was a late sleeper usually.

"You staying a while?" I asked him, moving past him to pour a cup of coffee.

"Nah, gotta get back. Checking in a few days from now and I head out again the following week."

"The excitement never ends," I said. I didn't miss that life, that world. It was exciting and terrifying. And for a guy like Brigsy, it was fulfilling—he was saving people, or fighting for ideals, all the time. But I'd joined for other reasons, and once I'd exorcised some of my personal demons and had a chance to dig deep in my soul for what I really wanted and needed, I knew it was time to get out.

"True," he said, flipping a pancake on my griddle.

"I'm gonna grab a quick shower," I told him and went to do it.

When I returned, I watched him cook for a minute, marveling at how comfortable he seemed in any space he filled—a gift he certainly took for granted, kind of like Amelia.

"So, my sister," he said, his voice tighter now, lower. "She's been through kind of a lot. She just needs some time in a safe, quiet place. I know it's a burden, but I appreciate you letting her stay."

I wanted to know what exactly she'd been through, what I might need to worry about keeping her "safe" from. But if Kevin wasn't volunteering it, I wasn't going to ask. "Of course."

"Just keep an eye on her, okay? I want to tell you to call me if anything comes up, but we both know that won't be possible."

"I've got it. Don't worry."

"She's going to tell you she's fine. She's not."

My curiosity piqued again. "Okay."

"Just . . . you know, pay attention."

I was starting to wonder if Heather was a suicide risk or something, if I'd taken on way more than I could handle—but before I could ask a question or raise any concerns, I heard her door open. A moment later, she appeared, wearing a long T-shirt and boxer shorts, her hair mussed around her face and her cheeks pink, and every inch of her looking far more beautiful than anything I'd seen in years. I pushed down whatever was brewing inside me, surely just a reaction to this unusual situation, and forced myself to smile.

"Good morning," she said.

"Morning," I said.

"You okay?" she asked, and I was taken aback. I was fine. It was her we were worried about, wasn't it?

"Uh. Yeah, fine." I felt my attempt at a smile pull down into a frown.

"You just looked, um . . . you know what? Never mind."

"I looked what?" There might have been a tiny defensive note in my voice.

Brigsy was watching this exchange with a half grin on his face, clearly enjoying whatever was happening here. Ass.

"Look, I'm a guest, and I owe you one for letting me stay, so it's totally not my place to comment on your facial expressions," she said, raising her hands and moving past me to the kitchen, where Kevin handed her a mug, and she poured coffee.

"My facial expressions?"

"His murdery face?" Kevin asked helpfully.

"No, it was like when you saw me, you made an angry face."

I shook my head, extremely uncomfortable at being the subject of such deep and thorough analysis.

"I think he was trying to smile," Brigsy suggested.

I stood up abruptly. That was enough. I had been trying to smile—not something I did often, apparently—and I wouldn't make the mistake again. "Listen, I need to get to work," I said, my voice gruffer than I'd meant it to be.

"Didn't you just come back from work, man?" Brigsy asked, holding the spatula aloft as he slid a plate of pancakes in front of me. I sat back down. I was starving.

"Yeah, that's farm work. I mean at the Busy Bean. I've got a few shifts over there too."

"What's the Busy Bean?" Heather asked, leaning her head to one side and resting her hips against my counter in front of the sink. The sunlight coming in from the window behind her set her hair aglow.

"Coffee shop in town," I said, taking a bite of the pancake and shoving down the part of me that noticed how sexy Heather looked standing in my kitchen.

"What do you do there?" Brigsy asked, cocking an eyebrow at me.

"Make coffee, mostly."

This was apparently confusing, and they exchanged a look that stirred up the discomfort inside me to an ever-greater level. "I need some extra cash to make improvements around the farm. The place isn't doing great, and the last thing I need is to have to move my uncle off this land to sell it just as he's ready to retire." The words came out in a rush, and I felt a little like I'd just exposed myself. My face flushed.

"So maybe having my rent money will be a good thing," Heather said kindly.

"You're not paying rent." I couldn't charge my best friend's sister rent. "This is a favor, not a business deal."

Neither of them spoke, and when I looked up from the plate in front of me, I realized my words might have come out a little harsher than intended. I sighed. "Listen, it's fine. Thanks for the pancakes. I really need to run."

I stood and carried my plate to the sink, regretting my inability to be personable and polite as Heather took two big steps to the side to get out of my way.

"Hey, man, thanks again," Kevin said, clapping me on the shoulder. "I'll get out of here in the next hour or so."

"It's no problem," I told him, realizing as I said the words that I was lying. It was going to be a problem, I was pretty sure.

"So, I'll see you when you get back," Heather said, sounding scared and uncertain, and I knew she didn't need me snapping at her and being gruff and grumpy on top of everything else she had going on.

I blew out a breath and then calmly, in as kind a voice as I could summon, said, "Yes. I should be home just before six."

I let my eyes find her face then, and her expression fell somewhere between fear and sadness. Something inside me twisted a little bit. "Rascal will be here though," I told her. "And he's good company. Can you give him a treat around noon? They're in the cabinet."

She smiled, and I congratulated myself on managing normal human conversation.

"Sure," she said, turning to look at my furry mutt, where he lay curled on his bed next to the back door. "I'd be happy to."

"Okay. Well." Awkwardness had found me again, so before it could get worse, I picked up my keys and turned to my old friend. "Hey, man, it was good to see you."

Brigsy pulled me into a hug that felt a bit like the opening move to a wrestling match. "Thanks. Take care, Mase. Thanks for looking out for my sister."

I nodded and told him to be careful, then headed out to the truck.

All the way to the Bean, I tried to get my head back on straight.

The problem was that my life had been simple for a long time, by design. I had a minimum of attachments—mostly Amelia and Uncle Billy—and that was fine with me. I had routines that were comfortable and work that was predictable. Life was good. It was just the way I wanted it.

And having someone like Heather watching it from a front-row seat, analyzing my facial expressions and asking too many questions . . . It had the potential to upend everything.

# HEATHER

My brother left an hour after Mason took off in his old red truck. I stood out on the front steps, Rascal at my side, and waved as Kevin disappeared yet again. My chest felt heavy as I watched him leave. I realized that no one ever had guarantees, but as I watched the Range Rover turn out of the little driveway and vanish, I tried hard not to think about the kinds of things Kevin did at work, about the risks he was pushed to take with his life. A very uncharitable part of me wished that he had chosen to be a barista instead. Let grumpy unattached guys like Mason go off and save the world.

Though that didn't feel quite fair. I didn't know anything about my host. Other than that he didn't seem capable of smiling and had an affinity for books.

"Guess it's just you and me, Rascal," I said, looking down at the sturdy brown dog at my side. I knelt down next to him, running my hands through the thick ruff of fur at his neck. "That okay with you, buddy? I'm worried I'm gonna be in your space too, like I'm in Mason's."

Rascal nosed at my cheek and gazed at me with eyes like pools of amber liquid, and the tension inside me released just a little.

"Okay," I told him, "let's go inside. If I'm going to be here all day, I might as well make myself useful." The place could definitely use some tidying up. And I had a feeling that if Mason was working double-time, running between the farm and the coffee shop, he probably didn't spend a ton of time thinking about putting things away.

I stepped back into the airy little cottage and allowed myself to explore in a way I'd never do if Mason was home. I poked into all the rooms, sticking only my head into his bedroom, where I was charmed for some reason by the neatly made bed, the single hardback chair in the corner, and the closed book upon his nightstand next to a glass of water. This room wasn't cluttered at all. I squinted to see if I could make out what he was reading and chuckled to myself when I caught the title, *Principles of Geothermal Farming*.

So serious.

I wandered through what appeared to be Mason's office, Rascal at my side as I looked around. This room was neater than the living room, floor-to-ceiling shelves filled with binders, their spines explaining exactly what they contained—tax returns for the last seven years all neatly lined up, medical records for Mason, and another binder for someone named Billy—his uncle, I was pretty sure—and lots of other binders that were labeled according to date and subject. Mason had notes on everything from cheesemaking to hybridization of tomatoes, and I smiled to myself as I explored. It was a little like looking inside his head, I suspected, and while I did feel like I was invading his privacy a bit, I also wanted to know who exactly I was throwing my lot in with here.

The tidiness of Mason's room had me back in my room, making the bed carefully and hanging my shirts in the closet, tucking the rest of my things into the empty drawers. I hadn't slept very well the night before, but that was nothing new. It had been comforting knowing that both Kevin and Mason were here though. It was a lot different than the recent nights I'd spent in my apartment, worrying whether this would be the night someone actually acted on their threats.

I spent the rest of the day tidying up books and magazines, dusting shelves, and baking a loaf of quick bread from some bananas that looked well past their prime on Mason's countertop. Hopefully he hadn't been saving them for some mystical farming purpose.

As I moved through the shelves in the living room, I lingered in front of the few pictures I found. There were three in total. One of them was actually of my brother—he and Mason were glaring at the camera in full Marine gear, holding serious-looking guns in their hands, but the picture was given a bit of levity by the tiny brown dog at Mason's feet, one of his legs stuck out in front of him and casted while a huge cone rose up around his little head. "That you, Rascal?" I asked him as he sat at my feet, patiently following me through my exploration of my new space.

The other two pictures were of Mason's family, I thought. In one, he was just a kid, standing in front of two adults I assumed must have been his parents. There was a little girl in the picture too. His mother had her hands draped over Mason's shoulders, the man laughing as he gazed down at his children, and the little girl beaming up at him. Mason looked directly into the camera, his cheeks pulled wide in a glorious smile that I wondered if he'd managed since. There was a startling difference between this gleeful boy and the man I'd met last night.

The last photo was a young woman, a teenager who must have been the little girl from the family shot. She was wearing a crown and holding a bouquet of roses, and something about the photo made me think it was prom or homecoming. She looked proud and happy, and I wondered where Mason had been when this was taken.

I spent the rest of the afternoon exploring the land around Mason's house, Rascal trotting at my side, dutifully keeping an eye on me. The yard consisted of the walipini, a chicken coop I hadn't noticed before, and a little fire pit set back in the trees with a few low chairs around it. The chickens were cute and seemed curious about me, so I hung out for a while chatting with them, feeling a bit like I'd lost my mind.

In the pantry, I found some soup I could heat for dinner—I didn't want to assume it would be okay if I raided the refrigerator for a full meal, but it felt wrong to expect Mason to cook after he'd been at work since before I'd been awake. When his truck rolled back up the driveway, I had two bowls of steaming chicken noodle soup on the table.

"Hi," he said as he came in the door, spotting me setting the table.

"Hi," I said. My cheeks flushed for no reason whatsoever, making me hot and awkward. "I didn't know what your plans were for dinner. I found some soup in the pantry."

"Oh," he said, glancing at the steaming bowls. "Okay. Thanks. I'll just wash up." He disappeared for a few minutes and then came back to the kitchen, pausing as he walked through the living room, a deep frown on his face.

He sat at the table, not looking at me as he picked up his spoon and started eating.

"So, thanks again for—"

"Did you move things around?" he asked, interrupting me.

"I did tidy up a little bit. I thought maybe you'd appreciate it. I know you're super busy, and—"

"It's fine," he said quickly. "I didn't mean . . . look, I think I'm just really used to living alone. It's gonna take some getting used to.

"I'm sorry," I said. "I just . . . I won't touch your things." Well, this was going to be a fun few days. There was no way I could stay here a month. I'd lose my mind.

"What else did you do today?" he asked, his tone was soft, but I felt put on the spot. Was I supposed to have a good answer? What did he think I'd be doing?

"I explored a little bit around the property," I said. "Made some banana bread . . . not much, really." An uncomfortable laugh escaped me.

He just nodded, staring into his soup.

When we'd finished eating, Mason insisted on cleaning up. Then he picked up a book and deposited himself on the couch, ignoring me.

"Well, I guess I'll head to my room," I said, figuring maybe I'd borrow a book.

Rascal responded by jumping down from Mason's side and nosing at my thigh for a pat. Mason said, "Good night."

As I tucked myself in, I tried not to let my mind search through all the feelings I was having, all the doubts. At least in the city I'd been in my own space, my own world. Here I felt detached and unmoored, completely unwanted. I knew no one, had absolutely nothing to do, and no plan for how to spend my days. What had my brother been thinking?

I didn't sleep. My mind raced between worrying about the situation I'd left behind and discomfort over the situation I was in now. I hadn't looked at my phone all day—it had become a conduit for the crazy and angry constituents of Senator Andrews to reach me. But I powered it up now.

Morgan had sent me a few messages checking in, and there were texts from numbers I didn't know that I didn't open. Those were the scary ones, usually. I didn't pull up my email, but I did listen to a message from my brother, telling me to give it at least a month. I blew out a little laugh.

I listened to the next message too, thinking it might be work-related, something I needed to forward to Morgan—but it wasn't.

"Listen to me, you lying little bitch," it began, and I pressed the delete button and then practically threw my phone away from me, my heart beginning to race again.

I lay awake for hours. I listened as Mason went to bed and tried to will myself to sleep. But after lying in the dark for what felt like hours more, I finally pulled the quilt from the bed and stumbled out to the couch, turning on the ancient television more for company than for anything else. Rascal came over and curled up next to me, and eventually, I must have fallen asleep there.

# 8

## MASON

Prior to Brigsy calling me and delivering his sister into my care, my life had been relatively simple.

Now?

Now I lay in my bed staring at the ceiling and falling into a fitful sleep for the second night in a row, despite the fact that goats required my presence at the same early hour every day, whether I'd slept or not.

I woke in the middle of the night in a cold sweat, vestiges of a nightmare I hadn't had in years lingering at the edges of my consciousness. If I allowed myself to, I could still smell the smoke.

But there was something else—my senses switched into high alert the second I'd risen from the dregs of the dream. My house was isolated and quiet. And right now? There was noise.

I crept out of bed, slowly realizing the sound was the tinny audio track of some television sitcom, and as I reached the door of my bedroom, my wary alarm shifted to anger.

This was what I didn't need. My routine being upended, my schedule being impacted. And turning on the television in the middle of the night?

For fuck's sake.

I moved to the living room, making no effort to be silent, since it was clear my visitor wasn't asleep. The laugh track on the show skittered across what felt like my last nerve. But what I saw when I reached the living room stopped me cold and sent my building anger cooling immediately.

She was curled in a tight ball, the comforter from her bed over her, and something about the way she lay told me it hadn't been an easy night for her either.

My dog curled just beneath her on the floor, alert and protective, and when I stepped into the room, his eyes found mine. If I didn't know better, I'd testify that dog was trying to tell me he was worried. About her. He let out a soft whine and got up, coming to push his head into my leg.

"It's okay, boy," I told him.

And then I crossed to where the ancient television blared in the corner, turning the sound down but leaving the thing on, and turned to face my houseguest.

She looked childlike, innocent and small, the comforter slipping from her shoulders as she slept. Her bright hair reflected the glow from the television, and I was struck again by how pretty it was, how light and soft-looking, and I found myself staring for a long moment. Her hands were clenched into fists next to her chin as she lay on her side, and her pink lips were pursed into a tiny frown.

I pulled the comforter up higher, careful not to jostle her any more than I had to, and then I tucked the edges in around her. Rascal watched all this, standing between the living room and the darkened kitchen, where he usually slept. When we were both satisfied, he turned and padded off to his bed, and I told myself I should do the same. I'd be up again soon enough.

With one last look at Heather, I turned and went to my own room, where I climbed back into bed.

It felt like moments later that I woke again. I was certain there'd been a sound in the house—not the television this time. It was still dark out, but my body clock generally roused me before the alarm I set as a backup on my phone, and it was just a few minutes before I'd need to be up anyway.

I tugged on a shirt and followed the sounds back out of my room. The comforter was folded and sat on the edge of the couch, and the television was off. But the lights were on in the kitchen, and Heather was at the stove, her back to me, and all that bright hair pulled up on top of her head.

Irritation and wonder flooded me in equal measure, and I found it hard to sort through the dueling emotions. Why was this woman in my kitchen at four in the morning? Why was my life suddenly upside down? And wasn't there something strangely nice about not being so alone in these pre-dawn hours?

I pushed that last thought down, since it was the least comfortable of any of those I was having, and went with annoyance instead. "What are you doing?"

Heather jumped at the sound of my voice and spun around, the spatula held defensively in front of her. "Oh my god, you scared me," she said.

I lifted a shoulder, running my hand over the top of my head to try to calm the hair I was sure was sticking up everywhere. "I live here."

I was being a grumpy dick, but she smiled at me anyway and laughed lightly. "Right, I know. And I knew you'd be up soon to go milk. I thought you might want some eggs before you head out."

"You're making me breakfast?" I felt like even more of a dick suddenly.

"I woke a little early," she said, both of us seeming to agree not to mention her late-night television viewing. It appeared that neither of us was sleeping well now. "I thought maybe you didn't normally eat before you went because it's so early, and you probably wouldn't bother."

"I don't."

"But I'm sure you're hungry," she tried.

I wasn't. I was so used to working before I even thought about food that my stomach usually didn't even try to grumble before I got back from the barn. The smell of the eggs and sausages Heather was cooking, however, had my stomach betraying me in the same way my dog seemed to be doing. Heather was winning them both over.

"I don't really have time," I told her, digging my heels in for no real reason.

"It's ready," she said, and she slid some eggs and sausage onto a plate, pushing it across the counter.

It felt strange, being served in my own house, but I accepted the plate and took it to the small table, sitting down like a guest to eat. The goats could wait a few minutes, I supposed.

"Coffee?" she asked, placing a mug next to me at the table and then sliding into a chair across from me.

"Thanks," I managed around a mouthful of delicious scrambled eggs.

I ate, and she watched, which wasn't my preferred setup. Her big, liquid blue eyes tracked the motions of my fork, and after a moment, I put it down. "Aren't you eating?"

She shook her head.

"You need to eat," I told her, sounding like a scolding mother.

"I will. I'll eat later, I promise," she said.

I glanced over to where my dog still lay curled in his bed, unfamiliar thoughts chasing each other through my mind as I tried to get used to having someone else in my space, cooking and speaking and moving around.

It didn't take me long to finish the plate, and I stood, carrying my dish to the sink. "I'll clean up when I get back," I said, my back to my houseguest. "Thanks again."

"Sure," she said, and I could hear the uncertainty in her voice, the lingering exhaustion and fear over whatever had chased her to Vermont, put her on my couch watching television in the middle of the night.

I dressed and picked up my keys. Normally Rascal came with me when I planned to be at the farm all day, but I decided to leave him in the house again today—it seemed like he and Heather were bonding, and they could both use the company, I figured. "I'll be back late."

"Like, tonight?" Heather sounded worried.

"Six or seven, I'd guess," I said, wishing my own voice didn't sound so harsh and edgy. I'd used it more in the past few days than I had in months. Years, maybe.

"Okay. Have a good day." She stood in my kitchen in her soft-looking sweatpants and a T-shirt and lifted a hand to wave goodbye.

"Thanks," I said.

"Mason?" she said, her voice soft and tentative. "I really didn't mean to get in your way yesterday. I just . . . I'm feeling a little lost, I guess. I don't suppose you have a Wi-Fi password you might share with me?"

"Oh. Yeah." I wrote it down for her on a scrap of paper from the coffee table and handed it to her. I should have thought of that earlier. "There."

She took it, not saying anything else.

"Okay, well."

"Bye." She sounded timid and small, and for some reason, it was hard to turn and leave. But I had work to do.

I drove to the other side of the property, my thoughts alternating between scathing reprimands to myself about how I was treating her and considerations of how unfair her very presence was here, how unsettling it was, how it had upended every carefully balanced thing in my world.

"What's up your butt?" Uncle Billy asked me the second he saw me.

"Nothing." I shoved my keys into my pocket and moved to the barn doors to start pulling goats from the pens.

"Bullshit."

I stopped and faced the old man. He'd worn overalls every day I'd ever known him, and today was no exception. But today he also wore a wry smile on that grizzled old face that I found supremely annoying.

"You're late," he said, a tiny smile pulling at the edge of his mouth.

"Sorry."

"Why would you be late today when you've been here at exactly the same time, down to the minute, for the last four years?"

I checked my watch. I was fifteen minutes late. "I overslept." I lied because Billy would be too interested in the strange development in my life, and I didn't want to spend the morning answering questions.

He frowned at me, clearly not buying it. "If that's how you want to play it," he said, shrugging and shuffling into the milk room.

I let out a sigh and shook my shoulders. I needed to get myself right. If Heather was staying a month, I had to figure out how to keep my life on track in the meantime. One small woman should not have the power to unsettle me this much.

As we worked, I resolved that I'd just live around her. She'd live her life, I'd live mine. It would be fine.

It occurred to me that she didn't have a car, or any way to get around at all, and that she was a complete stranger here. How odd that must feel, I thought as I moved the livestock out to pasture—to know no one and nothing in the place you were expected to stay for the next thirty days.

I needed to go easier on her, be more welcoming.

Despite my resolve, I found myself just as annoyed and speechless around Heather when I returned home each of the subsequent days. We repeated the same routine—I got up early to find her making me eggs and coffee, then I worked until sunset, returning to find she'd made something for dinner. She'd gotten more resourceful, digging into the freezer for meat.

And each night, I'd rise in the pre-dawn hours to find her on the couch, the television on, the flickering blue light evidently keeping her company as she tried to chase away whatever demons were hounding her. And Rascal. Always there at her side, protective and silent.

"Good boy," I told him as I tucked Heather in more tightly, turned the television down so it wouldn't wake her.

I was beginning to believe there was really something missing from my genetic makeup, whatever it was that allowed people to be kind and understanding. I didn't seem to have it, at least not when those people were constantly in my space.

I reported for my shifts at the Busy Bean twice more after milking, slowly settling into the rhythm of the place.

"You're getting it," Zara had remarked on my third day, nodding encouragingly as I steamed milk. I found the place comforting, actually. Unlike my home, where everything was upside down, the Busy Bean was a place where procedure and routine were welcomed, required. When the line was long, I'd worked with Audrey and Zara to enforce an idea they'd loosely adhered to in the past. One person stuck to the espresso machine, and one person did everything else. Since the process of pulling drinks and foaming milk was almost constant when the customer rushes hit, it made sense for one person to focus there—and it made sense for that person to be me once I'd gotten the hang of it. I wasn't cheerful and chatty like Audrey, and I didn't have Zara's wry wit, which customers seemed to appreciate. But I could be precise and efficient, so I stuck to that.

"Hey, Mase," Zara said at the end of one long afternoon shift as we were cleaning up.

"Yeah?" I asked, finally feeling almost balanced again after hours spent pulling coffees.

"Did you write that?" She pointed up to where a new saying was chalked onto the beam over the window that looked over the river. It said: *The truth of the matter is that you always know the right thing to do. The hard part is doing it.*

I nodded, feeling strangely exposed. Roderick, the baker, had given me the chalk around noon when it was quiet and suggested I refresh the quotes. And it had been strangely satisfying to do, plus, this one was kind of a reminder to myself, I thought. "Yeah. Roderick suggested I do it. I can take it down if you don't like it."

"I like it a lot, actually. Who said that?"

"General Schwarzkopf."

"Smart guy," she observed, nodding.

---

On Sunday, nearly a full week after Heather had arrived, I had the rare opportunity to sleep in. Uncle Billy had told me the previous two days that I looked like hell and suggested he'd handle the Sunday early milking before taking the rest of the day off himself. I didn't argue. Between the farm, three shifts a week at the Bean, and my house feeling like a completely different place than the one I'd known, I was out of sorts and exhausted.

I stumbled bleary-eyed into the kitchen just after seven—for me, that counted as sleeping in—to find Heather there, as usual, with my dog curled in his bed watching her with wide gentle eyes.

"There you are," she said, and the smile she turned on me lit up the room and actually made something within me vibrate with warmth.

"Yeah, uh." As usual, I felt awkward and lost inside my own home around her.

Rascal stood, stretched, and came to my side, looking up at me with his big eyes, as if to give me strength to form actual words.

"Uncle Billy took the early milking today to let me sleep in. I'll still have to go over later this afternoon, but I've got the rest of the day off."

"Pretty rare for you, huh?"

"It is," I agreed, moving to pour myself a cup of coffee.

"I was making an omelet from some of the tomatoes and basil you brought in yesterday. I found this cheese in the fridge." Heather pointed at a little tub of Garden Goat I'd brought home a few days ago from the farm.

"Should be good," I said, part of me glad she was comfortable in the kitchen, even though it felt strange to have her in my house, in my things. "Those tomatoes were pretty ripe when I picked them. Glad you're using them."

She glanced at me over her shoulder, a half smile pulling up one side of her mouth. "Glad? Do you do glad?"

I felt the frown pull at my face. "Maybe not as often as I should." I didn't want to be grumpy and awful. But I'd had a lot of practice at it.

"So," she began, sliding a plate over the counter to where I stood, "I wondered if maybe you could run me into town today? I think I'll rent a car, get back to DC."

I had been in the process of raising the fork to my mouth, but now I lowered it. "What happened to a month?" Why was I fighting her? Wasn't that what I wanted?

She shook her head lightly. "Listen, I'm just . . . I'm a city girl. And I'm used to being busy and needed, and I have literally nothing to do here. I think maybe that's worse than a few threats here and there."

My spine stiffened. "Threats?"

Her eyes narrowed slightly, and I could almost see the wheels turning in her head. "My brother didn't tell you why he stuck me here?"

It was my turn to shake my head. "Just said you needed a safe place. I didn't want to pry."

She pressed her lips together into a line and then turned away, plating up her own omelet and moving to the table. I sat down across from her, waiting for her to explain.

"It's a long story," she said finally. "But the short version is that I testified against a powerful and popular man in DC, and his supporters think I shouldn't have done that."

"What happened to him?"

"He was convicted of sexual misconduct and statutory rape."

I froze, suddenly understanding that Heather's past was a little more traumatic than Brigsy had let on. Had she been raped?

Anger began to build inside me at the thought of it, but she went on.

"He didn't touch me," she said lightly. "In case you were wondering. We were friends. Colleagues. He was very popular in the committees where I was working on pushing through some education reform in urban areas, and we shared ideals in that realm."

I nodded my understanding.

"So I walked in on him in the midst of one of his misconducts, and made the mistake of mentioning it to a coworker. When some of the women came forward, and they went looking for other witnesses, my name came up."

She leaned back in her chair and blew out a long breath. "And my life has been a disaster since then."

"What kinds of threats?" I asked, knowing my friend would not have called in this favor if things weren't serious.

She lifted a shoulder, but her face was grave, and her eyes took on that haunted look she'd had when she first arrived. "A lot of sexual slurs and a couple death threats. One guy figured out where I lived, and that's how I ended up here. Kevin happened to be home right after it happened, and I told him."

"You can't go back yet then," I said, feeling certainty slide into place within me. It might be annoying to have her here, but I was not going to send her back into harm's way. And besides, annoying wasn't quite the right word. It was . . . different.

She let out a humorless laugh, pushing her plate away. "Listen, as much fun as I've been having being a prisoner here, I do have an actual life waiting for me."

"You're not a prisoner."

"I don't even have a car, and we're in the literal middle of nowhere. I have nothing to do, and all your books are either nonfiction or mysteries. And you don't have cable." She trailed off in her list of complaints, staring down at her hands in her lap.

"We can fix all that." I didn't mind buying a few more books and hooking up cable if it meant keeping this woman safe. I found that as I pushed her to stay, some part of me really did want her to.

She glanced up at me and gave a little shrug. "Maybe another few days," she said, "but then I'm going to have to figure this out, or I'll lose my mind."

I swallowed down the guilt I felt at not being more welcoming. I would do better.

---

We cleaned up the dishes, and I went out to the greenhouse. I'd neglected it for a few days, and there was some tending I'd certainly need to do and probably things that needed harvesting.

A few minutes after I'd stepped down into the humid space inside, the door opened again, and Heather stepped in. "What are you up to?"

I kicked myself. I should have invited her out here or found something for her to do. I was so accustomed to doing my own thing, on my own schedule, that even after our conversation, I hadn't thought to offer.

"Just a little maintenance and some harvesting," I told her. "The tomatoes here are ripening a little earlier than I'd expected them to." I pointed out the row of tomatoes bursting in green and red around the cages I'd set up at one side of the space.

"It's warm in here," she said. "I guess that's the point."

"Pretty much," I agreed, checking my figs with satisfaction. I'd planted three varieties, kept in huge pots to allow me to move them in the winter when they'd go dormant. Now, with the burgeoning heat of summer amplified by the setup of my greenhouse, there were hard fruits sprouting.

"Those are the figs?"

I nodded, showing her the little tear-shaped fruits beginning to swell on the limbs beneath the wide green leaves.

"Why are you so devoted to growing something like that out here? Why not things you know will succeed?"

The answer was a little bit sentimental, and I wasn't sure how much I wanted to tell her. I settled for something halfway to the whole truth. "I told you how I lived on a farm as a kid. My dad grew figs, and I always really liked them. I guess they kind of remind me of home."

"Here in Vermont? You grew up here, right?"

I shook my head, an image of the wide, brown California valley nestled up against the foothills of the Sierras flashing through my mind like a ghost. "No. California."

She nodded. "Well, that makes sense then. Your folks still out there?"

"No."

Heather watched me, clearly expecting something more, but I'd said about all I could manage at the moment. Luckily, the increasingly tense moment was interrupted by a loud squawking commotion from outside.

I moved to the door and climbed out, heading for the chicken coop with Heather just behind me.

"Ho!" I yelled, seeing the branches arching over the coop populated by dark forms, preparing to launch an attack. "Ho! Get!" I waved my arms at the crows, sending them shrieking and scattering, and then went into the coop yard.

"Are they okay?" Heather asked, trotting up beside me. "Do the crows bother them?"

I took inventory, seeing that the girls appeared to be intact. I'd recently hatched a few bantams, and it was likely the crows were after them. They rarely bothered adult chickens. "I think so. They go after the young ones sometimes."

The chickens were upset, stating their concern loudly and scooting around the edges of the little coop yard. Heather stepped inside and knelt down, and to my surprise, she began talking to the girls.

"Hey now, Miss Rosie, it's okay. You're fine, little lady. Shhh," she said to my white hen. "Shhh, Dottie. It's okay."

My chickens, as far as I knew, didn't have names. "You named my hens?"

Heather looked up at me, a brilliant smile on her face as the sun shafted down through the trees, casting her in a warm glow that loosened up something inside me.

"I've been a little bored."

## 9

# HEATHER

"This is Dottie and Rosie and Molly," I told Mason, pointing at each of the hens as I stood, then brushing off my jeans. "And that's Hester and Allie and Ina."

He looked utterly mystified, his eyes narrowing slightly as if he was trying to understand why I would name the chickens.

A thought occurred to me. "Oh! Did they already have names? Maybe I've just confused things out here."

"No. They didn't have names."

"Oh good. Okay, well, they do now."

Mason looked at me for a long moment, his mouth slightly open and his eyes holding that same look—like a confused fascination. It was the way I imagined he might look at me if I told him that his dog and I had been talking. Which we had, in a way, but I didn't need Mason thinking I was legitimately crazy.

"Hester can do tricks," I told him, amusing myself by watching his reactions. That one made his mouth snap shut.

"You taught my hens tricks?"

"Hester is the only one who seems to have the aptitude," I explained. "So far. But if I'm out here for another three weeks, I'll have these ladies tending the greenhouse for you."

Mason said nothing to this. He was not exactly a jovial, chuckling kind of guy, but I worried I might have actually broken him with this news of chicken training. Still, when the tiniest glimmer of amusement lit in his eyes, I was addicted. I wanted to see more. What would it be like to hear the guy laugh?

"Show me," he said softly.

"Sure." I scooped a bit of feed from the corner and shook it in my hand. "Hester, come here, girl."

The little brown bird glanced at me and then cautiously stepped her way across the yard to where I stood. She twisted her head from side to side, eyeing me suspiciously.

I shook my hand again, letting her hear the food I held, and lifted my arm parallel to the ground over where she stood. "Okay, girl. Come on. Jump up!"

It took a couple coaxing suggestions, but after a moment, Hester leapt into the air, landing on my arm, and was rewarded with the feed I held. A moment later, I lowered my arm, and she walked down it like a ramp to the ground.

"See?" I asked, smiling up at Mason.

He was as handsome as anyone I'd ever seen, but it seemed to take an act of god to make the man smile. This, however, almost did it. A tiny hint of an upturn pulled at the sides of his mouth, and he let out a breath that could have been a little laugh. A surge of delighted pride rolled through me.

"So do you raise chickens for eating or just for eggs?" I asked as we left the coop.

"Eggs," he said. "Part of my diversification efforts."

As we stepped back into the house, Rascal on our heels, I realized this might have been the first real conversation Mason had allowed us to have since Kevin left. Or maybe the first one his schedule had allowed.

Mason paused in the kitchen, peering out the window over the sink at the wide grassy fields between his house and the big red barn on the other side of the property. The sun washed the land, and a gentle breeze set the green stalks to swaying. "You want a beer?" he asked, sounding like he thought maybe a beer was actually a bad idea. But I remembered the one he'd given me the night I'd arrived, and I definitely thought I'd like another.

"Sure."

"Nice day," he said. "Maybe we can sit out on the deck for a few minutes."

"I'd like that," I said, realizing only then how terribly I'd been missing company and conversation. I wasn't expecting much based on what I knew of Mason so far, but I would take what I could get.

A few minutes later, we sat on the back deck in the afternoon sun, looking out over the fields and sipping Goldenpour.

"What did you mean when you said 'diversification efforts'?" I asked.

Mason took a long drink of his beer and set the glass on the table between us, his eyes fixed on some point in the distance. "This used to be a cattle operation," he said. "But milk prices have been falling for a while, and cattle are expensive to feed. We had to borrow to keep the place going, betting things would turn around." He shook his head.

"They didn't?"

He gazed over at me then, a sad look in his dark eyes. "They did not. So we sold the cattle and bought the goats, started making cheese and adding vegetable crops on some of the old grazing acreage."

"What vegetables?"

"Beets and spinach so far," he said. "Hoping to add beans next spring."

"And what about the stuff you're growing in the greenhouse?"

"I sell that at farmers' markets, mostly, with the cheese. Because those products are a little more exotic here in the North-east, they bring a premium. Not a lot of folks selling locally-grown citrus or local strawberries up here."

I nodded. "So things are getting better then? I mean financial-ly?" It was a little invasive, but he'd brought it up.

He chuckled, but it was a mirthless sound that made me cold

despite the sun warming my cheeks. "If things were better, I wouldn't be working at a coffee shop."

"Ah," I said. "I guess not." My mind began turning. I couldn't help it—I was a problem solver, and people in need were the one thing that got my gears moving. I wanted to help Mason. I knew of a few grants for agriculture but didn't know a lot about Vermont initiatives. "Have you looked at grants at all?"

Mason shook his head and finished his beer. "I barely have time to eat, let alone run around begging the government for money." He sounded almost angry.

"Right," I said, not wanting to push him further. "So what can I do to help while I'm here? Clearly teaching your chickens tricks isn't going to help save the farm."

"It's not your job to save the farm."

"But I'm here. And I can help. And I'm dying for something to do."

"Careful what you wish for—we'll recruit you to make cheese before long."

"Yes. I'll totally make cheese!" The idea of being useful—even making cheese, which I didn't have the first idea how to do— sounded incredible.

"You're serious?"

I nodded eagerly.

"Well, it would help if you'd collect the eggs in the morning, since you like the chickens and they seem to like you."

"I can do that." I took his request as a sign of trust, and a tiny glow of purpose ignited inside me.

"And if you really want to, you can pick the ripe tomatoes and strawberries out in the greenhouse. Sometimes I let them go too long because I get busy."

"Sure." I could collect eggs and pick fruit for a few days—it would make the remainder of my stay pass more quickly. I was still feeling a little desperate to get back. Despite Morgan's assurances, work was busy, and I knew I couldn't just hide out forever. Besides, now that I was here—away from the city, away from the noise and rush of that life—it was hard to imagine there had ever been any real threat. Maybe I'd overreacted. My brother certainly had. I knew I'd been legitimately scared, and I thought I'd had reason to be, but from the idyllic green fields of Mason Rye's farm in quiet, pastural Vermont, it was difficult to find the fear and worry that had consumed me. Yes, I was still having trouble sleeping—darkness seemed to summon the shape of my fears if not the fears themselves—but I hadn't been a great sleeper in years. I'd learned to live with that.

I went inside that afternoon when Mason headed back over to milk the goats again, feeling more optimistic than I had in a while. I had a few other ideas about things I could do to help Mason's farm too, but I wasn't going to mention them to him for now. I was just glad I'd gotten the Wi-Fi password and brought my laptop along.

---

The next morning, I rose again before Mason did. Rascal eyed me from his bed in the corner as I made coffee in the little pot, probably wondering why I made such a racket in the mornings. It was dark out, and despite the fact we were moving into the middle of June, a chill hung in the air.

The scent of coffee was strong in the little kitchen by the time Mason came out to join me for breakfast. To his credit, he didn't say a word about me being up and completely dressed, which was a change from my usual sweatpants and T-shirt, but maybe that was more due to the hour than a lack of curiosity. After a few minutes, each of us sipping at steaming mugs and staring out the window at the landscape still draped in its bedclothes, Mason said quietly, "Going somewhere today?"

It wasn't a question at all. So I didn't explain. "I am." Perhaps I'd taken his invitation to help out a bit too far, but I wanted to get a feel for the rest of the farm.

So when he moved to the door and picked up his keys after

swallowing a few bites of eggs and toast, I was at his side, pulling on a sweater.

He frowned down at me over his shoulder. "What are you doing?"

"Coming to help."

"You want to milk goats?"

I shrugged. "If that's what you need help with, then yes."

He turned back toward the door and rubbed a hand over his face, then pushed it open with a sigh. "Come on then. Let's go, Rascal." I was relieved he didn't put up a fight.

Mason's truck was old but functional. It reminded me of a favorite ball cap or sweatshirt, worn in but nowhere near worn out. Rascal bounded out to the truck and jumped in ahead of me, making himself comfortable between us on the bench seat.

We drove along the edge of the fields I'd stared out at the previous night, the boundaries of the small life I suddenly had, and I felt as if my horizons were opening as we ate up the miles between the little house and the big barn that grew bigger in the windshield as we approached. Mason pulled to a stop just outside the huge, white structure, and I found myself grinning as I looked around. It was a goat farm, I knew, but it sure was pretty. I felt like I'd walked into a Charles Wysocki painting.

Mason headed for a large door on the front of the barn, and I followed him, feeling more than a little like an unwanted tagalong since the guy barely acknowledged my presence as Rascal trotted beside us. He pulled the door open, and it practically slammed shut with me in it as I scooted through behind him.

There were goats in pens along both sides of the barn, and as we passed them in the near darkness, they greeted us with grunts and wails, creating a strange cacophony. At the end of the long space, there was another door, and Mason pulled it open, turning to me and saying, "Milking parlor."

"Fancy," I commented.

He shot me a look that I swore was almost a smile, and my stomach leapt in a tiny victory dance. I wasn't sure why I was so determined to make this grumpy farmer like me, but it had become important to me. And a smile was a good start.

Mason switched on the lights to reveal a small, sparse room with a raised wooden platform in the center and a ramp at one end of it. One side of the platform had some long wooden pieces coming up perpendicular to the bottom, and each had what looked like a space for a goat's head, with a little platform just on the other side of the space.

"Billy should be here in a minute," Mason said. "He brings the sanitized gear."

I nodded. "So, the goats go here?" I asked him, pointing at the platform.

"Yep. Once we get them situated, we put some feed down in bowls for them. They don't mind being milked if they're eating." He stepped back, gesturing to a machine sitting on a rolling cart in the corner. "Billy will clean the teats with an antibacterial solution and then attach them to the milker."

I looked at the machine, suddenly glad I wasn't a goat. There were tubes from the machine that I guessed got attached to the goats and a tube at the bottom that ran into the wall. "Where does the milk go?" I asked.

"Bulk milk tank on the other side of the wall chills the milk as soon as we get it. That's critical with goat's milk. The sooner you chill it, the better the quality."

"You talking to yourself again, Mase?" A crackling voice like a paper bag preceded a grizzled old man through the big parlor door. He shuffled in, wearing a flannel shirt and overalls, holding a crate full of what looked like funnels and beakers, and he stopped with a start when he looked up and saw me. "Oh. Hello there." He swung his gaze to Mason, a wide smile on his wrinkled old face. "Remind me to talk to you about the kinds of dates ladies like, son. Goat milking ain't gonna get you far."

"Uncle Billy, this is Heather."

Billy regarded me with kind light blue eyes and nodded his head a couple times. "Well, I'm pleased to meet you. A little confused, if I'm honest. We don't get a lot of company for milking." He grinned to himself but didn't ask for any further explanation as he moved to where the milking machine sat and began rolling it toward the platform.

I realized that this entire week I'd been here, Mason must not have even mentioned me to his uncle.

"It's nice to meet you," I said. "I'm staying with Mason. I'm sure he told you."

The old man was busily checking connections on the machine, but he paused and looked up at me. "Of course he didn't. You've met the guy, then. You know you have to practically wrestle him to the ground to get him to tell you good morning."

Mason blew out a breath that was halfway between amusement and annoyance, and I looked up to meet his eye over his uncle's bent head. I gave him my best *what the hell* look, and he actually shot me a tiny smile and shrugged.

Billy didn't seem to notice any of this exchange and went on prattling as he pulled up a stool to the edge of the platform. "Nah, this one ain't never said much, not since him and his sister moved out here—"

"Let's get the goats," Mason said loudly, his eyes on me. There was a look in the darkened depths I hadn't seen there before, a plea almost. He moved to the door of the room, and I followed him out, wondering suddenly about the boy Mason must have been. I followed him out into the barn, and we went to the far end, saying nothing more about Mason's mysterious past.

"I bring them in two at a time," he said simply, handing me a lead and then opening the stall door just wide enough for us both to enter.

The goats inside the stall moved around us, making a racket and dancing, and they seemed to recognize Mason, butting him with their heads as if they were seeking a pat. Their ears were long and drooped at the sides of their heads, and intelligent eyes gazed up at me as Mason attached a lead to two of the goat's collars.

"These are Nubians," he told me, and I smiled to myself, noticing again that as long as you had Mason talking about farming and goats, he was happy to chat.

"That sounds exotic," I said, leading one of the goats from the stall behind him, mimicking what he did. The goat stepped up close behind me and rammed me in the butt with her head, nearly sending me crashing into Mason's broad back. "Hey!" I cried.

"That's Annalee. She's a handful," Mason said. "Just trying to make friends."

I gave Annalee a look suggesting it'd be better not to knock me over as we headed into the milking parlor where Billy was waiting.

Both goats were led up the platform, and I watched, fascinated, as Billy efficiently dipped their teats into one of the cups he had set on the rolling cart, then attached the milking tubes as Mason set feed bowls on the other side of the head holes. A moment later, the machine was doing its job. Both goats seemed pretty used to this, happily munching away as they each got milked. The whole process didn't take long, and Mason moved around the room constantly as Billy focused on the milking.

"These girls go out to graze now," Mason told me, handing me Annalee's lead again and holding the milking parlor door open for me. "Rascal will keep an eye on them out there. And we'll get the kids and send them out too."

We took the goats out the main door of the barn and let them loose in a small pasture just beside it, where Mason checked to be sure they had water before securing the gate again.

Then we went to a bigger stall inside the barn, from which a good amount of noise was coming. I peered over the door before Mason opened it, and my heart nearly burst. Inside the stall were seven or eight little goats, all jostling each other to get to Mason as he swung the door open and we stepped inside.

"They're so little," I said, the awe evident in my voice. These tiny goats were smaller than I thought goats could be, almost like puppies. But they were dancing around on strong legs and even leaping in the air as they cried at our presence. "So cute," I said, reaching down to pet a couple. They nuzzled my hand eagerly.

"We keep them separated from the big goats when they're this small," Mason told me. "Once they're eating hay, they don't need to be with their mothers all the time, and the larger goats can be a little rough with them. But I don't like to put them out in the pasture without a few of the bigger goats nearby to discourage predators."

I nodded, completely charmed by the antics of these tiny creatures.

"You ready? This will be a bit of chaos, but the barn will be quieter when we get them outside."

"Sure," I said, laughing as a little black and white kid turned in circles around itself before falling over.

Mason opened the door then and called the babies to follow him, which they actually did. I brought up the rear, herding a couple stragglers along, and they made their disorganized way out to the front, where Mason had the gate to the adjacent paddock open for them. Rascal trotted along behind me, herding the kids into their pen.

"Good boy, Rascal," Mason told him, glancing around the paddock and squinting in the early morning gray. "He'll keep an eye on them," he told me.

As we went back inside, I smiled at my host, who was proving to be a very interesting study in contrasts.

"You name your goats, but not your chickens, huh?" I said, elbowing him in the ribs. The action surprised us both—he froze for a half step, gazing down at me with his mouth partially open, and I realized too late that I'd touched him in a pretty familiar way that I probably shouldn't have. I did notice, however, that whatever was under that chambray shirt he wore was hard as a rock.

"Uncle Billy insisted on it. Seems silly to me. Guess it's different than livestock you're going to eat though." He nodded as we moved to the second pen of goats. "These girls do have distinct personalities, too, so I guess it makes sense."

I enjoyed the morning thoroughly. Goats, as it turned out, were playful and silly—and very noisy. Billy was fun to be around too. He seemed immune to Mason's grump and had no compunction in calling him out or teasing him. The old man referred to me several times as Mason's girlfriend, which I found funny, but Mason never bothered to explain to him why I was really there. I did correct him once, but he waved me off.

Mason had a shift at the Busy Bean to get to, but Uncle Billy invited me to stay a while, saying he'd feed me lunch and show me around the rest of the farm, which sounded like heaven compared to sitting in the little cottage alone again. Possibly to Mason's dismay, I took him up on it, and by the time Billy took me back to Mason's cottage, I was ready for a nap. I'd learned a little about Mason—that he'd lost his parents at fourteen and come out here because Billy was his dad's brother, and that he was evidently a handful as a teen. I couldn't imagine the Mason that Billy described, getting in fights and staying out all night drinking. Billy said joining the Marines had been partially his idea and partially Mason's, but that it had turned him around and helped him find his way.

Billy and I talked about the farm a bit too, and I was determined to help them find the funding they needed.

That night, I felt more relaxed than I had since arriving. I'd decided that Mason's gruff attitude was less about not wanting me here and more about him. He wasn't used to having people around all the time, and it wasn't like I was staying in my room, silent. But I thought he was getting used to me, and I'd done my best to make myself useful.

I'd roasted a frozen chicken he'd brought home from the store and some squash for dinner, and when Mason got home, smelling of coffee, he actually almost smiled at me. "How was the farm?" he asked. "Billy talk your ear off?"

I laughed. "No, he was great. I like him a lot. I think maybe he's a little lonely."

"It was nice of you to stay and keep him company today," Mason said. "He didn't make you bale hay or anything, did he?"

"No. He fed me lunch, and I helped label some of the cheese tubs," I told him.

Mason washed his hands, and then we sat down, the routine beginning to feel familiar and comforting. Rascal curled up just behind Mason's chair, as if he was quietly letting his master know he was glad he was back. The dog was good company during the day when Mason was gone, trotting around with me and giving me his lopsided smile anytime I spoke to him.

We were just about to eat when my phone vibrated from the counter beside me. "Excuse me," I said, worrying it might be work. It still felt odd to be away so long.

I stood next to the table and glanced at the number. It was a DC number, so it definitely could be work. "Heather Brigham, hello?"

"Your apartment is nice, you slutty little bitch. You get this nice place by spewing lies about upstanding men like Kenneth Andrews? You get paid off for making up stories to hurt good people?"

I sucked in a breath, pulling the phone away from my ear, my blood suddenly turning to ice in my veins.

The voice on the phone was loud enough to hear clearly without pressing the phone to my head.

"Your bed smells like shit, you fucking whore. I can only imagine how many men have been through here. And who's this in the picture here on your nightstand, huh? Is this slut your mother? She probably sucked—" Mason took the phone from my hand and ended the call. Then he put the phone on the counter and guided me back to my chair, his strong arm braced across my back.

I sat heavily. My mind felt frozen, my limbs numb. "He's inside my apartment."

## MASON

Heather's pretty face had blanched, and her hands were shaking visibly as I set her phone back on the counter. Her eyes were wide, but she didn't seem to be focusing—she wasn't looking at me.

"Hey," I said softly, squatting down in front of her chair so we were at eye level. "You okay?"

"He's inside my apartment," she said again, a sharp edge of terror lining the words. "Touching my things, looking . . ." She trailed off. "He called my mother a . . ."

I'd been with plenty of people in shock, a side effect of the kind of work I did in the Marines. But now, in my own home, I was at a loss for how to help. I had a strong urge to take this woman in my arms, to reassure her that nothing could hurt her while she was here, that I'd make sure of it. But her life was more complicated than mine by a mile—and if there really was someone inside her apartment, we needed to deal with that first.

I turned and picked up my own phone from where I'd set it next to the door when I came in. "I'm going to call 911 and explain what's going on. Hopefully they'll be able to send someone to your apartment."

She nodded slowly, her eyes still unseeing.

"Can you write down your address?" I asked her, putting a pad and pen in front of her.

I made the call, and the local dispatcher put me on hold briefly while she found a number I could call for the area where Heather lived. Once I'd reached the police there, they assured me they understood and would send someone immediately. I gave them my phone number and information, then hung up.

Heather hadn't moved the whole time I was on the phone, and I took one of her cold hands now, guiding her back to her feet. She was still shaking, and as I helped her to the couch, Rascal whined and rose to follow, settling at her feet as I motioned for her to sit at one end. I tucked the soft throw blanket Amelia had given me around her legs. She pulled herself into a little ball, wrapping her arms around her knees as she let her head lean back into the cushions of the couch, facing me. Her eyes found my face, and she whispered, "Thanks."

Helplessness raced through me—I wanted to do something to fix this, but there was nothing to do.

I sat with her, Rascal and I both standing guard against something we didn't quite understand, but a threat that was very real, given Heather's reaction. After what seemed like hours, my phone rang again. The police had been to Heather's and found the door standing open, her things upended and tossed around, but not destroyed.

"It will be difficult to know what's missing without the resident here," the cop on the line told me. "Will she be returning soon?" Not if I had a say about it.

Heather could hear the conversation through the speakerphone, and she shook her head at this question, her eyes widening again.

"No," I told him. "Unfortunately, she won't be returning soon. Can you possibly just secure the apartment?"

"We need her to file a report if there's anything missing. The sooner, the better."

"I understand," I assured him.

When I'd put down the phone, I turned to face her again, struck by how small and vulnerable she looked there at the end of my couch. "I'm going to make some tea," I said.

She nodded, and by the time I carried a warm cup over to hand her, she appeared somewhat recovered, if still shaken. She reached for the cup and said, "Thank you."

I sat beside her with my own cup steaming between my palms, trying to sort through the jangling emotions chasing each other through my body and mind. Seeing her frightened had done something to me, woken up something protective and fierce, and it was almost painful not to simply wrap her in my arms so I could reassure myself she was safe and whole. I wanted to tell her it was okay and then figure out how to make it true. It was jarring to realize, but something inside me was reaching for her, wishing for a connection, longing for her—and I couldn't let that feeling continue to evolve. Connections to people, as I'd learned over and over in life, made you vulnerable to the kind of hurt you didn't recover from. Losing people you loved changed you forever, and I never wanted to go through it again. I'd decided long ago to keep the connections in my life minimal, had promised my heart I'd never go out seeking that kind of vulnerability. I wouldn't survive another loss like the ones I'd already suffered. I was sure of it.

So I sat, hoping proximity and the quiet solace of my house and my dog were enough to relax my guest, to assure her she was safe.

After a half hour or so, Heather seemed better. She set her mug on the table and slipped down to the floor beside Rascal, cooing at him and petting him in a way that made me jealous, that longing rising in me again.

I sighed and put down my own mug, standing to stretch. "Are you okay?" I finally asked and was nearly knocked over by the bright smile Heather sent up to me from where she sat.

"Yeah," she said, still rubbing my dog's head. "Yeah. I will be." She got to her feet, picking up the mugs from the table and taking them to the kitchen. "Thanks for handling that. I'm sorry—I guess

I was just shocked. I'd been telling myself everyone was overreacting. I really did intend to head back to the city soon. But now . . ." Her nose wrinkled, and her eyes found mine. "Mason, I know it's hard for you having me here—"

"It's not," I told her. "It's fine. Stay as long as you need to." I had no idea where the words came from. Just a day or two earlier, I'd been wishing her away, wanting my space back to myself. But now, the thought of her leaving—especially if she was in danger—I didn't like it.

She looked down for a moment, the dark lashes fanning out against her cheeks and reminding me how she looked when I found her sleeping each night on my couch. My heart twisted in my chest as her eyes rose to meet mine again, shining with unshed tears. "I'm sorry, Mason. I never planned—"

"Stop," I said, stepping nearer without intending to consciously. "It's fine. You've been helping, and god knows we can use it. But if you stay, I just might find more work for you to do." I smiled down at her, the expression feeling stiff as I put it on, like an old pair of jeans that fit but that hadn't been worn in a while.

"Okay," she said softly. "I should call Morgan and see if he can check my house."

She took a deep breath, as if to steady herself, and picked up her phone. After a moment, she began talking, explaining everything that had just happened to someone on the other end of the call and letting him or her know she was hoping to take an indefinite leave from work. Evidently it was fine, because she hung up not long after and smiled at me, shrugging her shoulders in a way that made me want to scoop her up into my arms. "I guess you're stuck with me," she said.

Something inside me loosened as I realized she was definitely going to stay for a while.

That night, I heard the television again in the small hours of darkness before dawn. When I went out to the living room, she was there, curled into a ball on the couch, my dog standing guard at her feet.

I stood over her, realizing I might frighten her if she were to wake up, but unable to keep myself from staring in a way I couldn't do when she was awake. She was so beautiful. Her skin was fair and soft, and the glow that lit her face when she was excited or happy left a rosy tint on her cheeks, even as she slept. Her hair splayed out around her, wavy and silky, and I had a sudden urge to wrap a lock of it around my hand, to feel it between my fingers. Her lips were pink and full, parted slightly in sleep, and it took all the restraint I had not to press a finger to that little pout, to feel the softness of her skin.

Blowing out a frustrated breath, I leaned down and tugged the blanket up around her shoulders. As I turned to lower the volume on the television, she let out a little cry, and I turned back, worried I'd scared her.

But her eyes were still closed tight, only her face was contorted now, as if in a dream.

"Shhh," I whispered, "It's okay."

She cried out again in her sleep, and I stood in the center of the room, a silent war raging inside me. When she stiffened, tossing her head, my resolve broke, and I crossed to her again, sitting on the edge of the couch and pulling her into my arms gently. "Shh," I said, cradling her against my chest, letting my cheek slide against that mass of soft hair. "It's okay. Just a dream."

She whimpered once more, then nestled against me. For a long moment, neither of us moved. Her breathing slowed, matching mine, and I held her there in the darkness of my usually empty house, marveling at the softness of her, the warmth of her small body in my arms, the strange contentment seeping through my limbs as I breathed the scent of her.

Finally, I lowered her back to the couch, intending to go back to bed, but her arms slid around my neck before I could stand up.

I froze, my eyes finding her face. Her eyes were open, just a crack, and she gazed up at me, holding me in place for a moment that seemed to hang on the air, then finally releasing me. Her eyes shut again, and I moved away, turning down the television and going back to my own room where the scent of her still filled my senses, the feel of her in my arms flooding my mind as I took myself in hand and attempted to expel the sudden need I was ashamed to feel for her. I fisted myself roughly, angry that I'd let it get this far, that I'd let myself think of her that way. And as I released, shame flooded me at the knowledge that I'd crossed a line with my best friend's little sister—mentally, at least.

I'd need to do better.

---

I left earlier than usual to milk the goats the next morning, not wanting to confront Heather—or more specifically, the unwanted feelings I was beginning to realize I could have for her if I wasn't careful.

"That girl of yours is a spitfire," Uncle Billy told me as he pulled up his stool, the first two goats settling on the platform.

"She's not my girl," I grumbled.

Uncle Billy let out a laugh that only pissed me off more.

"She's not."

"Right." He was quiet a while, but Uncle Billy had never been a guy to keep his thoughts to himself if he had something to say. I could feel the words collecting in the dense atmosphere of the little room, and when I brought the next girls in, he went on.

"She's got some good ideas about how to help the farm," he said.

I stopped moving for a moment, narrowing my gaze at him. "What?"

"We talked a lot while she was here, and she suggested we dig into some kind of land conservation thing that the state offers to subsidize farms and help keep land undeveloped up here."

I shook my head. I hadn't asked her to do that. I'd told her I didn't have time for paperwork and long shots. "We need things that will help right now, not pie in the sky impossible ideas. She doesn't know anything about farming, Billy."

He nodded, taking this argument in stride. "Thinks we should change the labels on the cheese," he said, almost offhandedly.

I stopped moving, my arms crossing over my chest. "Oh really." I would never have left her out here with Billy if I'd known she was going to get her busy hands into every part of the business the same way she'd tried to reorganize my house.

"She liked the name though," he went on, oblivious to my rising irritation.

"I'm so glad," I said, the tone of my voice finally catching Billy's attention.

He narrowed his gaze at me. "Oh, I see how it is," he said, his voice sharp. "Big strong Mason doesn't need any help, is that it? Doesn't want any good ideas that aren't his own popping in and maybe making things a little better." He nodded, as if to himself. "Sure, better to just suffer in silence, let Garden Goat Farms fail on your terms."

Anger raged inside me, possibly because he'd hit the nail on the head. "It's not going to fail. I've got the farmers' markets lined up, and there are a couple local restaurants interested in the fruit I've been growing."

"Right. So when you're not working the farm, or pouring coffee in town, or helping your sister over at the school, you can head on out to make sales in Burlington, is that right?"

Shit. The school. I needed to get over there and start building the greenhouse I promised my sister. And Billy wasn't wrong. I didn't have time to shop the cheese and produce in town. I barely had time to harvest before things rotted on the vine.

"I'll figure it out," I bit out, the swirl of confusing feelings inside me threatening to explode.

We finished milking in silence, and I managed to keep my temper in check. "You going to mow today?" I asked Billy as I was leaving. We needed to harvest the alfalfa in the center fields before much longer.

"I might be old, but I can still drive a mower."

"I didn't say any different," I said.

"Only thing you haven't argued about so far today," he muttered. "I'll get it done, boss," he said, clearly annoyed with me.

"Okay," I said and headed for the truck. I had a shift at the Busy Bean and was already close to running late.

Billy was right. We needed help.

---

The line was out the door when I arrived at the Bean to find Audrey behind the counter, calmly chatting up customers and pulling drinks.

"You're on your own?" I asked her, looking around for Roderick or Zara.

"Roddy has the day off," she said, her tight voice giving away the tension she'd been feeling at running the place alone while I straggled in late.

I didn't waste time apologizing, instead, walked around the counter to the patrons waiting in line. "Anyone just looking for a drip coffee or something to eat?" I glanced up at the board over the counter, seeing that Roderick had made some of his onion quiche for the lunch crowd. "Sweet onion quiche and margherita pizza on the menu today," I added, knowing that Audrey liked it when we talked up the menu to the customers.

The line whittled some once I'd served the people not looking for complicated drinks, and Audrey relaxed a bit when things were a little more under control. I took over the Astra, and Audrey chatted with patrons as she served them.

I'd been working a couple hours when my sister came in the door during a slow spell, smiling brightly at me. She gazed around at the chalked sayings on the wooden beams and then frowned at me. "They let you write the motivational quotes now?"

"How do you know they're mine?"

"That Schwarzkopf thing. You've been saying it since you were fifteen. And this one"—she pointed to my latest addition —"'the only person you can really count on is you'?" She leveled a narrowed gaze at me. "Very pithy, Mase. Maybe you should add 'life sucks and then you die.'"

"Funny. I'll add that one tomorrow."

"No, you won't!" Audrey called from behind me.

My sister stood at the counter, smiling at me in a way I didn't like. I glanced behind her, hoping we'd get swamped again so I would have an excuse to avoid whatever it was she was dying to say. The shop remained quiet and calm.

"What?" I asked her.

"Is that how you take orders now?"

"'Melia," I said. "This is the first quiet moment I've had since four a.m. Just spit it out."

"Fine," she said, folding her arms across her chest. "Why didn't you tell me you had a girlfriend?"

I felt my mouth drop open. There were a lot of good reasons I didn't tell her. "Because I don't."

"Uncle Billy told me there's a woman *living* with you, Mason. Come on."

"There is. She's not my girlfriend. She's my best friend's little sister." That didn't sound as good out loud as it had in my head.

"Oooh, there's a romance novel waiting to be written," Audrey supplied from behind me, where she was organizing the display case.

That was what I needed. Both of them digging into my personal life.

"It's not like that," I said quickly, hoping maybe the vehemence in my words would make them convincing. Hoping I could convince myself. Images of the previous night washed through me—Heather in my arms, the scent of her flooding my senses.

"Hmm," Amelia said, squinting at me. "Well, I want to meet her."

"She won't be here much longer," I said, knowing it was pointless trying to hold Amelia off. It also occurred to me that Heather would like my sister and might need a friend. I sighed. "Fine, you can meet her."

She nodded as if she'd just won an argument. "Quiche and black coffee," she said, then added, "and when are you going to build my greenhouse?"

I plated her quiche and set it in front of her. "Soon. I'm sorry I haven't gotten over there yet. I'm running on fumes here."

Her face became sympathetic, and she tilted her head to one side. "I know. I'm sorry. I'll handle the markets this weekend, okay?" Farmers' markets were not my strong suit—but Amelia enjoyed them, and since she was off most of the summer, this was how we usually did things.

"Thanks," I said.

"And just let me know when you're headed to the school, and I'll help with the greenhouse too, okay? I can probably get some kids to help too."

That would definitely be good. I watched my sister settle into a table in the corner, happy to have her here, see her content.

## 11

# HEATHER

I had thought I could just go back home whenever I wanted. I'd thought everyone was overreacting.

But someone had broken into my apartment. What if I'd been home?

I'd been pushing away that particular thought since it happened. The police said they'd secured the door, but that hadn't stopped the guy before. Morgan had my extra key and had promised to swing by and see how bad things really were.

But the thought of going back now . . . I didn't know how I felt about it. I missed my life. But my old life had vanished in the span of a few months. I'd done the right thing, and now I was being punished for it.

Mason was already gone when I woke at four fifteen, and I suspected I knew why. As I collected eggs and tended some of the plants in Mason's greenhouse, Rascal trotting along faithfully by my side, my mind went back to the night before over and over again. When I closed my eyes, I could still evoke the sensation of Mason's arms around me, his hard muscular chest like a warm wall against my cheek, that scent of pine and coffee infusing my senses. I realized, as I thought back on those few moments when

I'd awoken to him holding me, that it was the safest I'd felt in months. Maybe years.

But as soon as I settled into the comfort of that feeling, another part of my brain raged a battle cry and rejected the idea that I needed any of it. I wasn't a damsel in distress. I didn't need saving. And I was tired of my brother and everyone around me believing anything different.

My mind went back and forth all day while Mason was at work, and by the time I heard a car pulling up out front—earlier than his shift was supposed to be ending—I was desperate for some kind of distraction.

It wasn't Mason who came up the steps to the door though. It was a woman. She knocked firmly on the door and smiled at me brightly when I opened it.

"Hi," she said, her wide smile setting me at ease immediately. "I'm Amelia, Mason's sister."

"Hi, I'm Heather Brigham," I returned, surprisingly happy for the company. "Come on in. It's nice to meet you." I pulled the door wide for her to step inside and silently marveled at the vast differences between Mason and his sister. She had dark shoulder-length hair and the same dark eyes Mason had, but her nose was scattered with freckles that made her look very young, where Mason sometimes looked much older than he could possibly be. Her face was unlined and rosy, and her smile stayed fixed in place, even as she stepped in and set her bag down on the couch. "Hey, Rascal dog," she said, kneeling to pet the dog's furry head and sink her hands in to rub the ruff around his neck.

"So," she said, standing to face me with a mischievous glint in her eye. "Let's grab one of my brother's beers and get to know each other. Mason told me you're going to be helping out on the farm."

I didn't feel like I'd been much help yet. I didn't argue, though, and handed her a glass of the beer I was coming to love as we moved out to the back porch where Mason and I had sat before. It was a little bit awkward, but Amelia had a way about her that told me it wouldn't last long.

"Mason told me you're a teacher," I tried.

Her face lit up. "I am," she said. "Third grade at Colebury Elementary." She practically glowed as she named the school.

"You seem to like it."

"Understatement. Yeah. Something about just getting to be with all those little minds, those little souls before they're jaded and loaded down with dogma and the media and whatever their parents believe. They're just like sponges, you know?"

I nodded. I remembered that feeling, that sense of wonder that kids could make you feel because they felt it.

"That's awesome," I told her. "I have a certificate too. I started out in a classroom in DC, but I had an opportunity to go work for a firm that was lobbying for education reform and I wanted to see if I could do more, work at the heart of the problems."

She nodded. "I know what you mean. Sometimes I feel so powerless when I see things happening, when I feel like the system isn't working for some kids."

"Exactly."

"So . . ." She glanced at me. "How come you're here?"

I laughed. "I guess I did kind of come out of nowhere, didn't I?"

She nodded, eyes widening.

For some reason, I felt comfortable with Mason's sister, and I let it all come flying out. I told her about the trial, about the threats, and about my brother. "So I'm out here because he swooped in to save me again, I guess."

"Again? Do you get saved a lot?" The question was asked lightly, jokingly, but it still struck a nerve.

"Unfortunately, yes. It's like a theme in my life, but one I'm trying to end."

"What do you mean?"

I sighed and leaned back in the sturdy wood chair. I realized that even if this wasn't my favorite topic, it was nice to have someone to talk to, and I liked Amelia a lot. "My dad pulled me out of a swimming pool when I was a little girl. Kevin and I were in the back of a friend's house while my parents socialized inside, and I fell into the pool. I was four, and I wasn't a great swimmer. I tried to get out, and Kevin tried to help. By the time he ran inside to get my dad, I wasn't conscious."

"Oh my god," Amelia breathed.

"So he basically brought me back from the brink. Kevin's been saving me over and over since then, even when I don't need him to. He kept me from getting hurt a million times as a kid, he beat up a guy I was pretty sure was about to rape me at a party in high school. I think he went into the Marine Corps because he had this idea that he could save more people, be the hero."

"Mason saved me once," Amelia said quietly.

I stared at her, not wanting to push her to say more than she was comfortable telling me.

She shook her head as if to clear it, taking another sip of her beer and leaning back in her chair. "So how long are you here?"

I shrugged. "Indefinitely, for now. Until it's safe to go home."

She looked at me sideways, and I realized that was completely vague. "So," she said slowly, a smile lifting one side of her mouth. "You can stay here, seduce my brother, and we can hang out."

I sputtered, nearly choking on the swallow of beer I'd just taken. "I don't think so," I told her. "I'm not in the market. At all." Men, as far as I could see, didn't tend to stick around. Maybe I was a little like Mason that way—I didn't want to get involved with someone who would probably just disappoint me or hurt me. My dad had broken my mother's heart, leaving her for another woman. And I'd been close enough to the senator to know that his scandal affected his wife and kids at least as much as it hurt him. I knew not all men were bad, but I hadn't met any I felt I'd be willing to trust. Not with my heart, at least.

"Well, maybe that will change."

We heard the door of Mason's truck slam shut, and Rascal, who'd been stalking through the yard, raced around to the front of the little house. A few minutes later, Mason stepped out onto the back deck.

"I see you've met," he said, his voice flat.

"We have, and Heather is delightful," Amelia declared, standing to face her brother. "You should not have kept her to yourself all this time."

He gave his sister an exasperated look, and then his gaze found mine. "How was your day?" His voice softened a bit, and I felt something inside me respond to the caring tone.

"Yeah, good," I said, getting to my feet.

"You staying for dinner then?" he asked his sister.

She looked at me. "In Mason-speak, that's a very cordial invitation."

We grilled some pork chops, and Amelia and I made a white bean and tomato salad with red onions and fresh oregano, and the three of us ate together. It was easy and comfortable, the closest thing to a family dinner I'd had in years.

"What are you doing this week?" Amelia asked as she was saying her goodbyes after the dishes had been rinsed and put away.

"My plans are pretty loose," I said, reminded suddenly that I didn't really belong here.

"Good. Let's have lunch in town. I'll show you around. Thursday okay?"

"Yeah," I said, feeling excited at the thought of having plans, of finally seeing the town where I'd be staying a while. "That'd be great."

Amelia frowned, glancing around the driveway as we walked her out. "Do you even have a car? How do you get around?"

I laughed. "I don't."

She shot a look at her brother. "Mason. You don't get a girlfriend by holding a woman prisoner."

He didn't respond, other than to huff out a breath.

"Uncle Billy has like three extra cars just sitting there. Why didn't you loan her one of those?"

"Oh no, I couldn't—"

"Of course you can," Amelia said. "Mason will take you over to get a car tomorrow. Won't you?" She poked Mason in the chest, and I watched him soften slightly as he looked down at his little sister.

"I honestly didn't even think about it," he said.

"Or you were trying to hold her captive until she fell in love with you," Amelia joked.

"Definitely not," he said, in a way that was almost too painfully clear.

As Amelia drove away, I pushed down the strange disappointment I felt at the knowledge that Mason definitely did not see me in any kind of romantic light. Not that I'd actually wanted him to, I told myself. And not that I was looking for anything anyway. My life was a disaster. The last thing I needed was a hot, grumpy farmer to turn my head upside down and then leave.

I went to bed early, intending to spend the next day at the farm. Billy had promised to teach me to make goat cheese, and I was oddly excited at the prospect.

# 12

# MASON

Heather was up and dressed in jeans and a long-sleeved T-shirt when I rose the following morning. She'd stated her intention to accompany me to the farm the previous night, and though part of me still wanted to protest, to keep the simple lines of my life straight and in place, another part of me was glad for the company.

I'd been doing so much on my own, I realized, and though I'd chosen that in a lot of ways, it had become lonely. Only, I hadn't identified the hollow feeling sitting heavily inside me as loneliness. It was nice to have an injection of life into my own predictable day to day, but I also couldn't help thinking about how much harder it would be to go back to my quiet isolation once Heather left.

"Billy's going to teach me how to make cheese after we milk," she said, smiling at me over the lip of her coffee cup. Her hair was tied up at the back of her head, though a few wavy pieces were springing free around her face, and her blue eyes shone as she smiled.

"Gird your loins, it's pretty heady stuff," I told her.

She put the cup down on the counter and stared at me in

pretend shock, her small pink mouth dropping open. "Mason Rye. Was that a joke?"

I filled my travel mug with coffee and turned toward the door, ignoring her jab. I knew I was serious and grumpy most of the time, but there wasn't usually anyone around to care. It annoyed me to find that something inside me cared what Heather thought. It annoyed me more to find that I wanted to make her smile, see her laugh.

"Let's go," I said, choosing straight and on task over any of the millions of other things I could have responded with—friendlier, gentler things. But there was no point letting myself become attached to her, to the friendly banter I knew we could have, to the simple comfort of company in the pre-dawn darkness. It was all temporary. She wasn't going to stay here forever.

Rascal was at my side as I picked up the truck keys, and Heather was right behind us, closing the front door as we stepped into the cool morning.

She smiled at the big brown dog next to her and wrapped an arm around his furry neck, planting a kiss on his head as I started out toward the barn.

That morning, milking felt like a completely different operation than the one Uncle Billy and I had been performing for the past couple years. Heather helped out, bouncing from place to place and bringing a lightness and fun to everything she touched. Her mood was contagious, and Uncle Billy laughed more than I'd heard him laugh in years. Even I found myself chuckling as she chatted up the goats while Billy milked them.

When the milking was done and the kids and goats were out in the pasture romping around, Heather rubbed her hands together expectantly. "Now we make cheese, right?"

Billy chuckled. "Wish you were this enthusiastic," he said to me.

"Come on," I said, smiling as I led the way into the room where we made the cheese. The bulk milk tank filled most of the far wall. "The milk can stay in here for a week or so," I said, pointing at the temperature gauge. "As long as it stays cool."

"But now it's time to heat it up," Billy said, starting the pasteurizer.

"You cook it?" Heather asked, looking extremely interested.

"We pasteurize it," Billy corrected. "Heat it to one hundred forty-five for about a half hour, then we cool it down to seventy-five."

"So there's not a whole lot to do for a bit," I pointed out.

Heather's face fell.

"There's plenty to do out in the yard," I told her. "Billy can come get us when the milk's ready."

She followed me outside and into the paddock where the kids were dancing around and jumping up and down the ramps and tires I'd put inside for them to play on.

"They're so silly." Heather laughed, watching one black and white kid jump on and off the ramp so fast I was surprised he hadn't fallen off yet.

"They are," I said. "It's good. Means they're happy."

"You worry about the goats being happy?" she asked.

I pulled out the hose and refilled the water trough as we talked. "It actually affects the flavor of the milk," I told her. "I want to do things right here, you know? It's important to me. So we take care of the land and the animals. And thinking about using sustainable practices and animal welfare are part of that."

"I love that," she said, smiling up at me in a way that made my chest feel tight.

We put out feed and swept up the paddock a bit, and then Heather helped me make the beds inside the barn by shoveling fresh straw and carting out what was soiled. For a girl who'd never worked a farm, I was impressed by the fact she didn't bat an eye at a single task I asked of her.

Soon, Billy called us back into the cheese room. "Ready for the magic?" he asked Heather, and it occurred to me that I hadn't seen him this gleeful in a long time.

"First things first," Billy told Heather, handing her a packet of freeze-dried culture. "Sprinkle this on top of this vat here."

Heather looked at the packet in her hand and then dutifully followed orders, sprinkling the culture over the top, where it sat on the surface of the milk, slowly rehydrating. After a few minutes, Billy handed her the stirring wand, and she mixed the culture in, sending it swirling beneath the surface.

The milk was beginning to thicken now, since we'd added the culture and rennet, and Billy brought over the cheesecloth bags we used for draining. We scooped the firming milk into the bags, and Billy and I showed Heather how we tied them to hang over buckets in the corner of the room. "This is how you separate the curds and whey," I explained.

"Like Little Miss Muffet," she said, and I couldn't suppress a chuckle.

"Right," I said.

"Come inside for coffee," Billy suggested when we'd finished, and we followed him to the farmhouse, where we each accepted a mug of steaming coffee and sat for a little while as the cheese drained.

Billy looked pleased to have company, and my heart twisted a bit, thinking about how much time he spent alone here in this big old house, and how quiet it must have been on his own. When my sister and I had joined him here, we'd been young and our aunt had been alive. The house had been full of noise and activity, a stark contrast to the dusty silence it held now.

"Cards?" Billy asked Heather hopefully.

They played Kings in the Corners for the better part of an hour while I excused myself to go check a few of the boards in the pasture fence I'd noticed needed repairing.

When we returned to the cheese room, Billy grinned at Heather. "Ready for the fun part?" He usually did so much of this on his own, and I could tell he was enjoying making it a party of sorts.

"Definitely!"

We squeezed the bags, draining the rest of the whey, and then turned out the curd into sanitized buckets, pulling on gloves before mixing the curd to a smooth consistency with our hands.

"This is so fun," Heather said, and I was surprised to see that she meant it. When Billy handed her the herbs to mix into one bucket, she watched with wide eyes as they were mixed into the cheese, dotting the creamy white product with studs of basil, thyme, and tarragon. "Smells incredible," she said, and a sense of pride filled me at her words.

It was a long morning, and we finished up by packaging up about half the cheese, scooping and weighing each tub before snapping the lids on.

Heather dove right into each task, following every instruction we gave her to the letter, always with a smile and a laugh. It was like having a ray of sunshine shining in our dark little world suddenly, and it was incredible to watch my uncle, who had been quiet and withdrawn lately, seem to spring back to life.

---

That afternoon, I dropped Heather back at the house, took a quick shower, and then headed into Colebury for a shift at the Busy Bean. I'd meant to pick up a car for her, but we'd spent longer than intended packing cheese, and I was close to running late. She waved off my apology and promised to head out to the greenhouse, where strawberries, oranges, lemons, and tomatoes were ripening faster than I seemed to be able to pick them. We were accumulating a large store of produce that would need to be sold this weekend, so it was a good thing we had a booth at the Capital City Farmers Market. It was the biggest market we attended, and though I hadn't secured a season pass to sell there, we had managed to get in for a few weekends this summer, and I'd planned my Bean shifts around those dates.

"Hey, how's it going, Mason?" Roderick asked as I tied on my apron and moved to the sink to wash my hands.

I glanced at him, trying for a friendly expression. I'd been working on the farm so long with Billy, this daily interaction thing was still new to me and still uncomfortable in some ways. But I liked Roderick, his easygoing nature, his enthusiasm, and his willingness to help me figure out how things worked around the Bean. "Pretty good," I told him.

He crossed his arms and leaned back slightly, his eyes narrowing as if he was evaluating me. "Something's different."

I glanced over my shoulder at him as I dried my hands. The shop was slow, which evidently gave him time to dig deeper into whatever he thought might be going on with me. "Nope."

"I'm very observant," he said. "It's a gift. And something's different. You're strangely cheerful today."

"Roderick, you've known me long enough to know I'm never cheerful."

He let out a laugh at that and shook his head. "Life is short, dude. Might as well enjoy the ride. Otherwise, what's the point?"

In a few words, he'd managed to puncture whatever good feelings I had held onto from that morning. Because he was righter than he knew. Life was short. People died. And there was no way to predict it or control it or stop it.

I sighed. "You're right."

He bumped me with his shoulder and then moved to the kitchen doors. "You okay out here? I have a couple more things to finish up in the back."

I looked around. There were a few regulars scattered at the little tables, Rita in her usual spot on the peach couch, but otherwise, the place was quiet. "I'll be fine."

He disappeared into the back, and I went to the big drip machine, noticing it was just about empty.

The shop remained quiet through most of my shift, and I spent most of my time cleaning things that were already pretty clean and organizing. Toward the end of the night, I picked up the chalk we used for the menu board and erased my Schwarzkopf quote.

In its place, I wrote, "Life's short. Enjoy the ride." I wrote Roderick's name next to it.

As we closed up, he glanced at the beam and grinned at me. "I always knew I'd be famous someday."

"Maybe you will be," I agreed. "But about that." I angled my head at his words. "I think you're right."

---

I arrived home to find Heather in the kitchen, chopping vegetables and talking to someone on her speakerphone. She heard the door and turned to look at me over her shoulder, and the smile she sent my way did something weird to my knees.

Off balance, I headed into the shower, both to give her some privacy for her call and to try to get a handle on the conflicting thoughts I'd been having all day.

When I emerged, I felt a little better. Heather was here for a short time, and yes, she was becoming really helpful at the farm and even here at the house. And yes, it was nicer than I thought it would be to have someone else in my space. But, I reminded myself, it was temporary. She needed my protection, not my attachment, and that's what I'd give her. Nothing more. Not that she was asking.

"How was the Bean?" she asked, hitting me again with that warm smile.

"Um. Good." I stumbled over my words, the glow of her skin and those dazzling blue eyes striking me speechless for a moment. Rascal pressed himself against my legs in greeting, and I reached down to pet him. "It was quiet today."

"I found this in the cabinet," she said, lifting a bottle of whiskey I'd had up there for a while. "I hope it's okay that I opened it. It's really good." She peered at the label again, frowning a bit at the image there of a disheveled looking cat with a wheeled contraption strapped to his rear half. "Half Cat?"

"Someone brought it to me. It's a little distillery in Maryland, I guess. They told me the cat is real. His name is Mr. Fluffy Knuckles or something."

"You're kidding." She laughed then, the sound bright and fluttering like butterflies of light dipping and spinning through the air.

I reached out to accept the glass she handed me, taking a quick sip. "Truth," I assured her.

"I made gnocchi," she said. "You had cauliflower and potatoes, and there was plenty of basil to make pesto. I added some of the walnuts I found up here."

"You're pretty resourceful," I said, enjoying the scent of basil and garlic in the air. Having her here was worlds away from my usual dinnertime rituals.

She shrugged as she sauced the pasta. "I like to cook, and I never really have time back at home."

I accepted the plate, moving to the table and sitting down. "This looks amazing."

"Thanks," she said, taking the chair across from me.

It struck me again how comfortable and natural it felt to have her here, and at the same time, that very thought set me to fiddling with my fork and clearing my throat nervously.

As we ate, making awkward talk about the farm, the coffee shop, and my greenhouse, I struggled to contain the unwanted emotions springing to life inside me. I excused myself right after dinner, helping clean up and then going to my room to read alone, to try to regain some of the contentment I'd felt in my solitude before Heather had come to stay.

Late that night, I went out to the living room again, tucking her in gently and lowering the volume on the television. This time, like the last, I couldn't help but linger a few minutes, my mind still spinning and twisting over itself. When Heather slept, I had the chance to really look at her, and tonight I felt a surprising sense of gratitude as I pushed a lock of hair gently from her forehead. Even though I'd been fine before, her presence had awoken something inside me. It was uncomfortable, and maybe it was even something I didn't want—but there was a chance Roderick was right. Maybe I'd been missing something all this time.

# 13

## HEATHER

I never planned to sleep on the couch. Every night I went to my perfectly nice room and tucked myself into the deep, soft bed, closing my eyes and even falling asleep there. For a little while. But inevitably, I'd find myself running in my sleep, chased by things I couldn't see or understand, but things that I knew with certainty would hurt me. I woke terrified and sweaty every single night, the dreams that had pursued me lingering with slavering jaws and burning eyes in the back of my mind. And then I knew I'd lie awake the rest of the night.

So each night, I'd wait for my heartbeat to slow, for my breath to come naturally, and then I'd creep out to the living room with my blanket and curl up on the couch with the television and Rascal to keep me company.

And each night, Mason would step out of his bedroom, his broad body shifting the atmosphere around us so that I could feel him nearby even if I couldn't see him. He'd lean down and tuck the covers close around me, lowering the television volume and then going back to his own room. I'd grown used to it, hoping each night he might take me in his arms again, that maybe next time I'd be bold enough to kiss him.

Last night he'd stood there a while, and softly pushed a piece of hair off my face. It had taken everything in me not to reach up to touch him, to pull him toward me, to take shelter again in the warm comfort of those sturdy arms.

But he didn't think of me that way. And the fact that I'd begun to notice little things about him—the way he checked on Rascal every time he saw him, offering a soft little rub, the way he gripped the back of his own neck when he was uncomfortable—was something I wasn't willing to think much about. Mason was hot. In an untouchable and off-limits way. I could only imagine what Kevin would say if I told him I was developing a crush on his best friend, the grumpiest goat farmer alive.

I needed to accept that to Mason I was mostly a nuisance, and I needed to continue to be as helpful as possible—to earn my keep, since he'd refused to let me pay rent. And I had to start formulating a plan to go back, to retake my life and rejoin the busy pace I'd kept for so many years before this crazy side trip to Vermont.

Amelia swung by Mason's house the following morning to pick me up, and I was excited in a way that surprised even me. I'd lived the last couple weeks essentially isolated in this little house. The idea of getting out, into a town—even one as small as Colebury was reported to be—was exciting.

We rode into town in Amelia's little Subaru, and she chatted happily the whole way about everything from the coming school year to her dating dry spell, which she said was beginning to feel like it was lasting centuries.

Colebury didn't have a lot of restaurant options, she explained, but she pulled into a parking lot in front of what looked like an old brick factory or mill.

"This place is called Speakeasy," she told me as we walked to the entrance. "It's got an amazing deck on the other side that faces the river."

We went inside the restored mill building, and I let my gaze wander through the space. Huge leaded glass windows filtered the afternoon sunlight, spilling it across rough-hewn, wide plank boards. The antique lighting and structural poles here and there gave the place a kind of funky, aged appeal that I loved. We followed the hostess out to the deck and ordered drinks to start. We spent a few minutes just enjoying the scenery as the river bubbled past and the sun dappled down through the tree branches.

"Is it tough to meet people here?" I asked Amelia as our wine arrived. "To date, I mean?"

She gave me an odd look over her menu and then whispered, "Why? You thinking of staying?"

I laughed. "No, of course not. My life is in DC. I meant for you."

She sighed and tilted her head to one side. "It is," she said. "I used to go to Burlington a lot with friends. You know, to fish in a bigger pool. But it's exhausting to keep putting yourself out there."

I thought about my own dating life . . . or complete lack thereof. "Yeah."

"What about you? Boyfriend?"

I felt myself roll my eyes, a habit I'd been trying to break. "Exes only," I told her. "I must have 'cheat on me' stamped across my ass or something because they always do."

She shook her head. "That really sucks, Heather. But you have to know not all men cheat."

I raised an eyebrow. That wasn't my experience. "That's kind of how I ended up here, actually. I think maybe it's just part of their DNA or something."

"The senator, you mean?"

"Exactly. I thought he was one of the good guys too."

"I hate that you think that. That you've had so many bad experiences you'd just write men off." She frowned and actually looked very sad about this.

"I mean, I'm ever hopeful," I quipped, feeling the jaded knowledge inside me prickle at the words. Was I hopeful? "I guess you just get enough examples of things being one way, and it's hard to see them any other way."

"There are plenty of examples of good relationships around though. It is possible." She sipped her wine and then grinned at me. "I'm reassuring us both."

"Thanks," I said, meaning it. "I haven't had a ton of examples of great relationships in my life. Mom and Dad were a mess, and then Dad cheated and left, and Mom died—my brother and I thought she'd died of a broken heart, actually. And when that's your first example, maybe it's hard to picture anything else."

"That's legitimately terrible," Amelia said, frowning. "But now that you're here, you'll see some really amazing couples. Have you met Zara or Audrey or Roddy at the Bean?"

I shrugged. "I haven't left the farm," I reminded her. "So if the great examples don't include Mason or Uncle Billy, then I haven't got much to go on."

"They do not," she assured me.

We ordered and chatted, enjoying the warm summer breeze wafting over the deck as the river gurgled and churned peacefully below us. It was a quiet and constant backdrop to our conversation, and it put me at ease in a way the noise and energy of Washington never had.

As we ate, Amelia asked me about my life in DC, listening carefully as I explained the education lobby I worked for, the constant rushing and drafting of memos, and optimistic legislation that occasionally got passed.

"It sounds exhausting," she said, and I laughed at her honesty.

But she wasn't wrong. "It is, actually," I said. "It funny though —until I left, I didn't even notice how tired I was. It's a little bit like coming up here and being forced to slow down woke me up a little bit."

"But you're definitely going back?"

"Yes," I laughed. "I have to. My entire life is there. I have a job and an apartment." As I said the words, I felt almost sad about them. It was true though, I had to go back. It wasn't like I could just hide here in the green, rolling hills of Vermont forever. This was not my life.

She traced a French fry through a puddle of mustard on her plate and then looked up at me for a second, as if trying to decide whether to tell me something.

"What?" I asked.

"It's just. I mean, you're going back to Washington, so there's kind of no point, but I'll tell you anyway."

"My curiosity is definitely piqued," I said.

"Well, you have a certificate, right? And you said you used to teach. There's a spot on staff at Colebury Elementary opening this fall. Fifth grade."

"That sounds so nice," I said. It did, actually. It sounded like a fantasy, and fantasies were definitely not possible in real life. "But I've got a million things going on in the city." Only, did I? Morgan had seemed fine with me taking as much time as I needed, despite the fact I knew we were heading into a busy season. And I didn't miss the hustle and churn of that life. At all.

I thought about leaving the farm, and Mason, and quickly pushed the thoughts aside. I definitely had to go back at some point. But I wasn't ready yet, and right now, Mason needed my help.

I told Amelia about the land conservation program I'd found through the state that might help Mason and Uncle Billy with some of the debt they were struggling under on the farm.

"That sounds incredible," Amelia said. "Did my grumpy brother agree to apply?"

"We talked about it once or twice," I told her. "But he's so busy, he said he didn't really have time to dig into it."

She nodded. "He's killing himself, and he thinks he has to do everything alone."

"Well, I'm helping out where I can, but obviously it's temporary. This, though," I said, thinking about the application I'd already put together for Garden Goat Farms, "this is something I could do pretty easily."

"It would be such a load off if they got it," she said. "So the state actually pays farmers to just . . . farm? They get paid to do what they're doing anyway?"

"It's a way for the Vermont Land Trust to help preserve land for things like farming and recreation. Basically, farmers sell their development and subdivision rights to pay down debt or add upgrades to their processes."

Amelia was nodding, her eyes bright. "Let's do it," she said.

I was thrilled at Amelia's easy agreement. "I need to get Mason to really understand it before I apply," I said. "And I need some financial information about the farm."

"I have all that," she said, surprising me. "I'm a third owner right now. And Uncle Billy's ownership splits between me and Mason. I help out when I can, but Mason understood that farming wasn't ever my dream." She swallowed a sip of wine. "So I'll get you whatever you need, and we'll submit the application right away. How long does it take?"

"I guess it can take a couple years," I told her. "But if you're selected, they sometimes let you know a lot sooner—it just takes a while to get the funding."

She nodded. "Okay."

"Okay," I said. "I just need a few things from you, and we can turn it in."

"I'll call you tomorrow when I've got my files together, and you can tell me what you need," she said.

As we finished up lunch, I was surprised to find that I felt happier and more confident than I had in a while. It might have been the excursion or the company, but I thought it was likely the sense of purpose I had now that there was something real for me to do here.

Amelia drove me back, but we didn't go straight to Mason's cottage. Instead, we drove to Uncle Billy's farmhouse, situated next to the barn and milking operation, and we went through to the workroom to help label the cheese for the weekend's market.

While we were working, Mason stepped in, his expression surprised when he found us side by side at the metal work table, pressing labels to plastic containers.

"Hey there," Amelia said merrily.

"I didn't know you were coming over today," he said. "I was just about to do that."

"Now you don't have to," she said. Then she looked at me and mock whispered, "Mason hates surprises."

Mason didn't respond to this but watched us for a few seconds, an odd expression on his face that was somewhere between a frown and a scowl.

"Your murder face is back on," Amelia told him.

"This is not a murder face. It's my natural expression," he argued.

"So sad," she sighed, and I laughed.

"Well, if you ladies have that handled, maybe I'll go take a nap." I doubted Mason Rye had ever taken a nap.

"I wish you would," Amelia said. "You work too much, Mase."

He dropped a hand on her shoulder then, his face softening. "I'm doing what I love, Amelia. Doesn't feel like work." They exchanged a look that made my heart twist a bit inside me—full of mutual admiration and affection—and I missed my brother for a second. But most of all, I missed having someone know me and understand me. Maybe I missed having someone looking out for me.

"You want to pick a car today?" he asked me.

"You make it sound like it'll be choosing between shiny new cars," Amelia told him, then turned to me. "It's basically a junk-yard of half-running beater cars."

"Anything that runs would probably be good," I said, excited at the prospect of being more independent. "You don't think Billy will mind?"

Mason shook his head. "Already talked to him about it. He loves the idea. They're just sitting there rusting. We need to sell them anyway."

"Okay," I said eagerly.

"You got this?" he asked Amelia, nodding at the label-placing operation we'd almost completed.

"I think I can handle it," she said, "Bye, Heather!"

I said goodbye, giving Amelia a hug, and I followed Mason out the door and around to the side of Billy's house to where a huge outbuilding stood. Mason pushed open a door to reveal four older model cars sitting inside, all of them in what looked like good condition to me.

"These are fantastic," I told him, wandering between a little blue Karmann Ghia and a pickup truck. There was also a Toyota sedan and a huge van. I smiled hopefully at Mason. "Think I could drive the Karmann Ghia? I've always loved these."

"If it's running you can," he said. "Be right back." He ducked out of the big space and returned in a few minutes, holding several sets of keys. He tossed me a set and said, "See if she'll start. I try to take 'em out regularly, but it's been a while."

I slid behind the wheel of the little car, not minding a bit that it wasn't plush and fancy like the new cars I'd been riding around DC in for the past few years. It was adorable, and after a few tries, the engine started right up.

I backed the car past Mason out the big door, and sat, engine idling, as he came out to lean in the window. "Will this work?" he asked me.

"Are you kidding?" I couldn't help the excitement in my voice. "This is basically my dream car."

A smile slid across Mason's face. It was brief, but it was bright, and it did something to my chest, making it tighten as my breath caught. God, he was gorgeous. "Then it's yours."

"Thanks," I managed to say, despite my racing heart.

"See you back at home?" he said, standing up and moving back a bit. "I've got a few things to take care of here."

Home. It was ridiculous how my already stuttering heart beat harder at the sound of that word from his lips. "See you there," I said, and I pulled the little car out onto the country lane that would take me to Mason's house.

I might have pretended—for just a brief minute or two—that the little cottage was ours. That we were together. That this was my real life.

But I knew it wasn't true.

## 14

# MASON

All afternoon I kept replaying Heather driving away from me in that car. It had been my Aunt Ivy's car—Billy's wife. As a teenager, I'd actually hated it—it was bright and fun, and my life at that time had felt dark and angry and cruel. But now, seeing Heather's glowing smile as she pulled the little blue car down the driveway—it had done something to loosen that ever-present tightness in my chest. The warmth had stayed with me as I'd finished up the chores on the farm.

I went home that night, thinking of that smile and even feeling a misplaced sense of pride that I'd put it there, that something I'd done had the power to make Heather happy. And she deserved to be, I thought.

But when I stepped through the door, I was met with a low whine from Rascal, and Heather was certainly not happy. She sat on the couch, her phone in her hand and tears running down her rosy cheeks. When she looked up at the sound of the door opening, her eyes were round and sad. My heart squeezed inside me.

"What is it?" I asked, moving to sit beside her.

She shook her head. "I should have known," she said, her voice thick with tears.

"I'm gonna need a little more than that," I said, pressing my shoulder into hers. I wanted to put my arms around her, try to take away whatever had made her sad and put the smile back on her face, the one she'd worn in my aunt's little blue car.

She sniffed and straightened her shoulders. "Sorry." She cleared her throat and then turned to face me, breaking the connection between our shoulders. "I haven't checked email or texts or looked at social media since I got here. I knew it would be bad. And I was so happy today, I just—I thought I could handle it."

"Bad how?" I asked. I didn't bother with social media and forgot about email except when I was making some arrangements for the farm.

She looked down at the phone in her hand and flicked her fingers across it a few times, then handed it to me.

A text message showed on the screen, the merry green bubble at odds with the hate-filled disgusting words within it.

"How do these people get your phone number?" I asked her, shock dropping my mouth open.

"I don't know," she answered miserably. "It started a few days before I testified. And they just get worse. I thought it would end when he was convicted, when the courts showed I wasn't making it all up, that there were other witnesses, other women." She shook her head. "Now I wonder if it will ever stop, if I can ever really go back."

A little thrill ran through me unbidden at the thought of her having to stay here, with me. But the reasonable part of me—and that was most of me—knew this wasn't the way she'd want to make an enormous life change. And that I wouldn't want her to stay only because there was nowhere else for her to go.

Surprisingly, I was growing more comfortable with the idea that I did want her to stay. But I chalked it up to loneliness and my own isolation. It had been nice having her here, that was all.

"It will die down eventually," I said, my voice far more certain than my mind. What did I know about Washington political scandals? "I'm sure soon someone else will get caught doing something terrible, and everyone will move on."

"But Senator Andrews's supporters seem like they'll never give up."

"Eventually, they will," I said, and my hand found her arm. I covered her smooth forearm with my palm, resting it there for a moment as both our gazes fell to that point of connection between us. I heard her take a quick breath as I touched her, felt her still beneath my hand. My own heart galloped suddenly with the contact, and a few seconds later, I pulled my hand away and stood awkwardly, trying to get control of my body. My cock had suddenly gotten ideas too, and I turned away from Heather, hoping she hadn't noticed. "I'm gonna get a quick shower," I told her and headed for the bathroom.

When I came out, having talked myself back into a more acceptable physical state, we made a quick dinner together—salad with greens from the greenhouse and grilled chicken. Neither of us spoke much, and there was a new spark in the air between us, something tight and tenuous that had us both edging around the other. We cleaned up, and Heather excused herself to go to her room, and I pushed down the strange twinge of disappointment I felt. I poured myself a glass of whiskey and took Rascal out with me to the back porch, where I watched the summer light fade above the treetops beyond the farm.

"What am I doing, boy?" I asked my dog, and Rascal got to his feet and laid his head in my lap, as if he understood my confusion.

I was having feelings for Heather—I could admit that much to myself at least. But what I didn't know was whether they were anything I needed to think about. Ridiculously, there were very few minutes during the day lately where I didn't think about her, and that hadn't happened since I'd had a crush on Melanie MacFarland in high school. But that had been schoolboy infatuation. This? Well, I didn't know what this was.

I sat out in the darkness for a long time, and I almost didn't hear it when Heather pushed the door open and moved across the wide planks to join me. She had the bottle and another glass in her hand. She raised the bottle toward me, her shadow visible in the light from the house against the near blackness of the moon-less night.

"Sure," I said, and she carried my glass closer to the light from the house to pour, then handed it back to me, taking the seat next to mine. Rascal moved from my feet to sit between us, letting out a little groan as he resettled himself, which brought a chuckle from Heather.

"What are you thinking about out here?" she asked.

Maybe the darkness made me bold, or maybe I was just no good at being confused and mixed up. "You."

She didn't say anything for a moment, and then her voice came softer. "Really? Why?"

I sighed and sipped my whiskey. What did I tell her? That I couldn't stop thinking about the way her blue eyes shone when she smiled? That her voice threaded itself through my thoughts, that her laugh was becoming my favorite sound in the world? That her presence here had brought a light into a life I'd forgotten was dark and lonely?

"I guess I'm just worried," I said, shoving aside all those things.

"About me?"

"Yes." And about me. About what would happen to me when she left.

"Mason," she said, and her voice was louder now, more direct. "What did you do out here before I came?"

"What do you mean?"

"I mean, now that I'm here, you work and come home. But you must have done other things when I wasn't here to worry about, right? Gone out with friends? Dated?"

I suddenly found that I wanted to tell her yes, that I'd done all those things. But I told her the truth. "Not really." I sipped my whiskey again. The darkness made it a little easier to be honest.

The burning heat of the drink helped too. "I guess I'm kind of a loner. And I'm busy, so there isn't a lot of time for that stuff."

"But don't you get lonely?"

"Maybe a little," I admitted, feeling like I'd just laid my soul bare for her to inspect.

"When was the last time you were in a relationship?"

I turned to look at her, but the darkness gave me little more than an outline at which to direct my surprised gaze. "Why do you ask?"

A light laugh escaped her, and she sipped her drink before answering. "You know almost everything about my life. I figured I'd learn a little about yours."

"I don't know when the last time you were in a relationship was," I pointed out.

"It ended a year ago. He cheated on me. So did my college boyfriend and my high school boyfriend."

"Shit."

"Exactly."

"Okay, well. The last girlfriend I had was probably Andrea Klein."

"Andrea. Okay. When was that?"

"We were together when I enlisted. And then she got fed up with waiting for me and moved away from Vermont while I was deployed the third or fourth time." For the best, really.

"Ouch." Heather was quiet a long moment. "Did you love her?"

"I was eighteen." I had been angry and headstrong. "I didn't know what love was."

"Do you now?"

I didn't answer, not sure what the answer actually was.

"That was a decade ago, right?"

"Yes."

She sucked in a breath, and I heard her move in the darkness, maybe turning to face me. "But you've been with women since then, right?"

"I have." I wasn't proud of it, though. One-night stands or weekend flings had been about all I'd managed since Andrea. "I just don't find that long-term relationships work out well in the end."

"If you do them right, I guess they don't end," Heather pointed out. "But I haven't mastered that part either."

"Also, this just isn't a life a lot of women would want to be part of," I said, thinking about it. "Goats and chickens, plowing and milking . . . it's kind of a hard sell."

"But then there's you," she said.

I waited for her to add to that. What did she mean? The part of me that longed for affirmation and acceptance wanted to hear whatever words she might put behind that. What about me? But she didn't say anything else.

We sat a few moments longer, listening to the night erupt around us in its quiet cacophony of animal, insect, and earth. And despite my loneliness, I knew this was something that I loved—this constant miracle of the land, of my home here. Maybe it was enough.

"Bedtime?" I asked her, rising. Though there wasn't much I expected could bother her here, I wasn't going to leave Heather sitting alone in the darkness. I had an unwanted thought about another dark night, about making a choice to stand by my sister instead of leaving her alone in the dark. I pushed it away.

"Yeah," she said, and the sadness in her voice wrenched my heart.

---

We went to the dairy together in the morning, and Heather stayed with Uncle Billy to make cheese as I threw supplies into the back of my truck and drove over to Colebury Elementary.

I had meant to dig in the walipini there in the spring, hoping to have it planted and producing by the end of the summer. But I'd had a lot of competing priorities, and sadly, things that didn't contribute to the bottom line had been shoved to the end of my list.

"Hi, big brother," Amelia said, turning to greet me as I made my way to the spot where we'd agreed to meet.

"Hey," I returned, handing her a stake and a mallet. There were two kids with her, scrappy-looking boys who grinned up at me unselfconsciously. They looked about eleven, so must have been former students of hers. "You brought some help, huh?"

"Mason," she said, "meet Eric and Jack. They're going to help us dig today."

"Great," I said, coaxing some false enthusiasm into my voice. These kids didn't look like they'd be much help, and I worried they might actually slow us down. Time was not something I had a lot of lately. "Well, the first thing we need to do is have Amelia —er, Miss Rye—hammer some stakes into the ground where she wants the corners of the greenhouse to be. Then we'll dig in the middle."

"Okay!" Jack burst out, his enthusiasm considerably bigger than the project at hand called for. He turned and ran to the edge of the blacktop, turning back to face us from a good twenty feet away. "How about here?" he asked.

I motioned for him to come back as Amelia laughed and handed a stake to Eric. When Jack trotted back to us, still grinning, I pointed to a spot a whole lot closer to where we gathered. "Jack, have you seen a greenhouse before?" I asked.

He shook his head.

"It's not going to be quite as big as a regular house," I told him. "Maybe about the size of a big garden shed."

His eyebrows climbed, and the other boy volunteered, "We have a shed."

"Okay, good," I said. "How big is it?"

"If you stand there," he told Jack, motioning him to a spot on the grass. "And I stand here," he said, stepping about ten feet from his friend. "It's about like this. And about the same the other way."

I nodded my approval.

Amelia hammered stakes into the ground where the boys stood and then again about eight feet from those stakes, forming a rectangle.

"Great," I said. "Now we dig in the middle. We'll put the dirt we take out into a pile on the side."

Luckily, the ground was soft and moist, at least until we got about three feet down. That's where the soil turned mostly to clay, and the boys weren't having much luck getting past it. I'd encountered the same hard-packed clay in my own greenhouse efforts and had resorted to bringing the little Bobcat over from the farm.

The sun was beginning to slide toward the horizon anyway, and I had work to do to get ready for the farmers' market in the morning, so I thanked the boys and began loading shovels back into the truck.

"Hang on a minute, guys," Amelia told Jack and Eric. "I need to pay you." She grinned and trotted back to her little car, digging inside for a moment. She returned with two paper sacks and money in her hand. She handed each kid a twenty-dollar bill and a sack, and their eyes were wide as they thanked her.

"See you later, Mr. Mason, Miss Rye!" Together, the kids raced off toward where two bikes lay on their sides on the blacktop.

"Good kids," I said when Amelia came to say goodbye.

"They're great," she said.

"What was in the bags?" I asked.

"Some goat cheese, a few apples, some rice, and a loaf of bread."

I felt my eyebrows rise. Amelia had told me that a lot of the kids she taught were struggling, and I knew there were probably folks barely making ends meet on the outskirts of Colebury, but it became real as I thought about Jack and Eric needing help getting food.

"I'm glad we're putting in the greenhouse," I said, a lump forming in my throat suddenly.

"Me too," she said, holding my gaze with her own, and I knew my sister saw what I felt without me having to say it.

"See you later?" I asked her, pulling her into a hug with one arm.

She wrapped both arms around me and held me tight. "Yes. Farmers' market tomorrow, right?"

"You don't need to come if you're busy," I told her. "Heather is really excited about it."

"Oh, she is, is she?" Amelia grinned at me as I released her from the hug.

"Don't do that."

"What?"

"You know what I mean."

"Fine. I'm happy to have my Saturday free. But maybe we can get this greenhouse going some more Sunday?"

I released her and nodded. "I'll bring the Bobcat over and finish the digging."

"Thanks, Mason." She grinned at me, and I watched her climb into her car and go. And for a moment, I stood in the schoolyard next to the giant hole we'd begun to dig and felt my heart fill.

But next to the happiness I felt at having done something good for my sister, at the closeness of the people filling my life suddenly, was fear. Because people—and life—were unpredictable. And enjoying having them near just set you up for the inevitable pain when they left.

## 15

## HEATHER

The farmers' market was amazing. For one thing, it was in Montpelier, and while it wasn't a big city—it felt like it, compared to Colebury.

Mason and Rascal and I had piled into his truck by eight and driven to the capital city, and I'd felt like a kid on a field trip the whole way, my eyes glued to the shifting scenery out the windows.

We arrived with a couple hours left to set up, and Bev, the woman who seemed to be in charge, directed us to our spot. Each vendor, she told us from beneath the brim of a floppy sun hat, had a ten by twelve space with a table and two chairs under a white tent. Any further personalization was up to us.

Mason pulled a dolly from the back of the truck, and I helped him load it with crates of cheese, oranges, strawberries, beets, and spinach, which we'd sorted into bags the night before. He also set up a cooler case, which I found the plug for along the back of the little tent space. Under the simple white tent, Rascal found a corner to lay down in, and Mason and I set to work arranging the wares on the table, which we draped with a simple white cloth.

"Do you have a sign?" I asked him, noticing that other

vendors had replaced the simple lettered sign provided with ones they'd brought featuring their logos and names.

He shrugged. "They always give us one."

I frowned at him as he continued shuffling produce around behind the table but decided to keep my thoughts about marketing Garden Goat's wares to myself. For now.

The market got underway quickly once ten o'clock arrived. Families and couples strolled the aisles, carrying reusable bags and dressed in shorts and hats. There were nearly as many dogs as people, and Rascal and I were both entertained by the wide variety of passersby.

Mason stood behind the table, and I suspected his gruff "hellos" might put a few people off. Because though I knew he was about ninety percent teddy bear, he sure didn't look it. He was broad and tall, his biceps bulging beneath the sleeves of the Garden Goat Farms T-shirt he wore. He was handsome—there was no doubt about that, and I definitely wasn't the only woman who noticed—but his intensity was always turned up to eleven, and it was a little much for a ten a.m. farmers' market.

I moved to stand beside him, smiling. "I have an idea," I said.

He looked down at me. "Go for it." He'd told me in the car that he really wanted to push his market strategy—go to more of these events and get the Garden Goat name out, and give people a place to count on finding his fruit and cheese. But right now, most people were walking right by after a glance at the imposing form behind the table.

"Sit down," I suggested, and though he gave me a quizzical look, he complied.

I opened a container of goat cheese, pulling a sleeve of crackers from the bag we'd brought. On a little plate, I arranged crackers with Mason's honeyed goat cheese on them, and then I stepped out in front of the booth holding it. Rascal seemed interested in my plan, and he moved to Mason's side, watching me around the side of the table.

Now I stood essentially in the increasing flow of traffic, and I put on my brightest smile.

"Hi there," I said, turning to a man with a child hoisted on his shoulders and a woman at his side with a bag clearly already full. These people were definitely shopping. "Have you ever tried Garden Goat's honeyed goat cheese? It's made just down the road in Colebury. This is the farmer right here," I said, gesturing at the handsome man in the booth behind me.

"No," the woman said, shaking her head and smiling. "I love goat cheese though. Can I try one?"

"Of course," I said, offering her the plate.

As she took a cracker, a few more people nearby seemed to be watching, and within minutes, I was offering samples to a slow-moving crowd, some of whom thanked me and moved on, but more of whom raised their eyebrows, smiled, and then moved to where Mason waited behind the table. I winked at him as he shot me a surprised look, getting to his feet to help all the customers.

I spent the next few hours offering cheese and oranges and talking about the farm's innovative use of geothermal energy to extend the growing season and produce fruit that couldn't be found many other places in the area. I explained the varieties of soft goat cheese Mason produced, and the farm itself, turning to Mason for facts when questions arose that I couldn't answer.

I loved every minute of it. I felt useful and alive, and engaging people in conversation came so naturally to me, it was like I'd just swapped out education reform for goat cheese and produce and was back in the swing of things. Being outdoors in this beautiful location, the fresh breeze off the river sliding by and taking the heat from the late June air as the sun warmed my skin, was an added bonus.

The Garden Goat booth was busy during the entire four-hour market, and though I exchanged a lot of smiles and nods with Mason during that time, we didn't get to talk again until we were folding the tablecloth and packing up our empty crates.

"That was like magic," Mason said. "We've never sold out completely before, even when Amelia is here."

The praise in his voice made me glow with satisfaction. I felt like I owed him something, and helping him realize success here was a start to paying him back. In the car, I pulled three business cards from my pocket and held them out for him to see as he drove. Rascal nosed at them and then licked the side of my face before settling with his head on my lap.

"What are those?" Mason asked, glancing at the cards in my hand and then back up at the road.

"Restaurant owners," I told him, hearing the smile in my own voice. "Looking to source local products for their restaurants. One of them manages a group of four farm-to-table restaurants from here to Burlington."

Mason's eyebrows went up, and he turned to smile at me. "That's incredible."

I nodded, feeling giddy. "I promised to visit them all next week and talk about how we can work together."

His smile drooped a bit. "I don't have time to do that," he said, sounding worried.

"That's what you have me for," I said. "I've been bored out of my mind. Now I can actually do something to help." I didn't mention that I'd also turned in the application to the Vermont Land Trust and hoped to have some initial feedback soon about the potential for an infusion of cash there.

Mason swallowed, his throat bobbing visibly as he frowned out the front window. But after a moment, he turned and looked at me, his eyes softening beneath the dark hair above his brow. "Thank you," he said, and his voice was low and gritty. "I'm not great at asking for help. But what you did today, what you've been doing . . ." He trailed off. "You're really incredible."

He delivered this last word while looking me right in the eye, and a pulse danced between us, filling the small cab of the truck with tension that felt like anticipation—like a bubble that would fill until inevitably it had to explode. Mason's dark eyes were pools of emotion, and I found my breath coming a little faster as I held his gaze.

"You're pretty incredible too," I said softly, meaning it.

We arrived home exhausted but happy, and after unloading everything, we'd each taken a shower. After an hour of gathering produce from the walipini and checking on the chickens, we fell onto the couch, Mason switching on the television and then handing me a beer.

"Good day," he said, touching the neck of his bottle to mine.

"It was," I agreed. "I really enjoyed myself," I told him.

"You were amazing," he said, shaking his head as he looked at me, the intensity in those dark eyes making my skin heat.

"Thanks," I said, pushing down the attraction I felt for him. "I'm just glad to be able to help out here. I know I'm in your way, that you never planned to have a long-term houseguest dropped into your lap. I'm getting up early tomorrow to help milk, okay?"

The room around us had begun to grow dark, the sun dropping behind the trees outside and casting the cottage in a late afternoon shadow that would give way to a cool summer night. The air felt charged, just like it had in the car, and I watched Mason's face as he processed my words or thought about his own.

"Heather," he said, catching my eyes and holding them with his own. "I didn't plan on having you here, that's true. But I'm starting to think some of the things that happen in our lives— some of the things we need—are things we don't go looking for. They just happen."

I was about to answer him when a voice on the television caught my attention. I snapped my head to look at it, seeing a newscaster and a photo of Senator Andrews in the corner of the screen. Fear and anger raced each other for a spot in the center of my chest. "That's him," I said, and I stood quickly and moved to turn up the volume on the television.

"The popular sophomore senator was recently convicted of several charges of sexual misconduct occurring during his last term in office," the newscaster said. "Multiple witnesses testified against the senator, resulting in his conviction, but now we're learning that the drama may not be over.

"According to sources, several of these witnesses have since suffered harassment and worse at the hands of some of the senator's more vocal supporters. We've had reports that at least two of the women who testified against Senator Andrews have left their jobs and fled the city, while another was physically assaulted in a parking lot after work. The senator's lawyer noted that Senator Andrews doesn't condone these acts and assures us that his client would request that his supporters stop their actions and allow the city to move on and heal."

The newscast moved to another topic, and the photo of the senator disappeared, and I reached out, turning the television down again, uncertain how to feel.

"Think that will help?" Mason asked.

I took my seat next to him again. "I don't know. I guess it can't hurt." I sipped my beer, my mind spinning. "Someone was actually assaulted." My heart ached, thinking about the poor woman.

"Yeah, I heard that," he said, and one of his big hands landed on my shoulder, the warmth and solidity of it comforting. His thumb rubbed a little arc over the top of my collarbone, sending chills skittering through me. "You're safe here," he said, his voice almost a whisper. "You know that, right?"

The combination of his warm hand and his low, gentle voice calmed my nerves and wound through me, and without thinking, I moved closer to him. His hand slid down my back as I leaned into him, and I gazed up into the dark softness of his eyes. Time seemed to stretch and suspend as he lowered his head toward mine, slowly, carefully.

Our mouths were just centimeters away from one another, and while a little part of me was busy throwing out cautionary guidance, a much larger part was caught in the moment, pulled toward Mason by a force I no longer had the energy or desire to deny.

I tilted my chin up a fraction, and in the next second, his soft lips met mine and held there, unmoving for a moment. But then his arm tightened across my back, and I felt myself give in completely, my arm sliding around his neck as I moved closer on the couch. The kiss deepened, our mouths plying and seeking, until Mason reached around me to set his beer down, and then his other hand found my waist, and he shifted me onto his lap.

My legs fell to either side of his, and I pressed myself into his chest as his tongue teased my bottom lip, sending a shiver through me. Our centers were aligned, and I pushed against him as my tongue met his.

A low groan came from somewhere inside Mason's chest, and I felt it rumble through me, goading me on. I tilted my head, and Mason responded hungrily, his kiss becoming demanding, insistent, hungry. I could feel the solid length of him as I straddled him, and I ground down, seeking the pressure and sensation that would eventually lead to release.

Mason's hands slid up beneath my T-shirt, and the warmth and roughness of his palms against my skin ratcheted my desire to another level as I let my own hands play with the soft hair curling at the back of his neck, feel the rough stubble of his jaw.

The kiss went on for what felt like hours, and it was both rough and careful, demanding and polite at turns.

But I knew it wasn't right. I'd wanted Mason almost since I'd seen him, but he hadn't come looking for me. I'd been forced on him by my overprotective brother, and now here I was, forcing myself on him in another way. His hands held my waist firmly as his mouth explored mine, and then kissed and licked its way across my jaw.

God, it all felt so good. But it couldn't happen. I took a deep breath and slid from Mason's lap, out of his grasp.

My chest was rising and falling rapidly, and I knew I needed to say something, to explain myself. But words weren't coming to my lust-addled brain. Only embarrassment. I'd basically climbed on my host and molested him—given into my ridiculous crush when he'd given me little indication he was interested. I'd basically taken advantage of the situation, and now I didn't know what to do.

"I'm sorry, I—" I stood, unable to meet his eyes.

"Heather, wait."

"No, I shouldn't have done that. I think . . . I'm just . . . I'm going to go to bed." I turned and closed myself in the little bathroom, splashing water on my flushed face as I tried to make sense of what had just happened.

We'd had a great day, and my desire for Mason had only deepened as I'd seen how grateful he was for my help. But I'd allowed it to get out of control, mistaking gratitude for something else.

But his hands had been on me, I remembered now. He hadn't pushed me away. And he'd responded—I felt the iron rod in his jeans as I'd pressed myself against him.

But he was a man. Of course he'd respond when a woman basically threw herself at him, right? And even if there was the potential for any mutual interest—what in the world did I think I was doing? I didn't live here. I had no right to start something with a man who was pretty clear in his desire for solitude and the simple life he'd built. There was no place for me here. And the last thing I needed was another man leaving me.

No. This couldn't happen.

I sighed, brushed my teeth, and left the bathroom, intending to say something to Mason, to explain myself if I could. But he wasn't on the couch when I walked back into the living room. I stood there for a long moment, looking at the spot on the couch where I'd basically jumped him, then turned and went to bed.

# MASON

I didn't sleep.

Historically, I didn't sleep well anyway. I guess that happened when you lived with guilt for most of your life. My sleep was generally something closer to the exhaustion that came as a result of pushing myself through hours of manual labor so that when I lay down, my body had no choice but to turn off, and my mind often followed.

But this time, I didn't sleep for entirely different reasons.

I'd slipped. I'd reacted to the fear and vulnerability I'd seen in Heather's eyes—along with my intense attraction to her—and I'd slipped. I'd pulled her into my arms and kissed her, allowing myself to act on the drive I'd been pushing away almost since the moment she arrived here.

And if I'd thought finally kissing her would help to staunch the desire I felt for her . . . well, that had been a moronic idea.

Instead, I'd spent the night reliving the way she'd felt in my arms, all softness and light. She was fragile and small but so full of energy and life—holding her was like catching a contradiction between my palms. And kissing her was the closest I think I'd ever come to actually losing my mind. From the moment our lips had touched, I could feel one world sliding away as something entirely different took its place. My daily life, full of goats and guilt and loneliness, became a sunny plain washed with sunlight and hope.

And then she'd pulled away and apologized.

That was the part I struggled with all night. Why had she apologized to me?

I had thought through every possibility.

I knew that I had not taken advantage of her. Yes, I'd put my hands on her first, but I hadn't misread the desire in her eyes or the way her body had pressed itself against mine. I was a master of feeling guilty, and this was not another thing to add to my load. The kiss had been consensual.

So why the apology?

I could only take a guess at what might be going through Heather's mind. She was frightened, I knew that. Her life had exploded around her, and she'd ended up here. And maybe I hadn't been very welcoming at first. And that message had probably stuck.

That was why this morning I'd gotten up early enough to make the little egg, ham, tomato, and goat cheese muffins I'd perfected and had them steaming on the counter next to a pot of coffee when Heather rose—true to her word—to help with milking.

"Good morning," I said, trying for a light tone. I needed to work on being more welcoming, less gruff. I tried to rearrange my resting murder face into something lighter—like resting vandalism face or annoying banter face.

"Hey," she said, not meeting my eyes. She wore a pair of jeans and a light blue long-sleeved T-shirt that looked soft. My hands itched to hold her again.

"I guess you were serious about milking," I said. "I made us something we could take in the car." I pointed to the egg cups.

"Wow, these look amazing," she said, pouring a cup of coffee, still not meeting my eyes. "Listen, Mason," she said. "I really screwed up last night. I crossed a line, took advantage—"

"I'm going to stop you there." I was glad we were going to address this, discuss it.

For the first time since she'd been in my arms the previous night, Heather met my gaze. Her blue eyes were wide, but a wrinkle of confusion appeared between her brows.

"I've been wanting to kiss you almost since you got here. I'm not the kind of guy who's going to try to weigh out if that's right or wrong. It just is. So there was no reason I can see for you to apologize about it to me. Maybe the other way around. Do I owe you an apology?"

She shook her head.

"Did I take advantage of the situation last night?"

"Not at all." Her eyes dropped. "I wanted to kiss you too."

The flickering little flame inside me glowed brighter, and I blew out a relieved sigh. "Okay. Then no more apologies, okay?"

She glanced up again, relief easing her features. "Okay."

"Let's go take care of the goats, and then I wondered if you might like to go into town. It's not huge, but there are a few shops, and if you liked the Goldenpour, we could go grab some more and taste a few of the other local brews at the Speakeasy. I just need to get over to the school before sundown with the Bobcat to finish digging." I hoped that if we were going to give in to whatever this was between us, maybe I could try to do it right. Plus there was less chance of me hauling her to my bed if we went out.

"That's where your sister took me for lunch," Heather said, her eyes lighting up. "It's so cool. I'd love to go there again."

The flame inside me burned a little brighter at the thought of spending time with Heather away from the farm, away from the house.

We went to see the goats and got through milking in record time, despite Heather's insistence on playing with the kids out in the pasture. The babies were pretty cute, I could admit, and goats enjoyed attention. Heather ran around the pasture with them, laughing as they chased her and butted their little heads up against her legs, bleating as they did it.

Uncle Billy watched all this with amusement and clapped me on the back as I asked if he thought he could handle the second milking on his own that afternoon.

"Mason, you go do whatever you have in mind," he said, shooting me a smile I was glad Heather didn't see. "If I was your age, I'd be trying to get that one in the sack too."

I elbowed him gently in the ribs, shaking my head. "It's not like that."

"Like hell, it's not," he said, elbowing me right back.

---

Heather and I went into town in the little Karmann Ghia she'd been driving. She said it was a more appropriate day-tripping car than my big ancient truck. She was probably right, and letting her drive allowed me the opportunity to watch her surreptitiously. She smiled as she drove—not an all-out grin, but a vague lift of the corners of her pretty pink lips.

"I love driving down these country roads," she said, glancing at me as we followed the winding pavement through the dappled sunlight toward town. "I feel like I'm flying. It's so different from driving around the city."

"Did you have a car in DC?"

She shook her head. "No, there'd be no real point. I Ubered or took the metro. I hardly ever left the city."

I nodded, though I really couldn't imagine a life like that. "I don't think I could live in a city," I mused aloud. "I'd feel penned in, kind of claustrophobic with all the buildings and concrete, I think."

"So you've been on farms in the country your whole life, huh?"

"Except when I was in the military, yeah. That's the only place I've really spent much time in a city. And in the cities we were in, there were a hell of a lot of explosions. Hopefully DC isn't like that."

"Not usually," she said, and her brow scrunched a bit.

"You worry about Kevin?" I asked her, pointing left at the fork in the road that would take us into town.

"All the time," she said.

"Would it make you feel any better if I told you that actual combat is about ninety-five percent waiting around in sheer boredom and only about five percent adrenaline and fear?"

"Not especially."

"Okay. Maybe we'll just change the subject then."

She glanced at me and smiled in a way that made my heart turn over in my chest.

"Speakeasy is just over there," I said, motioning to the parking lot just past the Busy Bean where the old mill building sat on the river's edge.

"This is such a cool location," Heather said, parking in front of the large brick building. "And I love the history of the place."

We got out of the car and walked to the front entrance of the building, my hand falling naturally to the small of Heather's back as we stepped inside. I got a strange thrill from the feeling of standing beside her at the hostess stand, seeing the eyes of other patrons register that we were here together.

Prior to Heather's arrival, the only time I really hung out in town was with Amelia, so anyone who recognized me certainly noted the change. I prepared myself for some questions about her next time I worked at the Bean.

We opted to sit outside on the patio overlooking the river, but the hostess walked us through the space first, because Heather asked about the brewing operations.

"We do make some of the beer here," the hostess said, indicating the huge tanks set to one side of the space behind a glass window. "And we're hosting more and more events," she went on.

As we moved to the doors on the other side of the bar, the hostess stopped us, her eyes huge. "Do you feel that?" she asked, crossing her arms over her chest.

"It's chilly," Heather agreed.

"But only right here." The hostess shivered. "It's Hamish."

We headed outside, and the warm air blowing in from the patio was welcome. It was cold inside suddenly. "Hamish?" I asked walking to the table she indicated. I pulled out Heather's chair and then took my own seat.

"Our resident ghost," she said, a gleam in her eye.

"Of course," I said. Ghosts were not on my list of things to believe in. There were enough terrifying things in the world that I'd seen with my own eyes and touched with my own hands. I didn't need to add any more.

The hostess left us, and we sat back in our chairs. I closed my eyes for a few seconds, enjoying the sun on my face.

"Mason?" I sat up straighter, surprised to find Audrey standing next to the table, smiling down at us.

"Hi, Audrey," I said, returning her smile. "Heather, this is Audrey. She's my boss over at the Busy Bean."

"Hi," Heather said. "Such a cute place. Mason's sister took me in when we were in town."

"Oh, thanks," Audrey said, looking between us, and I could see that she was making assumptions about our relationship as she smiled at us.

"Heather is one of my best friend's sisters," I said, realizing too late that it didn't explain anything and seemed like a really awkward interjection.

"Oh," Audrey said, her eyebrows climbing a little, probably connecting this to her earlier romance-novel suggestion when I'd been at work. "Well, it's nice that you could visit," she said. "Are you in town for a while, Heather?"

"I'm not sure," Heather said. "At some point, I will need to go home to Washington DC, but it's hard to leave all this."

Audrey grinned at that. "Well, don't be a stranger," she said. "I'll let you enjoy your lunch."

"See you at the Bean," I told her.

She smiled and gave me a little salute before heading back to her own table on the other side of the patio. Now I knew there would be questions later.

When the server arrived, we each ordered a tasting flight of beer.

I watched in amusement as Heather systematically sipped each one, her forehead wrinkling in concentration as she compared.

"Do you need a notebook or anything?" I reached for the one I usually kept in my pocket.

She put down her little glass and tilted her head to one side. "Making fun of me now?"

"No, it's cute how serious you look about tasting beer."

"That's the point, isn't it?"

I shrugged. "I was just going to drink them."

"Which one do you like best?" she asked. "You need to know."

"I like beer," I told her. "So they're all pretty good."

She shook her head. "Don't drink them. Taste them. That's the fun of it. Then we can compare."

"Fine." I liked her focus, so I sat forward and made a show of sipping each one. "This one," I said, putting down the first glass. "Tastes like beer."

She frowned at me, waiting.

"And this one," I noted after sipping the second glass. "Also tastes like beer. Different beer. But still beer."

"You're ruining this." She was grinning as she said it.

I laughed. "Okay, you tell me what you taste."

She straightened up. "Okay," she said, picking up the first glass of amber ale and tasting it. "This one is wheaty and light. I taste honey."

I raised an eyebrow.

She lifted the second glass. "This one is really hoppy. Not my favorite."

"Impressive. Hoppy. That's a good beer word."

She made a face at me. "This one," she said, lifting a much

darker glass. "Is my favorite. I taste chocolate, and it's a little bitter but pretty well balanced."

I picked up my own dark ale and tasted it. "I do taste chocolate now that you mention it."

"See?" she asked, grinning like she'd just won some kind of victory.

"So now can we just drink them?"

She sighed and sank back in her chair. "Fine." But then she laughed and leaned forward again. "It's fun giving you shit."

"Is that what you were doing?"

"Yes. You're so serious all the time."

"No, I'm not."

She raised her eyebrows at me as if to say, "Really?"

"I'm serious when the situation calls for it."

"You were super serious this morning when you were attaching suction cups to goat tits."

"Milking is serious business."

"Think about it, Mason." She pressed her lips together, but after a second, she broke into a laugh, unable to maintain the serious expression on her face. "You squeeze goat boobs for a living."

A chuckle escaped me before I faked indignance. "I do not. I'm a farmer."

"Who fondles goats as part of his responsibilities."

"That just sounds wrong," I told her.

"I know," she said, laughing.

"Okay, but the rest of the operation is pretty fucking serious."

She nodded, making a mock serious face. "Right."

"I am serious a lot," I began, and Heather met my eyes, her smile wide.

"Part of your charm," she quipped.

"Probably not super charming most of the time."

"You probably have your reasons for being so serious. You have a lot going on."

I wondered what she knew, whether she knew the biggest reason I wasn't a fun-loving, carefree guy. "Maybe, yeah."

We sipped our beer and eventually ordered food, making small talk about the farm, the markets coming up and even geothermal farming. The more I talked to her, the more I relaxed. And oddly, the way the sun glinted across the deck, the way I felt being with Heather, had me wishing for her to really know me, to really understand me.

She kept smiling, and I took a deep breath, wanting her to know about my past, about who I was. "Did Amelia tell you about our parents?"

Her smile faded, her eyes widening slightly. "Only that they died," she said. "So you came to live here."

I nodded. "They did," I said.

"I'm so sorry." She didn't say anything else, and I sucked in a breath, finding myself wanting to tell her everything. To tell her things I rarely spoke of, even with my sister.

"It was my fault."

She shook her head lightly. "What do you mean?"

I took a deep breath, the guilt I felt pressing outward against my lungs. "Our house caught fire. They think it was some kind of wiring in the walls."

"That wasn't your fault, Mason," she said, smiling.

"Not that," I said. "But I could have saved them. And I didn't."

Heather took a deep breath, waiting for more. I steeled myself and continued, pushing down the pain that came with the memories.

"We were asleep," I began, doing my best not to relive it as I spoke. "I was fourteen. I hadn't been in bed too long, so maybe I wasn't sleeping deeply. I don't know. But when I woke up, I heard something, and I smelled smoke." I squeezed my eyes shut hard, then opened them, going on. "I pulled open my door, and the fire was everywhere—climbing the walls, on the ceiling of the hallway."

Heather's eyes held mine, and she sat stiffly, listening.

"I climbed out the window. I didn't know what else to do. My sister's room was right next to mine, and my parents' was around the corner. I completely panicked. I ran between them—wasting time, basically. I thought if I woke up my parents, they'd know what to do, so I banged on their window, hoping they'd wake up. But they didn't answer, and I couldn't see them—the room was full of smoke. I broke the glass with a rock, hoping maybe it would let the smoke out. But when I'd looked into the hallway, the fire had been everywhere, covering their door. I knew about smoke inhalation, and didn't know if maybe it was already too late, and . . ." I trailed off, took a long gulp of beer.

"Mason, you don't have to tell me," Heather said, reaching across the table and laying a hand on mine.

I went on. "I wanted to go in, to get them out," I said. "But my sister was so little, and I knew she'd be terrified. I told myself I'd have time to go back. I knew my dad would tell me to help my sister, so I did. I climbed in her window, forcing it open. She was asleep, but I woke her up, and I pushed her out the window. By then it sounded like a freight train roaring down the hallway outside."

"Oh god, Mason." Heather's voice broke.

"When we got outside, I pulled her to the road, and we didn't look back until we were standing there, and by then the flames were everywhere. I was going to go back, but Amelia . . . she wouldn't let go of me. She was crying and terrified, and it was dark. We lived out in the country. There were coyotes and mountain lions . . . " I looked up and found Heather's eyes full of tears. "I had to choose," I told her. "I let my parents die in that fire."

"You were a kid," she said softly. "God, Mason. You were just a kid."

## 17

# HEATHER

I wiped my eyes and took a deep breath. My heart squeezed in my chest for the choice that fourteen-year-old boy had made, to protect his terrified sister, to keep her from danger. An impossible choice, knowing maybe there was a chance he could have saved his parents too.

"Mason," I said quietly, squeezing his hand. His eyes were bright, blazing, almost as if he was daring me to take in what he'd told me and stand up to walk away. He was watching me as if he expected judgment, blame. "You were a kid. It was a horrible tragedy. But it wasn't your fault."

"I might have saved them."

"If you'd gone back in, you might not have come out again. What would Amelia have done then?"

He shivered despite the hot afternoon sun, and I took a deep breath, understanding so much more suddenly about what kind of man Mason was. Why he was so intense, so closed off.

"I shouldn't have brought it up," he said, rubbing a hand over the back of his neck. "Kinda killed the mood, I guess."

"No," I said, but it was a bit of a relief when he let go of my hand and sat back, lifting another of his tiny glasses to his lips and drinking. I did the same, and after a few moments, the intensity of the story had faded, the day had washed back over us, soft and light. And eventually, we laughed again.

As Mason and I sat in the early afternoon sunlight on the back patio of the Speakeasy, it was easy to forget my embarrassment over the night before. I felt close to him as we shared a couple appetizers and talked of lighter things.

I found myself enjoying this version of Mason.

Don't get me wrong, I was wildly attracted to the stern, serious guy who seemed to want to protect anyone he thought might need it. I loved the way he concentrated when he was working at the farm, and the intensity with which he approached pretty much everything was compelling. But this man—this broad, dark-haired, handsome man laughing across from me at the table over a row of tiny beer glasses—was something else.

When he smiled, dimples appeared in the stubbled cheeks, and those deep ebony eyes glowed with fun.

His laugh was rich and hearty, and warm. And I wondered for a moment what Mason would have become if his parents hadn't died in that fire, if he hadn't spent his life trying to make amends for something that wasn't his fault.

There was something so deeply rewarding about having brought out this lighter, more carefree side of Mason too.

And despite my earlier embarrassment about it, my mind kept wandering back to the night before. To the kiss. To the way my body had ignited as he'd touched me, held me. All that intensity had been directed right at me, into me, and it was heady.

"If you were back in DC right now, what would you be doing?" he asked me at one point as we sat soaking up the sun and sipping our beer.

I thought about that. It was Sunday, so I wouldn't be working. "I guess it depends on if we're talking about before or after the trial," I said, remembering recent Sundays when I'd holed up at home, doing my best to be invisible and small, to hide.

"Let's go with before." He was watching me intently, waiting for my answer, and I felt it again—the thrill of being the focus of this man's singular attention.

"I'd probably be out and about," I said, thinking back to what the previous summer had been like. "I used to really embrace the whole work hard, play hard thing. So I'd probably go to the gym in the morning or for a run around the Mall if it wasn't too crowded out there. Then I'd spend the rest of the day with friends."

"Doing what?"

"Honestly? Doing something like this, I guess." I glanced around the big, wide patio, and for the first time in as long as I could remember, I felt content. Not scared, not worried, not tired. Just content. "I didn't have a huge circle of friends," I went on. "But we were pretty devoted to each other. My boss, Morgan, and his husband, Sam, were my two best friends, probably. And there was a girl I used to teach with who would hang out with us sometimes, but she got married a few months ago." I hadn't gone to the wedding, which had taken place just a few days after the trial ended, when Andrews's supporters were at their most vocal.

"You're talking about your life in past tense," Mason said.

"I am?" I hadn't even noticed.

"You are. But I can attest to the fact that you're living it in present tense."

"That's good," I said, my mind rolling over that idea. "I guess I sort of feel like my life in DC is past tense."

Mason's eyebrows climbed toward his dark hairline. "What do you mean?"

I shook my head, letting out a little sigh. "I'm just not sure it will ever be like it was. I'll go back, but I can't imagine walking around the city now or going for a run without being afraid someone will step out into the path to scream at me. Or worse."

"That's not going to go on forever. It can't."

He was right. "But still. It's almost like it's all tainted by that. Like all the places I used to love have lost their shine."

He pressed his lips together for a moment as he watched me

and then picked up a glass and drained it. "You don't have to go back."

"Of course I do. I have a job. I can't just stay away indefinitely."

"Isn't that what you're already doing?"

"Well. Yeah, but I do plan to go back."

"Or maybe you don't."

My stomach twisted over itself, and I wasn't sure quite what he was saying. His face had returned to its usual serious mask, and those dark, penetrating eyes gave nothing away.

"I'm not suggesting you stay here," he added, just as I'd begun to think that was exactly what he was suggesting. "You could go anywhere."

"Right." I could definitely not go anywhere. The idea of moving to some distant unknown city sent a shiver through me. "I don't think so."

"I'm just saying, you've got marketable skills and experience. Especially now that you know how to milk a goat." The tiniest hint of a smile pulled at one side of Mason's mouth, and I felt the heaviness that had settled over our table lift.

"That'll take me places."

"Definitely."

We were silent a few minutes, each of us focused on the thoughts circling inside our own heads. I was relieved he hadn't suggested I stay here—I could definitely not do that. People didn't run away from their realities forever. Especially not to tiny towns and goat farms in Vermont. The strange thing was, even as I considered how ludicrous it was, part of me wanted to live in that little fantasy for a while. What if I could get the teaching job Amelia had told me about? What if I could build a new life here?

The rush of the water in the river and the fathomless blue of the sky felt comforting, welcoming. And the man sitting across from me was intriguing too. I could imagine a life where I lived to make Mason Rye forget his serious side, where days were spent rewarded by his gorgeous smile or that deep rolling laugh I'd heard once or twice now.

But that was all just a fantasy, and I knew it.

"Grab a coffee and head back?" Mason asked me.

I hated to end what had been the nicest day I'd had in months, but I knew he had work to do. Mason always had work to do, I was quickly seeing.

"Sure."

Mason left some bills on the table, refusing to even let me leave a tip, and we went out to the parking lot together, agreeing silently to walk over to the Busy Bean.

The sun beat down on us, and I was able to linger in the warmth flooding me inside and out a bit longer. Mason pulled open the door of the Busy Bean for me, and I stepped inside, where I was hit immediately by the rich scent of coffee layered with the smell of baking cookies.

"I'd gain forty pounds working here," I said, stepping up to the glass case displaying quiche and cupcakes, cookies and bagels.

"It's a hazard for sure," Mason agreed.

Behind the counter, a dark-haired woman smiled and addressed Mason. "Just can't get enough of us, huh, Mason?"

He smiled at her. "Hey, Zara. Yep, guess I can't stay away." He turned to me, stepping back a little to include me in the conversation. "Zara, this is Heather."

Zara's warm smile turned on me, and there was a long beat of silence before she said hello, like she was putting things together in her head. I knew that Audrey had assumed we were a couple as we sat out on the restaurant patio, and now I could see Zara jumping to the same conclusion. It'd be easy enough to believe that a guy like Mason had a girlfriend he'd never mentioned. He didn't make small talk easily.

"It's so nice to meet you, Heather," Zara said. "Mason's been getting us all on track around here since he started working."

I laughed. "What do you mean?"

"Efficiency," Zara said, her face taking a serious cast. "He's got us running the place like a well-oiled machine. Like a tank or something."

Mason shot Zara an amused look. "A tank?"

She shrugged. "It's actually been great. He's got some good ideas, and things are going a little more smoothly now that we've installed the hot water tap and the rapid order system back here."

"That's great," I said, glancing at Mason, who looked bashful suddenly.

"What can I get you guys?" Zara asked. "Roddy made some fantastic artichoke and spinach pizza today, and I think we've got one left."

"That does sound good," I said, though I was full from the food we'd had.

"Just a black coffee for me," Mason said, turning to look at me.

"Tea?" I asked, and Zara pointed at a selection behind the counter. "Orange spice, please."

As Zara moved around behind the counter, I let my eyes roam the interior of the shop. It was bright and airy, strewn with funky, mismatched furniture that offered several comfy-looking places to sit.

"You're working tomorrow morning, right?" she asked Mason, handing him his coffee.

"I'll be in as early as I can. Just gotta milk first."

We said goodbye to Zara and headed back to where the car was parked.

Behind the wheel, I looked around for a cupholder, but my new old car didn't seem to have any, and without a word, Mason reached over to take my tea so I could drive.

"To the farm?" I asked.

"Yeah," he said. "I got the Bobcat loaded on the flatbed earlier. Just need to get it over to the school to finish digging."

"Can I drive the Bobcat?" I asked, pulling the Karmann Ghia out of the lot.

"Ever driven one before?"

I laughed. "Not a lot of opportunities for that in DC, no."

"Then no."

Mason's face was serious again, but a little spark of humor glinted in his eyes when I glanced over at him, and I felt that satisfaction glow inside me again. Making Mason forget to be grave and dark was one of my favorite pastimes.

We switched cars at the farm, Mason taking over driving as we headed out with the Bobcat on the back of the truck toward the school. He called Amelia on the way, and she said she'd meet us there, and true to her word, she was waiting when we backed into the spot closest to the partially dug hole.

"Hey!" she called as I got out of the truck.

"Hi," I said, hugging her. We turned to watch Mason lowering the bed to get the Bobcat down. "Mason won't let me drive the tractor thing."

She laughed. "I'm surprised he'll let you drive your own car," she said. "He likes to control everything, you know."

"I know," I said. A warm sensation filled me at getting to know more about my host.

We watched as Mason made quick work of the hole he'd begun digging, the Bobcat's shovel cutting through the hard earth like butter as we chatted about her plans for the school year.

"Guess you didn't really need my help," Amelia laughed when Mason had put the machine back up on the truck.

"Always good to have moral support," he told her.

"Have you changed your mind yet and decided to stay?" Amelia asked me, nudging my shoulder. "They still haven't found a fifth-grade teacher."

Mason's eyebrows shot up as he turned to me.

"No," I assured them both. "Lovely as that would be, I'll have to stop pretending not to have any responsibilities pretty soon."

Amelia frowned, but then she turned to Mason. "So what's next here?"

"I'll get some sheeting down under the soil to prevent any water seepage, and then we'll need to build up the walls with the bricks I've got piled up at the farm." He turned to us both, rapt in his explanation now. "Since we're not digging into a hillside here, we'll mimic a hill by building up the northern side and berming it with the soil we've collected." He pointed at the big pile of dirt they'd removed from the hole. "Then, when I put the plastic sheeting over the top, it'll face the right way to maximize the sunlight."

"So I have a question," Amelia said. "When it's legit freezing out here, won't everything in the hole freeze too? How does a piece of plastic over a hole keep things growing?"

Mason smiled at her, clearly in his element now. "We dug down six feet here," he said, pointing at the hole. "It's deep enough to take advantage of something called the thermal constant. Even when it's ten degrees outside, it'll be fifty in here. And we can add some water drums to maintain the warmth when it gets colder than that. We'll put the door on this end." He pointed to one side of the hole.

Amelia just shook her head, smiling widely at her brother.

He looked proud and completely invested in his explanation, and seeing his passion did something to me, made me want to stand a little closer to him. I knew what it was like to have that intensity directed at me, and I found myself wishing for it again.

We said goodbye and took the Bobcat back to the farm. Once we'd returned to Mason's, and he'd taken a quick shower to wash off the dust from digging, we found ourselves at opposite ends of the couch, Rascal on the floor between us.

## 18

# MASON

I didn't have a lot of days I'd volunteer to relive again and again, like Bill Murray in *Groundhog Day*. Most of my days were very much the same anyway, filled with goats and coffee, Rascal and the quiet simplicity of my house. But today? I'd live today over and over again if I had the chance.

Today had been sunny and warm, filled with Heather's bright smile and laughter, my sister's snark and attitude, good food and drinks, and work that would benefit someone else.

And the part of it that stood out most in my mind when I considered what had made it incredible was the woman sitting on the other end of the couch from me as the night crept in, bringing the familiar background of cicadas and owls through the open windows.

"So you line it," she was saying, repeating what I'd told her about building the greenhouse, "so water doesn't get in? But isn't water good for plants?"

"Yeah, but when you dig several feet into the ground, you're running the risk of two things. You might dig close to the water table—though here that's not the case. It's a few feet deeper, and we don't need to worry about that. But natural drainage after a rainstorm is something we do have to worry about. The land over there is pretty flat, but when the ground is saturated, it could end up flooding the greenhouse floor, so I line it to make sure that doesn't happen."

She nodded, understanding lighting those clear blue eyes. "Got it," she said. And then she smiled brightly. "It's so cool that you're doing that for the school. And that the kids are going to learn about it this year. It's pretty simple once you dig the hole, I guess. And they can grow cool exotic produce."

She stretched her legs across the couch, her feet coming to rest against my thigh. Without thinking about it specifically, my hand fell to the top of one of her small feet.

"For the school, it's less about growing exotic produce," I explained. "They'll use it to grow basic crops that the kids can take home for dinner. And it's a way for their families to learn to produce some staples even during the winter months when a backyard garden is not usually a thing."

"Like what?"

"Like peas, spinach, kale, beets, carrots."

My hand rubbed the firm arch of Heather's foot as I talked about my favorite topic, and it felt as natural as sitting here in my own living room with her. She wiggled her toes against me and stretched, her arms pressing upward, and the T-shirt she wore pulled across her chest, revealing a shape I was beginning to think about more than I wanted to.

"I had a great weekend," she said, and there was something in the air between us suddenly, something tense and uncertain. I wanted to pull her into my arms, to hold her again, to feel her against me.

"I did too," I said, my voice unnaturally deep.

She stilled beneath my hand. I lifted my gaze, meeting her eyes, and found them darker than usual, something expectant there, waiting for me to acknowledge it.

I let my hand rest on the top of her foot, and then ran it higher, pressing my palm lightly to her ankle, up the line of her shin beneath the leggings she wore. Her sharp intake of breath spurred me on, and when I glanced up, her pink lips were parted slightly, her chest rising and falling visibly.

Without allowing myself time to think, to second-guess, to be the careful person I spent my life being, I shifted my weight, moving onto my knee on the couch and bracing my other foot on the floor, so I was hovering over her.

Her eyes met mine, and there was no resistance there, only anticipation. My hands found her waist, and I tugged gently, until she was on her back beneath me. And then, bracing myself against the back of the couch, still above her on one knee but with Heather's body basically between my legs beneath me, I stared down at her, trying to catch my own breath.

She was perfect—ambitious and optimistic, smart and capable. And in the way that light rushes in to banish darkness, she'd spilled into my life, illuminating the things I was missing, the things I wanted.

I let a hand rise to her forehead, pushing back the light blond strands of hair there, and then I raked my fingers into the length of it, trailing them down through the silky gold, marveling at the way it slid across my skin. Her eyes never left my face, and as I traced the curve of her jaw with my fingers, studying her, one of her hands reached up, cupping the back of my neck.

She pulled me into her, and I lowered myself carefully until our lips grazed. It was the briefest of touches, but my body responded as if I'd been touched by a bolt of electricity. Every nerve jumped to life, every fiber of me leaning in, working to get closer to the heat of Heather's light.

I let myself kiss her then, one hand pushing into her hair as her hand pulled me closer, her lips parting beneath mine. She was soft and delicate, and I forced myself to hold back, to go slowly, teasing her bottom lip with the tip of my tongue until she moved beneath me, pulled me even nearer and met my tongue with her own.

She let out a breathy little moan, and it unlocked something deep inside me, a desire I'd ignored—maybe for years. But as our mouths tangled, pulling and pressing, our tongues sliding together as our bodies began to meld, I stopped trying to control it.

A deep low groan escaped me, and I swept my other arm beneath her, pulling her into me as I pressed the length of my body against her on the couch.

Her hands found my back then, pulling my shirt up until soft, slim fingers slid over the planes of my skin, igniting tiny fires everywhere they touched.

Heather was moving beneath me, pressing her hips into the hard thickness of my cock, which was rapidly becoming impossibly stiff as she ground herself against it.

I felt like a teenager, desperately kissing a girl as I sought the friction that felt better than anything I'd ever experienced before. But when Heather stilled in my arms and dropped her head back, asking me one question, my world shifted. This was not high school. And I already knew I'd do just about anything this woman asked of me.

"Mason, will you take me to bed?"

There was no confusing her request for anything chaste or innocent, and there was only one answer. I swept her into my arms, pulling her body against my chest as I stood. Rascal seemed to sense that whatever was happening wasn't his concern, and he turned and padded off to his bed in the kitchen as I carried Heather to my room.

I laid her gently on my grey comforter and switched on the bedside lamp. She lay, her hair splayed out around her and her eyes dark with lust, looking up at me with a faint smile on the lips I'd been imagining touching all day. Heat bloomed in my chest, and something that felt a lot like happiness exploded in my mind.

"Come here," she said, reaching for me.

I climbed onto the bed, and for a few seconds, I hovered next to her, staring down at her.

"What?" she asked, laughing.

I shook my head, feeling a smile overtake my lips. "Nothing. I'm just . . . I'm happy."

"I think I can make you even happier," she said.

Heather pulled me to her, everything about her welcoming and warm. She tugged my shirt over my head and then pushed me until I rolled onto my back, and she climbed onto my hips, straddling me. I struggled to maintain control—I loved this demanding version of Heather.

Her hands traced the lines of my pecs, her fingers trailing down my stomach and toying with my waistband as her eyes watched the tracks they made. She played with the hair on my chest, her lips in a smile as her eyes glowed, and I lay there, enjoying the attention and trying desperately to memorize everything about the way she looked, the way she felt.

"You're perfect, you know that?" she said, running her hands up my sides and pressing one into my hair as she lowered herself over me. "Strong and manly, intense and stoic—always looking out for everyone else."

"Manly?" I laughed as she pressed her lips to mine.

"Yes," she said, raising her head and looking down at me with a grin. "Manly. Look at all this muscle."

In most situations, the term might have embarrassed me, but in my own bedroom with a gorgeous woman pushing herself against my cock, I was a little beyond humble. I liked her praise. I liked her acknowledgment of the things I tried to be. I was not at all sure about "perfect," but I'd take the rest.

Heather kissed me, and when I tried to push her gently to her back, she resisted, sliding down my chest, trailing her lips the whole way to my waistband. I watched in fascination, every nerve ending jolting beneath her mouth.

Her hands made quick work of the button of my jeans, and then her fingers were slipping beneath the elastic of my briefs, pushing both layers of fabric down. I toed off my shoes and helped, and soon I was utterly naked beneath her, her eyes huge and fastened to my penis.

"Perfect," she said again, and I glowed in her admiration.

She sat astride me again, still fully clothed, and my hands went to the hem of her shirt, lifting it gently. She responded immediately, pulling it over her head, revealing a simple pink bra beneath, holding the two plump globes of her breasts.

Before I could fully appreciate the sight, she wrapped one of her hands around my length and pressed her core against the base, and I felt my eyes roll back in my head as she pumped me and simultaneously ground against me. I could feel every slide of her hands on my cock, and the heat of her center at my root had every nerve inside me lit like a Christmas tree.

"Holy shit," I bit out, reaching to still her hand and managing to focus my eyes enough to find her face.

"You don't like that," she said, sounding disappointed.

I pulled her to me, practically forcing her to lie down along my body, and then rolled her to her back. "I like it way too much," I told her.

And now that our roles were reversed, I took my time, gently sliding her leggings and panties from her body, revealing inch after inch of silky pale flesh. I worked my way down her body with my lips, my tongue, rewarded with breathy moans and throaty gasps. And when I reached her wet, pink center, where I teased her before finally pushing my tongue hard against her hot nub, she moaned in a way that had me almost losing it.

I pulled her legs up so that her knees were over my shoulders as I lay propped on my forearms between her legs. Her hands found my hair as I explored, and when I slipped two fingers into her slickness, she cried out, her clit pulsing against my tongue. She tasted like salt and honey, and as I tongued her, it felt like something clicked shut inside me, some kind of completion or certainty. I didn't have the mental capacity to explore the sensation just then, only to feel that this—everything in my arms at this moment—was exactly what I wanted.

My tongue worked in small circles and long strokes as my fingers pumped slowly, curling up to tease the little spot inside her, and Heather became more and more vocal until, as her body spasmed around me, she ground out my name like a plea. When she was regaining her breath, I climbed along the length of her, resting my weight to her side as I let my hand splay over the silky skin of her stomach.

"God, that was . . ." She trailed off, her hand coming to the back of my head and urging me in to kiss her. The kiss was tender and gentle, but within a few minutes, I could feel the urgency returning to her movements. She pulled away and looked at me, an intense fire in her eyes. "Do you have a condom?"

I retrieved one from my bathroom, and I watched in rapt fascination as Heather opened it and slowly rolled it down my length as I knelt over her. She slipped her hand beneath me then, her fingers wrapping around my balls and squeezing gently before her other hand came up to grasp my aching cock.

I sucked in a breath, unprepared for the sensation of her fingers rubbing down the seam of my sack as her other hand's warm pressure engulfed me. A tiny smile played across her lips when I managed to open my eyes, and then she guided me lower, positioning me at her entrance.

I wanted to say something, but my ability to form words had left me the second she'd put her hands on my body, and I went with a kiss instead, hoping she could feel how much I wanted this. How perfect her body, her hands, her being were.

As I pressed inside her hot, tight space, she sucked in a sudden breath, and I stopped. "You okay?"

"It's so good," she said, her voice a breathy moan. "Just taking a second to adjust."

I waited, every bit of my focus concentrated on the tip of my cock as it throbbed inside the fiery squeeze of Heather's body. When she began to push her hips upward, taking in more of me, I couldn't hold back any longer. Heat and sensation pooled inside me, and a tingling sensation started to build at the base of my spine.

"Fuck," I breathed, thrusting as gently as I could into that incredible warmth, pulling out again slowly and then pressing back in as Heather's body rose to match me.

She began to moan with each thrust, every cry from her lips spurring me on, sending me higher and higher until my vision blacked out, and the tight coil in my spine shattered, releasing every bit of feeling outward in a series of ecstatic shocks unspooling through my limbs.

Afterward, it took a few seconds for me to come back to myself, to find her face beneath me, to press a soft kiss to her lips.

"God, you're perfect," she said again.

And in that moment, in the glow of what I had to agree was pretty fucking perfect, I ignored the fear that crept into the room and crouched nearby, the danger that lay in letting another near to your heart. I let myself embrace the woman in my arms, the moment in my life, and the happiness I felt. I let myself imagine a world where I could have this, where it would be safe to love someone, and I ignored the fact that she was leaving—one way or another—and that she would never be mine.

# 19

## HEATHER

It's very possible that I let myself get lost inside the fantasy of being with Mason, of living this life, of staying here. How could I help it though? After the day we'd shared, his careful attention to every little thing—no one had ever treated me like that. Like a prize, like a delicate but treasured discovery. I'd been treated like a possession, sure. I'd felt the fire of someone's jealousy, the grip of a man wanting to show me I belonged to him. But this was different.

Mason was, as I'd managed to say too many times, perfect. He was masculine and capable, protective and strong—but I never felt as though I didn't have a say. He took care of me, he looked out for me, but I was coming to see that his brand of protection and my brother's were different. Kevin always thought he knew best. It was how I'd ended up here in the first place. But Mason— he worked on a different level. On instinct, maybe.

And I felt safer with him than I ever had in my life. Not just physically. Mason was different from other men I'd known. There was no external striving for acceptance or need to impress others, which I'd started to think was at the root of infidelity for a lot of men. They needed to prove something to themselves or to society at large, demonstrate their desirability by ensuring they 'still had it'—even when they had a woman at their side telling them they did. Maybe they didn't believe it themselves, I decided, and they needed constant outside validation.

But Mason. The man was many things, and I knew he wasn't really perfect. But I also knew he wasn't the kind of man to look outside himself for validation. He didn't doubt himself. If anything, I wondered if maybe the world wasn't a constant source of disappointment for a man like that.

His strong hands held me now as we lay in his bed, my head tucked against the warm solidity of his chest. Our breathing was synchronized, and there was something so peaceful and comforting in the simple rise and fall of our bodies. I let my fingers tangle in the curled hair on his chest as we lay quietly, but after a while, I pulled my head back to gaze up at him.

Mason's eyes were closed, but I knew he wasn't asleep by the way he held me, his hand sliding slowly up and down my side. His dark lashes fanned out against his cheeks, his full lips were parted slightly, and his jaw had begun to show a dark stubble through the soft, smooth skin. I raised my hand, letting my finger trace the line of his jaw, and his eyes opened sleepily.

"Hi," I said.

His arms tightened around me a bit. "Hi." A light smile touched his lips as he looked at me. "Are you getting cold?"

The room was warm, but the nights didn't hold on to the heat of the day like they did in Washington. I nodded, and Mason pulled the comforter over us, wrapping me against him.

His hand rubbed my back, making me feel sleepy and content as the warmth settled into my bones. I had a fleeting thought that this was just about perfect, and for an instant, I could imagine myself here, in this life, with this man. But I put the mental brakes on. This, nice though it was, was basically make-believe. This wasn't my real life, and though I had a good reason for staying away from that life for a bit, I would definitely have to go back. People didn't just walk away from jobs, apartments, friends. They just didn't.

So it was easy to linger here in Mason's embrace. Because I knew it didn't mean anything. He knew as well as I did that this was just temporary. So for once, I would let myself just enjoy something, and I would not think about what my brother would say if he found out.

After a while, Mason began to stir.

"Is your arm falling asleep?" I asked him, my hand rubbing a line up his chest.

I'd felt another stirring against my thigh too, but Mason didn't seem to be in a hurry to acknowledge it if he was hoping for round two. I had a feeling he might be stuck inside his own head, questioning our decision to sleep together, which was probably not the best choice, all things considered.

"No," he said, his voice a low rumble I felt through my body. "I'm getting hungry."

I looked up at him, and he smiled at me, a sleepy, beautiful thing that made my heart ping inside my chest.

"I am too, actually," I told him. We really hadn't had dinner. "I guess we better get up."

"I'm pretty sure Rascal will be in here in a few minutes anyway if we don't get his dinner down for him."

I smiled at the thought of the patient brown dog that was Mason's quiet shadow. He definitely deserved his dinner. "Okay," I said, beginning to untangle myself from Mason's embrace.

"Just a second," Mason said, his voice still deep and languorous. He pulled me into his chest once more and dropped his chin as I tilted mine up. Our lips met, and I felt him stir against my thigh again, and I pressed into him in response.

As he kissed me with slow, deliberate movements, his hands sliding down my back and coming to rest on the globes of my ass, I could feel his desire growing in intensity—and my own matched his.

I slid a leg over him, inviting him in, and he shifted, notching himself at my entrance. The heat of his cock combined with his passionate kisses had my body beginning to tighten in arousal, and I rubbed myself over his length a few times, building the friction I was craving.

"Poor Rascal," Mason said, his arms tightening around me as he pushed his cock back into position at the center of my need. Then he stopped, his mouth stilling on mine. "Let me grab a condom," he said.

But I didn't want him to go. "I'm on the pill," I told him. "And I'm clean—I haven't been with anyone in a long time."

His eyes met mine, a question there. "You're sure?" Then, seeming to understand that I needed to know his history too, he added. "I don't even remember the last time I was with anyone. Years. I'm not on birth control though."

I slapped his shoulder, laughing, and he retook my mouth with his own, but I pulled away. "You actually know how to joke?" I asked, teasing him.

He responded by sinking his teeth gently into the side of my neck—not a bite, but a nip that sent my arousal spiking. "Be good," he growled.

I reached down, gripping him in order to put him where I needed him, and he growled again, but this one was a needy, deep groan that lit every one of my nerves. When I had him where I wanted him, I pushed myself down, taking him in, inch by inch as my hands braced against his shoulders. And I watched him, our eyes locked as I worked him inside me until he was seated there, his full length enveloped in the wet channel of my desire.

"Fuck, you feel good," he whispered, and then one of his hands came up to trace the line of my face, to push a lock of hair behind my ear. "You're so beautiful," he said, and the way his voice broke on the sentence made me wonder if it was hard for him to say. Mason wasn't the kind of guy who handed out compliments freely, and the words meant that much more to me as a result.

"Thank you," I whispered, and then I began to move, sliding up and then pushing myself back down, Mason's iron length becoming the focus of every cell in my body.

He let me set the pace but matched me, thrusting up as I pushed back down. I could feel his restraint as his body began to shake beneath me, and there was something so heady in knowing I'd done this to him, that I'd driven this strong, stoic man to a point where he had to fight for control.

My own control was slipping, and I let my chest meet his as I thrust against him, welcoming the warmth and strength of his body bracing mine as my release began to coil itself in tight rings around me.

"Oh," I heard myself say, almost in surprise, as I felt the inevitable rise of sensation inside me. "Oh god," I moaned, my body beginning to feel like a foreign object, something I couldn't control.

"Yes," Mason said beneath me, the sound an encouragement and a signal that he was close too. "Fuck, yes."

My senses shattered then, my body desperately clutching and throbbing around Mason as his own release took him, and he let go of control, thrusting up into me relentlessly as his hands gripped my butt.

When the orgasm began to fade, I lay on his chest, enjoying the aftershocks of his release as his body began to slowly relax.

"What were you saying about feeding the dog?" I asked him, laughing.

"Right. Yes. In one minute." His arms banded across my back, holding me to him, his cock still inside me.

We lay for a long minute, breathing each other in, and then we rose by some silent agreement, to find food and feed poor Rascal.

After I'd cleaned up a bit, I met Mason in the kitchen, giving Rascal a couple long strokes on the back as he ate his very late dinner.

Mason had turned on the television, and the news was droning behind us as he worked in the kitchen.

"Can I help?" I asked him.

"Chop tomatoes?" he suggested, pushing a cutting board and knife my way.

He'd pulled a couple flatbreads from the breadbox and was making what looked like pizzas with tomato sauce, spinach, olives, and cheese. I chopped the tomatoes and listened to the news, feeling like I'd been away from the world for a very long time.

My attention was only half on the television until I heard the newscaster mention Senator Andrews by name, and then I turned to watch, the pleasure of the day sliding away. Mason stopped moving and listened too.

"Senator Andrews, clearly upset by the actions of his constituents on his behalf, has issued a statement through his lawyer. The statement was read on the steps of the Capitol at a press conference this morning."

The camera footage switched to the press conference, a man in a suit with glasses on reading from a sheet of paper as he faced a small crowd.

"While I appreciate your loyalty and your faith in me," he read, "I am ashamed to tell you that it is misplaced. Though my lawyer cautioned me not to admit guilt because of the appeal he's working on, I feel that I have no choice but to be brutally honest in light of the actions my constituents have taken against those brave enough to testify against me. I did things I am not proud of, things I will learn from, things I will not repeat. I hurt my family and this great nation, and I've disappointed all of you, who believe in me so completely. Please, I beg you to stop retaliating against those who told the truth. The women who bore witness to my indiscretions should be allowed to move on with their own lives, and should suffer no punishment for doing the right thing according to the laws of the country we all serve.

"I want to be clear: stop harassing those who testified at my trial. It doesn't help me, my family, or our country. Instead, turn your attention toward helping to find a better representative of your interests, someone who will deserve the great faith you've placed in me."

The camera moved back to the newsroom, and the newscaster continued.

"Hopefully that heartfelt message will be enough to put an end to the terror some of the witnesses from the senator's trial have had to endure.

I had dropped the knife somewhere in the midst of that—hearing the lawyer speak took me back to trial in some ways, and a cold discomfort spread through me.

Mason stepped around the counter and pulled me into his arms, his solid warmth acting as an immediate antidote. "That should help a lot, don't you think? If the guy these nuts think they're helping tells them in no uncertain terms to stop?"

"I hope so." Relief was beginning to move through me. Mason was right, I thought. If the senator himself told people to stop, it seemed like they would. They'd thought they were working on his behalf, but that message made it clear enough he didn't support their actions.

"You okay?" he asked, holding me and looking down at me, his handsome face etched with lines of concern.

I nodded. "Yeah. I feel better, actually. I think maybe that really will be the end of it." I did. The more I considered the words I'd just heard, the way the senator's following listened to him, the more I was certain it would help a lot.

But another thought registered just as I'd begun to feel better about things: this meant it was probably time to go home.

## 20

# MASON

Heather had been quiet after we'd seen the newscast and the senator's lawyer had read the statement from his client. She hadn't seemed upset or worried, just lost somewhere in her own head.

We ate, watching a rerun of *The X-Files*, which I remembered watching as a kid. I'd had a thing for Gillian Anderson once, thanks to that show. Any tiny little redhead who could kick alien butts and keep Mulder in his place . . . well, she did it for me. But that was a fantasy I'd had as a kid. And the woman beside me now was the real thing.

I'd broken every rule I had for myself, tossed every caution I gave my heart right out the window. I thought I'd been preparing my whole life, protecting myself, building up my defenses to make sure I could never feel the kind of pain again that I'd felt as a kid. And it had worked. Until my best friend had asked for a favor I couldn't refuse.

How did you plan for having a long-term houseguest who ticked every one of your boxes when it came to the kind of woman you'd choose if you were the choosing type?

You didn't.

And so we ate, and then after I'd taken Rascal out for a bit and turned off the lights in the kitchen, I'd come back to the couch and stood in front of where Heather sat, unsure how to say what I wanted. But she made everything easy—it was part of what I loved about her. She didn't need me to ask, to speak. She just stood up, slipped her arms around my neck, and rose on her toes to push her lips to mine.

Every time she touched me, it felt like coming home. It was comfort and pleasure, reassurance and contentment.

And it scared the living hell out of me.

A wise man would not have led her back to his room. He would not have spent half the night inside her, his hands roaming the miles of soft, pliable skin, his fingers twisting through those silken strands of hair. He would not have let his heart open a little bit more with every sound she made, every sigh he wrought from her lips, every glint of mischief he caught in her eyes. And he would not have spent the remainder of the night curled around her protectively, sleeping the most peaceful sleep he'd found in years.

When I rose to go milk the goats, Heather didn't stir. She lay in the near darkness, her bright hair splayed out around her like an angel's halo. She was tiny, I thought as I pulled on my jeans. She took up just the smallest of spaces, curled up under the blankets of my bed. But the space she'd filled inside me felt much bigger.

Once dressed, I stood quietly for a moment, watching her. One of her hands was tucked up beneath her cheek as she lay curled on her side, and her breath moved her back in a regular rhythm, calm and steady. She was so vulnerable there, sleeping innocently in my bed, and my heart twisted painfully at the thought. We were all so vulnerable when we slept, so trusting of the universe to deliver us safely to morning, to another day.

A dark fear spread through me as I thought about my parents, about that night out on the road listening to my sister sobbing and the crackling greed of the fire. My parents had gone to sleep that night, trusting and faithful that morning would come.

Watching Heather sleeping, I couldn't ward off the fierce

desire to protect her, to stop anything that might hurt her, to be ever vigilant now, since I hadn't succeeded before. But a small part of me realized it wouldn't matter. You could not protect the people you loved from everything. And the things you couldn't foresee were the things that would tangle your emotions and shred the tender pieces of your heart.

I heaved a sigh and turned, quietly leaving the room and moving out to say goodbye to Rascal after letting him out for a moment.

"Look out for her, boy, okay?" I ran my hands through my dog's thick coat, and as always, I felt like there was understanding in those big amber eyes, like he knew what I needed and he'd do his best to provide it.

---

Heather was still sleeping when I returned from the farm, and I took the opportunity to collect a few ripe oranges from the greenhouse and make some fresh orange juice. I might have smiled as I picked the fruit—the success of my walipini was still surprising to me. I'd understood that it would work in theory, but seeing ripe citrus on the little dwarf trees at the start of July was still gratifying. I'd kept the trees inside all winter, after planting them the spring before in preparation for this year. And seeing the literal fruit of my labors was amazing. The figs were coming along too, and as each little teardrop fruit swelled, my sense of accomplishment grew alongside an uncomfortable longing for a childhood I spent most days trying to forget.

Fig trees have a particular smell, and in the small, warm space of the greenhouse, the scent wafted thickly in the air, mingling with the oranges and tomatoes and unleashing memories that came at me suddenly now and then. My mother, laughing at the kitchen counter at something I'd said or done, her eyes glowing with a love I'd never questioned, one I'd neglected to treasure. And my sister and me, running between the trees in the fig grove as my father walked along behind us, checking his crops. Those big old trees with their wide canopy of branches and huge leaves had made a kind of jungle for us to enjoy, sheltered from the blazing sun of the San Joaquin Valley.

I shook off the unwanted memories and went back inside, making eggs and bacon and waiting for my houseguest to rise.

## 21

# HEATHER

I woke up slowly to the smell of bacon and coffee, and I stretched luxuriously beneath the soft blankets that covered me. And then I realized where I was.

Mason's bed.

I'd become used to waking on the couch as soon as I heard a sound anywhere in the little house. But this morning, I'd slept in, and now the sun was streaming through the high windows along the wall in Mason's bedroom, and I felt miraculously well-rested. No nightmares. No huddling on the couch. No fear.

I didn't know if it was the senator's statement on television the night before or, more likely, the time I'd spent in Mason's arms. But my body and mind felt calm and clear for the first time in months.

After ducking into the bathroom for a quick shower and pulling on some leggings and a T-shirt, I joined Mason in the kitchen and was nearly knocked over by the smile he offered me.

So he did know how to smile.

This one wasn't awkward or painful-looking. It was wide and natural and glorious, and it lit his dark eyes with merriment while revealing the adorable dimples in his cheeks. My heart swelled inside me.

"Good morning," I said, returning the smile. "You let me sleep in. Did you already milk?"

"A while ago," he said. "I hated to wake you. You looked so adorable curled up in my bed."

Did Mason Rye just use the word 'adorable'?

"I slept really well," I said, my voice carrying a bit of the wonder I felt at waking to find this relaxed version of my intense host. "Did you?"

He grinned at me again. "Better than I have in years."

"We're good for each other." It was a joke, but as soon as I'd said it, I wished I could take it back, say something less assumptive about our situation. We were not a couple. We did not have a future. We were two people who'd had sex, and it was probably only going to complicate things. I didn't want to make Mason think I needed to put a title on it now or that I'd become clingy and expectant just because we'd slept together.

I knew that wasn't what this was.

"We are," he said softly, as if thinking about it for the first time.

I was grateful when Mason slid a plate of eggs and bacon in front of me, along with coffee and orange juice, leaving off the embarrassing verbal slip-up to begin talking about his plans for the day.

"I need to get a few hours at the Bean," he said, sitting down with his own plate. "But I wanted to start construction at the school too, now that we've got the hole dug."

"No farm work today?"

He shook his head. "Tomorrow."

"I'll help out today if you want," I said, eager to spend another day feeling useful, needed.

"That'd be great. Not sure you want to bale hay, but there are probably labels to be printed and placed, and I could definitely use help at the school."

"Sounds good."

"Hey there," Uncle Billy greeted me as I made my way down the aisle between the empty stalls in the barn to the little workroom attached to the milking parlor. "Annalee's been asking after you."

I laughed, thinking of the playful gray goat I'd made friends with last time I was here. The goats and kids were all out grazing now, and the barn was quieter than usual. A low drone filtered in on the warm air—a distant farmer driving the baler over the mown fields of alfalfa, probably.

"How are you, Billy?" I asked him as he held the door open for me.

He pressed his lips into a firm line, his eyes gleaming as he looked at me frankly. "Well, I'm pretty damned old," he said. "And I'm tired a lot of the time. I miss my wife like hell."

I nodded, unsure how to respond to his bald honesty. A stack of labels had already been printed and sat next to the printer in the corner of the room. I picked them up and moved to the work-table along the wall. "I'm sorry," I managed.

He waved off my words. "Mason's got you back to work, I see."

I moved to the big refrigerator and retrieved a stack of plastic tubs filled with cheese. "I don't mind. I like to stay busy."

Billy's head bobbed, and he watched me as I settled onto a stool to begin placing labels on the little tubs. It was mindless work, but I enjoyed it. Seeing the stacks of labeled tubs grow at the end of the table felt like an accomplishment, albeit a small one.

I worked, and Billy watched me, but it wasn't uncomfortable. He had an easy, unassuming way about him, and I was happy for the company. But he kept opening his mouth, seemingly about to speak, before closing it again.

After a few long minutes, I put down the sheet of labels I held. "I get the feeling you might like to ask a question," I tried.

He shrugged, and a sheepish smile crept across his face. "It's a strange situation," he said. "I love that boy." He gestured to the door, as if to indicate Mason, out there in the world. "But he's about as smart as a bar of soap sometimes."

A laugh escaped me at the expression and also at the idea of Mason being dumb. A guy who read physics books for fun was probably not. "I think he does okay," I said.

"Oh sure," Billy agreed. "If you want him to solve an algebra problem for you. But that's not what I mean. I'm talking about the kind of smarts that happen in here." He tapped his chest, and I felt my face begin to heat. "Look at the situation," he went on, against the table across from me. "You show up here, pretty and smart, friendly and eager to help. You're staying in his little house, single—if I'm not mistaken."

"You are not." I cringed a bit. I should have been having this conversation with Mason, but it seemed I was going to have it with his uncle instead.

"And he's figured out how to get you helping with everything from digging holes to escorting goats to be milked. But he can't seem to figure anything else out."

I considered letting him know that Mason seemed to figure out plenty the night before when his hands and mouth had explored my body, but that didn't seem appropriate. My cheeks grew hotter, and I took a deep breath, trying to flush my embarrassment.

"And if he doesn't see things clear soon, you'll be leaving, and he'll go back to being the lonely, miserable sunovabitch he's been all these years."

"You think Mason was lonely before?" I asked.

"I know it. But the damned fool has this idea that if he lets himself depend on anyone, they'll die in another fire."

A lump formed in my throat at that. "Can't blame him really," I said. "You don't just get past something like that happening when you're a kid."

"Amelia does okay, and she was a lot younger. The man was my brother, for chrissakes."

I thought about that. Amelia was single too. I wondered if that was more to do with the difficulty of meeting men in this small town or if it was by choice. Was she protecting herself? Was that what Mason was doing?

"I'm so sorry that happened," I said, not sure what else I could say.

Luckily, Billy seemed to be finished, and he excused himself to go out and attend to the animals.

I spent another hour labeling tubs, thinking about his words.

By the time I heard Mason's truck coming back from the Busy Bean to pick me up, I'd talked myself back around to where I had begun. I hadn't come here looking for anything except time to let my situation in DC settle. I didn't need a relationship and certainly didn't want one, given the way they tended to end. I told myself the last thing I needed was to add heartbreak to my list of recent emotional issues.

I just wasn't sure if I'd already let myself get too close to Mason. Even if it was just a fling, or a mistake even, it would still be hard to leave.

"You ready to head to school?" Mason asked, stepping through the workroom door.

I sucked in an involuntary breath when I caught sight of him. His broad shoulders filled the doorway, covered in a gray T-shirt that clung to the muscles of his chest and biceps. The jeans he wore weren't tight, but they strained around his thighs all the same, and the rough, stubbled skin of his jaw made me want to rub my fingers across it. He wore a ball cap now, no doubt to keep the sun from his face, and it gave him a more boyish look than usual. Despite my best efforts to keep it in place, my heart jumped a little in my chest at the sight of him.

"Yeah," I said, dropping my gaze. "Just need to get these back into the fridge."

He helped me stack the labeled tubs in the bottom of the refrigerator, his shoulder bumping me gently as he leaned down. He smelled like coffee, sunlight, and grass, and as his skin brushed mine, he gave me a smile that melted every rational thought I'd been feeding myself about not becoming too attached here.

I was already attached.

---

Amelia met us at the school, along with a gaggle of five kids, boys and girls who she said had been students of hers. They looked to be anywhere between ten and twelve, and their eager smiles and energy were contagious. I even caught Mason grinning at them as he explained how we were going to build walls for the greenhouse.

He'd had a load of big, dark brown adobe bricks delivered from the farm, along with bags of gravel and some bigger river rocks, and they sat in a pile next to the dirt he'd excavated with the Bobcat and the topsoil they'd dug out earlier.

The kids listened intently, captivated by the passion with which Mason talked about the project. He showed us how he'd dug on an incline, so the floor of the greenhouse was higher in the center and sloped to a ditch at either side of the space. He explained how the rocks we'd be putting in today would assist with drainage and why plants couldn't grow if the roots were too wet. Mason might not have been a teacher, but he seemed to have a knack for connecting kids to what he wanted them to learn. I was impressed.

The kids were enthralled, and once he'd finished explaining how we'd fill the floor with rocks and gravel, lay the big adobe bricks up the side walls, and then shore up the sides with dirt, they exploded into activity.

At one point, I'd become the designated scooper, helping kids fill buckets of gravel that they'd transport to Mason, who would help them lay it in the big hole. As I stood there, watching the project progressing before my eyes, I saw Amelia greet an elegant Black woman who emerged from the main school building with an air of authority. She smiled widely as they talked, and after a moment, Amelia walked her in my direction. I wiped my hands on my jeans and smiled.

"Heather, I want you to meet Principal Franz," Amelia said.

"Hello," I said. "It's really nice to meet you."

"And you," she said. "Please, call me Anita." She turned to survey the flurry of activity around us, a wide smile on her face. "You've made great progress here. The children are very excited about this project and the addition of maintaining the greenhouse to their usual workload this school year."

"Mason is pretty ingenious," I agreed, catching his quizzical look as he gazed our way over the top of the ditch.

"Amelia speaks highly of you too," the principal told me. "And she happened to mention that you have a teaching certificate and some multi-subject teaching experience."

"I do, but not here in Vermont. I'm just here for a little bit—I live in DC. And I haven't been in the classroom in a few years. I work in education reform." I battled the part of me that wanted to impress her, that thought it would be so easy to look for a job here, to settle in. To never go home.

The woman nodded, a satisfied smile on her face at hearing this. "Well, I know Amelia mentioned to you that we're looking for a fifth-grade teacher."

"She did," I said, a part of me wishing I could entertain the idea of applying for the role, staying here. "But I can't really apply. I have to head back to my job soon, and I'm not licensed in this state anyway."

"That's remedied easily enough," Principal Franz said. "What's harder is finding qualified and motivated teachers. I'm sorry to hear you won't be staying."

"It was very nice to meet you," I said, shaking her hand.

As the principal made her way over to inspect the progress of the walipini, Amelia bumped my shoulder with her own. "You could stay, you know. It'd be so nice having you here. And I know my brother wouldn't complain." She waggled her eyebrows at me.

I gave her a look that I hoped would stop her speculation.

"There's something going on, right?" Evidently my look was not as hard-hitting as I'd hoped. "With the two of you?"

I didn't think Mason would appreciate me sharing anything too intimate with his sister. But I also thought of Amelia as a friend. "I don't know," I said, trying to avoid admitting anything. "I mean . . . I definitely am attracted to him. Is that weird to hear? I mean, he's your brother."

She shook her head, a wide grin overtaking her face.

"It's just that, well, it doesn't matter. I have to go home soon, and it just . . . it wouldn't work out. Long-distance is impossible. And it's not like we've talked about that, either."

"Talking is not Mason's strength."

My mind flashed unbidden to the image of Mason's muscles rippling above me as we'd rolled around in his bed the night before. He had other strengths, but I was pretty sure his sister didn't need to hear about those. "Right," I said.

"Well, for what it's worth, I think you should stay." She smiled again and then headed back over to help distribute the rocks and gravel in the big hole.

She made it sound so easy. As if my life was so easily transported from place to place, like I could just decide to move to a different state on a whim. I shook my head to clear it of the idea, to erase the images of Mason that kept sliding across my memory's projection screen, to remind myself that I had a life.

And it was not here in Vermont. I needed to go home. Didn't I?

## 22

# MASON

Even as Heather began to talk about making plans to head back to Washington, we fell into a rhythm that made me wish she could stay. I worked—and so did she, often staying at the farm after I'd milked and then headed over to the Bean for a shift. We'd meet up again at the cottage, and Heather usually had something cooking that filled the place with a scent that I'd started to think of as comfort, as home.

Rascal had fallen into a rhythm with our long-term houseguest too, greeting us in turn each morning and then heading out the door any time Heather went outside to collect eggs or just get a breath of fresh air.

Over the course of that next week, we went to the school a few times, shoring up the walls and finishing the more complex details of building the sump and irrigation system for the greenhouse, and finally stretching the plastic roof over the top with Amelia and some of the kids.

Each night we found ourselves in my bed again, Heather nestled into the space between my arms after we'd had sex, her hot skin pressed against my chest. And for the course of that entire week, we didn't talk about what was happening between us, and I did my best not to think about it.

I knew that with Heather here, in my arms and in my bed, I felt a strange contentment I hadn't experienced before. Despite the mounting pile of debt Billy had walked me through again this week, despite my inability to make enough money to secure the future of Garden Goat, no matter what I did, my mind remained calm.

My nightmares—usually filled with smoke and flame and terror—had ceased since she'd been in my bed, and I did my best not to think at all about what that might mean. Heather's late-night wanderings had also stopped, and it seemed we'd both traded our fears for the comfort we found together.

It was a good break from the usual rhythm of each of our lives. But it couldn't last. Love was temporary enough in the best of situations, but ours was built to be temporary from the start. And I didn't think this was love. Something closer to convenience.

Still, I'd begun to realize there was more to it than the soft intimacy of hands sliding over skin, finding release together. My heart lifted when she laughed, and I had begun trying to think of ways to surprise her, to make her smile. I'd brought cupcakes from the Busy Bean and stopped by Speakeasy to pick up the burger she kept telling me was the best she'd ever tasted.

One evening she'd gone into town with Amelia for drinks, and I had the cottage to myself. Rascal and I sat on the back deck with a beer, and I felt oddly unmoored without her there but was doing my best to feel glad to have things back as they should be. When my phone rang, I jumped to answer it, thinking it might be Heather before quickly admonishing myself for the assumption.

It was Kevin.

"Hey, brother," he said when I answered.

"Brigsy. How are you?"

He let out a wry chuckle, and I could almost picture the austere space from which he was probably calling—a tent or a freight container made into a comms center. "I'm fine," he said, and the words offered the assurance that we wouldn't talk about where he was or what he might be doing. I remembered offering the same words, in the same tone, to my sister when I'd been in uniform. "How's Heather?"

"She's good," I said, my stomach churning. Kevin would probably not appreciate the most recent developments in my guardianship of his little sister. "Yeah, she's uh, she's better."

"She didn't answer when I called."

"She's in town with my sister," I told him. "Having drinks. Might be loud."

"Oh yeah?" He sounded surprised. "That's good," he said. "So she's staying put?"

"I think she's actually starting to think about going back. The senator made a statement, and it seems like things have calmed down." I hated the words even as they came out of my mouth.

"Good," he said. "No chance she'll just stay up there? Maybe settle in podunk? Sounds like she's already made friends."

"She seems to want to get back to the city." I tried to keep the sound of disappointment out of my voice. The idea of Heather staying here, of seeing her regularly, made me hopeful in a way I didn't want to examine. "For the best," I added.

"Maybe." A loud jostling noise came at Kevin's end of the line, and I heard him respond to another male voice before coming back on the line. "Hey, man, I have to go. If I don't get to talk to Heather, tell her I love her, okay?"

"I will."

"Thanks. Take care."

"You too." I hung up and stared off into the dark green of the trees at the edge of the farm.

What would it be like to have Heather stay, I wondered. But as quickly as I allowed my mind to consider it, my heart jumping into the fray in a hopeful leap, I squashed the notion. She had her life. I had mine. The two didn't intertwine beyond the short time she'd spent here.

I reminded myself how it felt to be alone and tried to push myself back into the quiet headspace I'd occupied before she had arrived. By the time she arrived home, laughing and smiling from her time out with Amelia, I thought I'd managed to shore up my emotions. I was going to suggest she sleep in her own room. But when she stepped close, smiling and bringing the sunlight and joy she carried inside right up against me, I couldn't stop my arms from circling her and trying to hold on to some of that joy for myself.

And as I made love to her that night, my entire body desperate to get closer to her, to hold her tightly to me, I told myself it needed to end. I was getting in too deep, and if I didn't pull away now, I would suffer that much more pain when she left. And it was certain she was going to leave. Any other ideas were just fantasies.

## 23

# HEATHER

Mason crept out of bed before his alarm went off and slipped from the house more quickly than I would have thought possible. As the warmth began to fade from his side of the bed, I lay still, my mind slowly turning through thoughts like pages in a photo album.

The last few weeks had been strange and wonderful by turns. I'd arrived terrified and alone, essentially banished from the life I'd built, and untethered since my work was what had brought my life focus and purpose. Now here I was, in a place I hadn't even known existed, finding myself more fulfilled than I ever had before.

It wasn't just about Mason. It was the work I'd gotten to do. Helping at the farm, knowing they were short-handed and needed me, was fulfilling in a very grassroots way that my own work never could be. Helping Mason and Billy was immediate and fruitful—we sold products, we reaped and baled fields—results were obvious, at least in a physical sense.

And then there was the school. It had been gratifying seeing the kids so engaged in helping Mason build a structure that would ultimately benefit them. Hearing their questions and watching their eager hands carry bucket after bucket of gravel and soil as their bright, curious eyes took it all in—it reminded me why I'd entered the education field in the first place.

And Mason.

His quiet constancy, his gruff protectiveness—they'd felt abrasive at first, maybe because I was used to the noise and action of the city. But after some time here, with his steady strength at my side, I knew I'd come to rely on him. But it was more than that. Yes, I felt safe when he was near, but I felt other things too. Things that scared me.

My stomach flipped when I watched his strong hands work, whether in the kitchen, the milking parlor, or out in the garden. His quiet capability and stoic nature made his occasional laughter and wide smiles feel that much more precious. And earning those smiles felt like an accomplishment greater than any others I'd secured. I loved watching those dark eyes dance and hearing the low roll of his amusement, and I loved knowing that, in that moment at least, the pain of his past wasn't forefront in his mind. Mason had saved me in a way, but I found myself wanting to save him too. And that worried me.

His absence this morning worried me too. We'd spent the night together again—in a week, it had become a habit. But he'd been quieter and more withdrawn last night. And now he'd left without waking me, without allowing me time to wake up and come help him milk.

I stretched and watched the gray light of dawn begin to color orange and yellow across the planked ceiling of Mason's room, and I tried to stop the worry growing inside me. But it was no use. It was too familiar. Every relationship I'd ever been in had waned at some point—I'd become more invested, more convinced this was the one, while the other party inevitably began to decide the complete opposite thing. And then started to move away, to withdraw.

Mason and I were not in a relationship. I knew that. But our circumstances had forced whatever this thing was between us to grow rapidly, to advance more quickly than it would if we were simply dating. And now I felt him pulling back, just like men always did.

I sighed and sat up, letting my legs slide from the soft sheets of Mason's bed. And then I padded out to find my phone and call Morgan. I'd been talking about planning to go home for the past two weeks, but I hadn't actually planned a thing. Now, as I felt Mason pulling back, it was the wake-up call I needed. This was not my life, not my man. This was all a nice little game of make-believe and a great diversion from the life that had begun to feel stifling and scary. But I'd spent my month, fulfilled my promise to my brother, and waited out the crazy constituents. There was no longer any reason for me to stay here.

"Heather," Morgan said, picking up on the first ring. "How's Vermont?"

"Good," I said, staring out the window over the fields to the trees lining the horizon. "It's good, but I think I'm ready to get back."

"Yeah?" He sounded relieved. "In a nick of time, actually."

"What's up?"

"We really need you. There's a meeting we're trying to get on the agenda. I think we've found a new champion for the urban educator reward legislation you and Andrews were working."

My heart lifted a tiny bit. I'd pushed that idea hard—that those working in some of the more difficult environments should be incentivized over those in less demanding positions. It was controversial and nuanced, and we needed an articulate, conservative supporter. "Really?"

"Yeah, but you're the one with all the finesse on that issue. Your timing is perfect."

"That's good," I said, but as the idea settled over me, it felt like weight I didn't want.

"When will you be back?"

"I'm not totally sure," I said. "Soon. I'll call you when I know for sure."

We hung up, and I struggled to assure myself I was doing the right thing. That my life was in DC, not here.

"Hey, boy," I said, greeting Rascal as I moved out into the kitchen to make coffee.

Rascal made a low noise of greeting and came to rub against my thigh. I would miss him. Maybe I'd get a dog, I thought. But then reality set in. My life was fast-paced and demanding. I didn't have time for a dog.

I dropped to a squat as the coffee brewed and dug my hands into the dog's soft ruff, rubbing the thick fur of his neck as my mind rolled on. I'd miss this guy. And I'd miss the farm too.

"I'm going to help before I go," I promised the dog in a whisper. "I'm hoping to hear back soon from the land conservancy, and I've got a few other ideas too. You guys will be okay," I told him, saying the things I knew I couldn't say to Mason. I wanted that—to know that I'd helped, to know that me staying here hadn't just been one more example of me needing to be saved. I wanted to save someone else for a change—and I would.

---

After breakfast, I drove myself over to the farm, Rascal enjoying the ride in my little borrowed car. I'd miss that too, I thought, but pushed the idea away. I didn't need a car in the city. I wasn't in a rush to get back, despite what Morgan had said. I wanted to make sure I finished things here.

"Hey there!" Billy called, catching sight of me as he came out of the barn.

"Hey, Billy," I called back. "How are things today?"

"Good, now that you're here. Mason's in a mood." He shook his head, and I wondered what kind of mood Mason could be in. It clearly wasn't a good one, since Billy didn't look very happy. "Maybe you can cheer the guy up."

I sighed, wishing I didn't have a driving desire to do just that on hearing he wasn't happy. But I couldn't be responsible for the way Mason felt—he wasn't mine, and he was just as aware as I was that whatever had happened between us was temporary. Over before it really even began.

I found Mason in the workroom, finishing up the cheese he and Billy had made the day before. I washed my hands and stepped to his side, helping to press lids to the little plastic tubs.

"You made more than usual," I observed.

"The goats are producing more right now for some reason."

"Maybe they're happy," I suggested, shooting him a smile.

He raised an eyebrow at me. "What do my goats have to be extra happy about?"

"They have a pretty good life here, I think. They've got plenty of reason to be happy. You and Billy take good care of them, they've got lots to eat and a beautiful farm to graze."

"For now." His voice was dark and ominous, and I knew he was thinking again about the farm's debts, about his uncle's future. And his own.

"Farmers' market tomorrow, right?"

He looked at me for a long second, something deep and unhappy moving through his brown eyes. They lightened then, and he inclined his head. "You don't need to worry about that."

"I'd like to go. I enjoyed it. And I called a couple of those restaurant managers we met last time, plus the guy at Speakeasy. And I made a few cold calls to other restaurant groups in Burlington and Montpelier."

He shook his head, and I could see him struggling between wonder and confusion. "Why?"

"The greenhouse has been producing well," I said, parroting the words he'd told me just the night before. "You have more than you can sell and will for the rest of the summer. So I made some calls to invite those guys to come by. They didn't make a commitment to buy anything, but the one guy manages a group of several restaurants, and he said if you can supply him with citrus for the rest of the summer, he'll buy whatever you can produce. And same with the beets."

Mason just shook his head, and I couldn't tell if he was shocked or upset.

"They want to buy local, Mason. They just needed to know you were here."

He was quiet a moment, turning back to the cheese. He worked silently, pushing the tubs my way to press lids to, and after what felt like forever, he turned to face me again, a little smile on his full, plush lips. "Thank you." It was almost a whisper. "We'll have figs tomorrow too. Maybe they'll be interested."

"I'm sure they will," I said, relief and happiness mixing inside me even as I chastised myself. It shouldn't make me so happy to win Mason's approval, to see that smile.

---

That night I got ready for bed, planning to go to my own room, to put an official end to whatever had transpired between Mason and me—there was no sense dragging it out. But he didn't give me a choice.

Just as I turned to head to my own room, he stepped into the hallway.

"Where are you going?" he asked, his voice rolling like distant thunder.

"To bed," I said, feeling off-balance and uncertain in the velvet darkness of the hallway.

"Heather," he said, taking a step closer. His voice was rough and low, full of need and longing, and it sent heat pooling to my center. I wanted to touch him, to make him smile, to hear him say my name like that again.

I sucked in a breath, my determination to be strong slipping away as my body reacted to his proximity. He was still a foot away from me, standing there in the near-blackness, but I could feel the burning intensity radiating from him, and it drew me closer. I took one step forward, tentatively, and the next second I was in his arms again.

Mason pulled me to him roughly, as if he'd been trying to tell himself he wouldn't or that he shouldn't. He kissed me, hard and demanding, even as a rumble escaped his chest.

The strong arms I'd come to crave drew around me, pressing me against the hot solidity of his chest, and my own hands found their way to the hem of the white T-shirt he wore, sliding up the hard planes of his back.

His mouth was demanding and careful at once as he kissed me there in the hallway, and I found myself pressing against him, needing every inch of contact I could find. We staggered together, and my back hit the wall behind me as Mason spun me and then held me there, his mouth and arms keeping me captive as the hard length of his need pushed against my belly.

A needy want had built inside me as he'd kissed me, something desperate and wild, and I tried to contain it even as a moan left my throat, carrying every bit of the desire I felt for him.

Mason undressed me, there against the wall, his mouth leaving mine only to trace and nip down the length of my neck and across my collarbone as he slid my shorts from my legs. My own hands found the waist of his jeans and unfastened them, pushing them down his firm hips until he took over the action, breaking contact for the briefest moment to kick them free.

And then he lifted me until our mouths were even, and my back found the sturdy solidity of the wall again, the cool wood planks a contrast to the driving heat of Mason's body against my chest and stomach.

He devoured me like a man seeking water after a long trek, his hands moving as if he was trying to memorize every bit of my skin. And when he entered me, it was slow and steady. He impaled me inch by slick inch as a groan built in his chest, leaving him in unison with my own cry, which ripped from me as he filled every single one of my senses until I couldn't breathe.

Mason's thrusts became as demanding as his mouth, and as I rode him against the wall, my legs helplessly splayed to the sides as my hands clutched at his strong back, a wild tumult of sensations tore through me. Part of it was the near-violence of our sex, greedy and hard and frenzied as Mason took me there against the unyielding wall of his house. But part of it was purely emotional as I waged a battle within myself, every bit as violent and frenzied as what we were doing in the hallway. I fought to keep away the need I felt for this man, the desire I held for him, the way he made me feel safe and needed and so completely wanted. I tried to keep from acknowledging the longing I felt when he wasn't near, the way I wanted to ease his burdens, to help him through the pain of his past.

As my body spasmed and heaved with release, senseless words streaming from my lips while Mason cursed and grunted through his own climax, I tried to deny the desire to stay here, to remain wrapped around this man, to be as close as I could possibly be to Mason Rye. And I tried to tell myself it was only physical, that when I walked away, we would both be fine.

And when he carried me to his bed and then cleaned me gently with a warm cloth before pulling me into his arms beneath the covers as his breath was soft in my ear, I closed my eyes hard and tried to pretend the tears prickling my eyes were only fatigue.

---

The farmers' market was even busier than the weeks before. We had citrus, tomatoes, and beets, in addition to the multiple varieties of Garden Goat cheese, and once I let people sample the figs and cheese together, word spread. The stand was packed, three people deep, for most of the time we were there. Four of the five restaurant managers I'd spoken to stopped by, and I took orders—with Mason's help—for the following week. Mason agreed that we could deliver the produce to two of the restaurants, and two others had no problem driving to the farm to pick it up.

By the end of the day, we had tripled what Mason made at a normal farmers' market, and he was grinning from ear to ear.

"That was incredible," he told me. "You. Were. Incredible." He shook his head as we climbed back into his truck, his eyes dancing as he looked at me like he couldn't believe what we'd just done.

"You were there too. It's your produce," I reminded him. "I just helped people discover it."

The truck rumbled to life, and Mason muttered words like "brilliant" and "amazing" as we pulled back onto the road to the farm.

## 24

# MASON

In just over a month, Heather had managed to bring more weekly money into the farm than I'd been able to do in the past year. "But it's not like I wasn't getting there," I explained to Billy as we milked on Monday morning while Heather slept in since I was heading straight to the Busy Bean from the farm.

"Getting there don't pay bills," Billy said, and irritation flared within me.

"Right, but I'd diversified the produce already and added the new cheese varieties. It was just a matter of finding the buyers."

"Which that girl of yours did," Billy pointed out.

I sighed. He was right. She deserved the credit. Why was it so hard for me to admit?

"She tell you any more about the land trust?" Billy asked as we prepped the next two girls for milking.

I had to pause before I could answer because one of the goats I had on the platform was Annalee, and almost as if she could sense us talking about her new favorite human, she decided to join the conversation, calling out loudly in an admonishing tone.

"That right?" I asked her, placing the bowl of feed in front of her as the milking machine began to pump.

She looked at me and let out one more bleat before turning to her food.

"Haven't heard much. I guess she sent the paperwork in and is waiting to hear. It'll be fine either way." I knew it was a Hail Mary, and without it, there was a good chance we would not be fine.

Billy stopped what he was doing and narrowed his watery eyes at me. "No, it won't."

"Sure, it will. We were fine before."

"That's why you're working at the crazy coffee?"

"Busy Bean. And no, I'm working there to give us a little cushion while I turn the rest of the operation around."

Billy sighed, and I knew he was right, but it was hard to admit someone else had accomplished what I'd been struggling to do for so long. That maybe she'd even saved us in a way—she'd definitely bought us a bit more time by bringing in an infusion of cash to the farm. And if the Land Trust really did want to buy the development rights? Well, depending on what they paid, that could put us in the black again.

"Well, you better skedaddle," Billy said, looking down at his watch. "You said you had an early shift, and by my watch, it's early now."

I did have an early shift. Audrey and Zara usually worked around my schedule at the farm, but today they'd both had things to do early this morning, and I'd agreed to open for them.

As I prepped the Busy Bean for opening, my stomach growling at the scents coming from the kitchen as Roderick baked bread, muffins, cookies, and something that smelled like garlic and heaven, I realized I felt better than I had in a long time. Hopeful, even. At the same time as I felt this relieved sense of hope roll through me, I recognized that I'd been switching wildly back and forth. I was veering between determination to stand apart from

Heather, to not rely on her, and acknowledging that my need for her actually made me happy. I couldn't make sense of it, and for the time being, decided to live in the moment.

I used the menu chalk to scratch a new saying in an empty spot on the beam near the front door and felt myself settling inside in a way I wasn't sure I ever had.

Was it Heather? Her actions here, or her presence in my life, at my house? Was it the feeling of connection, of understanding, I was beginning to recognize?

The morning passed quickly, regulars taking their places on the scattered furniture like extras filling in the set of a sitcom, and the line moving steadily past the counter as I pulled coffees and served up little plates of baked goods. Roderick helped during the busiest times, but I'd become adept at multi-tasking.

"Dude," Roderick said, turning to me with a wide smile once the rush had died down. "Did I just hear you making cheerful small talk with Mrs. Browning?"

"I just complimented her hat, that's all."

"That's cheerful small talk, friend."

It was. And it was a skill I'd never possessed before coming to work at the Bean or before a certain bubbly blonde had come into my life. "Just being friendly," I said, beginning to be uncomfortable under his attention.

"And what about this? 'I may not have gone where I intended to go, but I think I ended up where I needed to be'?" He gave me a quizzical head tilt.

"Douglas Adams."

"*Hitchhiker's Guide*?"

"Close. *Long Dark Tea-Time of the Soul*."

"Interesting." Roderick leaned one hip on the counter as he narrowed his gaze at me, and it felt like he was seeing far more than I would have shown him if asked. "Mason, I daresay you seem happy."

Was I happy? Had I not been happy before? I wasn't sure I felt happier—just more awake, alive. It was almost like I'd been hibernating for a long time. "Maybe." I shrugged and turned to empty grounds and start fresh coffee for the lunch crowd.

I was preparing to head home—Audrey had come in to relieve me just before lunchtime—when Heather stepped through the door of the coffee shop. Though I tried to push down my reaction, I swore I felt my heart lift inside my chest at the sight of her.

Her hair was a tousled knot on top of her head, and she wore jeans with tall brown boots and a T-shirt that clung to her lithe frame in a way that my body took notice of immediately.

"Hello," she said, her cheery smile lighting the space as she moved toward the counter.

I had just removed my apron but moved to wait on her. "Hi." I felt strangely shy here, seeing her in town, out of our usual routine. "Can I get you something?"

"I wondered if you'd have time for lunch," she said, and while part of me jumped at the invitation, something hesitant in her voice suggested her motivation for visiting me might not be her desire for a spontaneous meal together.

"Sure," I said.

"You staying here?" Audrey asked. "The goat cheese and onion pizza Roddy made with the cheese from your farm is insane."

"Let's go sit on the deck at Speakeasy," Heather said. "Though I can smell the pizza," she told Audrey. "Is that the honey drizzle?"

Audrey nodded. "I'm so glad you brought that stuff in." She shot me a look. "No idea why Mason was keeping it a secret. I think I'm addicted to it."

"I wasn't keeping it a secret," I said. I just hadn't thought to offer it to my employers, but now I realized I just didn't have a marketing mindset. Not like Heather seemed to.

"Can you spare him?" Heather asked Audrey.

"He's off now anyway. Go enjoy the sunshine," she said,

patting my arm as I turned to join Heather on the other side of the counter.

We headed out into the warm street, a light breeze wafting by as we wordlessly agreed to walk, heading for the little path through the woods just beyond the Gin Mill.

There was an unfamiliar urge in me, pressing me to take her hand, to pull her closer, but I fought it, shoving my hands deep in the pockets of my jeans instead.

It was warmer in the trees, the summer day making the woods feel close and private, like a world apart from the relative business of the streets of Colebury.

"How was work?" Heather asked, turning her head to look up at me with the shining blue eyes I'd started to see behind my own lids at night.

"Good, actually," I said, surprising myself. Working at the Busy Bean had been a means to an end, but today I'd enjoyed the rhythm of working side by side with Roderick and the quieter moments where I got to appreciate some of the efficiencies I'd suggested Audrey and Zara adopt too. "It's something different than the farm, a different rhythm. But still a rhythm, you know?"

"You like your routines, huh?"

It wasn't a dig, just an observation. "I do. I guess I like to know what happens next."

"That's security, I suppose."

It was. "Kind of the opposite of my childhood," I said as we slowed our pace a bit, ambling between the narrow trunks. I didn't usually talk about my parents, about the terror I'd felt as a kid, wondering what would happen to Amelia and me after we'd lost them. After I'd let them die in that fire. "We had a lot of uncertainty right after the . . ." I still couldn't easily discuss the way I'd failed my parents. Guilt climbed my throat and stole the words.

"It must have been terrifying, especially as a kid. You didn't know for sure that your family here would come get you?"

I sighed. "We were kids. I mean, I was fourteen, but I was self-absorbed and selfish. I kind of forgot we had family out here. We didn't see them often, and I had no reason to assume Billy would come get us."

"But he did."

"Yeah." I tried not to think about the two weeks my sister and I had lived in a foster home, waiting for Billy to arrive. We'd known it was temporary, and the family that took us in was nice enough. But all I really remembered was my sister's constant tears, my own guilt, and the dogged fear of the future. Of not knowing if things would be all right.

We were quiet as we exited the woods and entered Speakeasy, following the hostess to the same table on the deck we'd had before.

After we'd each ordered an iced tea, Heather leaned in a little, and I could almost feel her words coming before she spoke. "I talked to Morgan back at the office."

My own visceral reaction to her words surprised me. I had an urge to spring up and run away, not to hear that she was done here, that she was going to go back to DC. I pushed down the sudden insanity I felt and swallowed hard, keeping my voice neutral. "How are things there?"

"Well, I'd spoken to him a week or so ago, and he'd assured me that things with the senator had died down, even in the city. He'd also said he didn't need me back right away."

Relief rolled through my limbs, cool and refreshing. He'd told her not to come back.

"But today he said it'd be best if I got back as soon as possible. I guess the senator who replaced Andrews is seeking to overturn some of the progress we made over the last year within the urban schools, and Morgan needs me to come strategize how we'll gain support in other places now that our ally is in prison. There's another conservative we might be able to win over, but I need to be there."

My blood stopped moving through my veins. I nodded, but

my mind wasn't on her words. I was hung up on the idea of her leaving, of being suddenly flung backward into the life I'd hidden in before she arrived. It was a terrifying feeling, and I hated how weak it felt to admit I was afraid—afraid that if she left, I'd never find this kind of calm happiness again. I didn't know what these feelings I had were exactly, but I knew they related to Heather, and I knew I wasn't ready for her to leave.

"Sounds like they need you," I managed as Heather sipped her tea.

She nodded, and her eyes stayed fixed on my face, like she was waiting for me to say more.

"You sure it's safe to go back though? It sounded like the senator's supporters were pretty die-hard. You feel okay about returning?"

Heather sat back in her chair and gazed around her, taking a deep breath and then meeting my eyes again. "I have to, right? That's my life. That's where I live. This has all been . . ." She trailed off, holding my gaze. "I mean, Mason . . ." She sighed, and I found myself hanging on her words. Would she tell me how she felt about the way things had changed between us?

"Mason, you have to know how grateful I am for this time, for the chance to escape and hide out for a while. And to meet you."

I waited, wanting to hear something from her that would confirm my own feelings, solidify my idea that there might be something real between us despite my best efforts to avoid just such an entanglement.

But she fell silent.

"You could stay," I said, surprising myself.

Her eyebrows shot up as she met my eyes again.

"They need a teacher at Amelia's school, right?"

"Yes, but . . . I mean, why would I stay?"

Her words were like a dagger. Was she asking me to give her a reason? Or telling me she didn't feel the same? My defenses rose. "You like it here, don't you?"

She let out a laugh, but it was a dry resigned sound. "I like

Disney World too, but I've always known that visits there were temporary. This has been a break. Like a vacation. I need to step back into the responsibilities I have in my life. I can't keep hiding."

My stomach churned uncomfortably, and I pushed away the burger I'd only begun to eat. "So when will you go?"

"Morgan wanted me back as soon as possible. I guess I'll go tomorrow? I just need to rent a car."

"Right." The afternoon seemed to darken around us, the river suddenly too loud as it rolled over the rocks and swept around the bank just off the edge of the deck. "We can do that now."

"I mean," Heather's eyes widened in surprise. "We can finish lunch."

"Sure," I said, though I knew I couldn't eat another bite. I watched her pick at her burger and paid the check as soon as the server came by again.

The walk back through the woods was silent, and where they'd felt close and intimate before, the overhanging branches and dark trunks now felt ominous, dangerous, and the close warmth of the day felt sticky and oppressive.

Heather wouldn't let me take her to the gas station on the edge of town that rented cars, but I gave her directions, and then I headed to the elementary school to work on the greenhouse. I didn't want to be home when she came back, didn't want to watch her pack her things tonight or hear her saying goodbye to my dog.

I didn't want her to leave.

But it was for the best, I told myself as I tried to hide in the hard work of moving earth and pulling plastic sheeting over the roof, securing it down the walls of the structure.

Losing people was a pain I already knew too well. Better that Heather go now, when I really didn't even know her, than wait until something inside me shifted and her loss might break something critical I could never fix.

This pain, I told myself, was just surprise. It was only the alarm of being caught off guard. Heather would leave the next day, and I would finally get back to my regular life, quiet and controlled and alone.

## 25

# HEATHER

From the moment I told Mason my plans, I felt sick.

I was doing the right thing. I knew I was. I was doing what anyone would do. I had a life to return to. People didn't just run away and stay that way. This time in Vermont had been temporary from the start, and it made me angry and confused to know that somehow, when it was time for it to end, it felt like a surprise.

Mason's face had turned to stone the second I'd told him. We'd sat on the sprawling deck by the river, and as I'd explained my plans to him, his mouth had pressed into a hard line, and he'd leaned back, as if he wanted to get away from me.

And every second after that had felt like an eternity, full of loaded tension.

I knew it was unrealistic, but some part of me had hoped Mason might say something else. Might ask me to stay.

He had suggested I could, in a way—he'd asked about the teaching job anyway. But I wouldn't uproot my entire life for a job that in some ways seemed like it could be a step backward. I'd left the classroom to do other things, to have a more direct impact on kids and communities, to make things better for them at a higher level. But still, the idea of being back at a small school like Colebury was appealing in some ways.

But without other reasons to stay here, to uproot my life, it wasn't enough.

I drove to the farm after lunch and said goodbye to Uncle Billy, and I called Amelia to thank her for everything. She sounded hurt and surprised too, which only made everything harder. That night I was in bed in the guestroom before Mason even came home. The next morning I waited until he'd returned from milking to say goodbye to him.

"Okay," I said, dropping my bag next to the front door as Rascal came to sit on my feet and stare up at me with his huge, liquid amber eyes. "I know, buddy. I'm going to miss you," I said, squatting down and petting him.

Mason stood in the kitchen, watching us, and the look of simmering hurt in his eyes made my heart twist inside me. I didn't really want to leave him, but it was time. And he hadn't given me any indication of there being an alternative.

So I hugged the big brown dog, tears clogging my throat as I pushed my face into the thick fur at his neck. "Bye, little dog," I told him, pulling myself together as I stood.

Mason was driving me to the gas station at the edge of Colebury where I'd pick up the rental car I'd arranged the afternoon before. He'd gone to milk in the morning, and I'd packed up, collected eggs one last time, and harvested tomatoes. Then I'd sat on the couch and waited for him, feeling an awkward disconnect somewhere inside me.

"Let's go," Mason said, stepping close and picking up my bag. On the doorstep, he paused and looked back. "One more ride in the Karmann Ghia?"

I nodded wistfully at the little blue car, and Mason moved to put my bag into the back seat. I'd miss this car too. In some ways, it had been a physical representation of this little jump off the tracks of my regular life. And it was time to let it all go, to get back on my path.

Mason drove, and as the now-familiar fields and trees slid across the windshield, a deep heaviness settled inside me. Mason hadn't said much to me since lunch the day before. I knew I owed him a lot, but I was also a little bit hurt. We'd had something, I'd thought. Something beyond just a physical connection. But now it was almost like it had never happened.

As he drove, his jaw set and his gaze straight ahead, I gathered my courage to say some of what I needed to say. "Mason," I ventured, my voice unsteady.

He turned to acknowledge that I'd spoken but still said nothing.

"I just wanted to thank you. For everything."

"No need."

"No, there is. You opened your home without a question, took me in, and made me feel safe. I had nowhere else to go, and while I know I didn't seem excited to be here at first . . . I really liked it here." I paused, frowning as I searched for better words. Words that captured how my heart was flooding with emotion as I looked at him, words that could explain the sense of heavy sadness that came when I thought about my lonely apartment, my lonely life.

"I found something here I didn't know I was looking for," I said finally, knowing it wasn't enough.

He looked at me then, his expression softening for the duration of the long gaze, and a shiver passed through me as our eyes met. But then I watched as he swallowed and set his face again into the determined expression he'd worn since the day before. "I'm glad you enjoyed your time," he said, sounding as if each word pained him.

"I enjoyed meeting you," I said, forcing myself to say the difficult words, but they came out so quietly I wasn't sure if he'd heard.

He nodded, just once, acknowledging my statement. But he didn't say anything back, and the heaviness inside me grew.

"And I'm sorry about not getting to help you finish with the greenhouse. I meant to see that through," I said. "But you should be good with the produce pick-ups from the restaurants, right?"

I'd left so much hanging there, had hoped to solidify things before I left.

Mason just nodded and muttered, "We'll be fine," as my stomach sank.

We pulled into the gravel lot of the gas station a few minutes later, and I stood, pulling my bag from the back. "Well, thank you," I said, expecting Mason to pull away, drive out of my life forever.

"I'll make sure you get on the road okay," he said stiffly, stepping out of the car.

He followed me to the counter of the rental place at the side of the gas station and watched wordlessly as I collected the keys and directions to where the Prius I'd rented was parked. When I'd settled my bag in the trunk, I turned to face him, surprised to find him standing just inches away.

That dark intensity was back, vibrating the air around him in a way that was both compelling and daunting, and I wasn't sure what to do.

"Well—" I started, the keys gripped in my hand.

Mason's arms went around me suddenly, his mouth finding mine, and all that dark intensity was channeled through the kiss he wrenched from me without warning. It was fierce and desperate, and as he kissed me, he pressed himself to me so that I could feel every hard edge of his body, and my need for him spiraled immediately.

And then he released me, both of us breathless.

"Drive carefully," he said softly.

"Mason," I said, but he was already turning away. "You could visit me . . . in DC," I tried, my brain still not quite catching up to my mouth. "It's not that far. People make longer distances work all the time."

Mason stopped, glancing at me over his shoulder, and then turned away again and walked back to the tiny blue car.

The drive back to the city was long and silent, and I filled the time and space with self-recrimination. What had I thought I was doing, sleeping with Mason Rye? What had he thought we were doing? The fact he hadn't even responded when I'd suggested we could see one another still was all the indication I needed that it had been nothing more than a convenience for him.

Only, I didn't believe that.

He'd been upset when I told him I was leaving, and you didn't get upset unless you wanted someone to stay.

I knew Mason was a man of few words, but I suppose I had expected more. I had hoped maybe he would ask me to stay. Really ask me. Not for a job or because of some no-longer-existent threat to my well-being in DC, but because he wanted me to stay. Because he cared about me. Because maybe there was something worth exploring between us besides a shared physical comfort in the late hours of the night.

And I'd been with enough men who weren't all in, who found it easy to turn to the next thing that came along. If Mason wasn't sure we were worth a try, then that meant we were not.

"There she is!" Morgan greeted me with a huge bear hug as I stepped into the office the following day. My first night back had been rough. My apartment felt foreign and sterile, and also like a once-safe space that no longer belonged to me. I tried not to think about the man who had been here, going through my things, but it was impossible.

"Here I am," I agreed, trying for a jovial tone. Unsurprisingly, I hadn't slept well, and I hadn't been able to muster up much enthusiasm for returning to work either.

"You look gorgeous," he said, walking me to my office. "Rested and rosy-cheeked. Vermont agreed with you."

My stomach churned, and the mention of Vermont made my heart feel too big, too heavy inside me. "It was beautiful," I said.

"I bet you're glad to be back though, back to your mission in life, right? And away from grumpy goat farmers?"

Morgan knew better, and he was poking at me, trying to get me to talk. But there was no point spilling my confusion here at the office. I'd made a choice, and it was time to move forward.

My best friend raised an eyebrow when I didn't respond to his baiting, then let out a sigh. "Okay then. You're back. Let's get you up to speed."

The rest of the day, and the week that followed, were filled with long days at the office, compounded by sleepless nights. In between the two were harrowing excursions out into a city that felt too big, too frenetic. Cars flew by, horns blared, and people moved with a careless ferocity that made me feel like I needed to stake some kind of claim on the very air I intended to breathe.

I spent the nights huddled on my couch, the television keeping me company as I tried to eat, but everything felt wrong—like a favorite sweater that had shrunk in the wash.

We worked hard during the days, but Morgan didn't give up trying to wrench information about Vermont from me. And when I admitted that I'd gotten involved with my host, his eyes lit up.

"Tell me everything," he said, plopping himself down on the edge of my desk.

I did. I managed to tell him everything, from the farm stands to the school, goats to nights spent in Mason Rye's bed. Talking about it only made me miss it more.

"And you're back here, why?"

I stared at him. "Because you called me and said you needed me to come back. Because this is my real life. That was all some kind of temporary fantasy."

"Why wouldn't you want to stay in the fantasy?" Morgan looked shocked, like he couldn't understand my choice at all. As if I'd really had one.

I tilted my head, uncertain. "I did." This might have been the first time I'd really admitted this to myself.

"But you're here."

It was pointless trying to explain it to him. Morgan was my boss, but he was also my overly romantic friend, and once he found out there'd been anything between my host and me, it was all he wanted to talk about.

I lasted two weeks. Two weeks of forcing myself through the motions of a life that felt like it belonged to someone else, two weeks of sleepless nights and a dogging sadness I couldn't explain to myself. It wasn't about Mason, I told myself. I wasn't willing to be the girl who wasn't enough for the man again. We hadn't been like that anyway, I reminded myself. It had never been a real relationship.

During that time, I began to replace the sadness and discomfort with something more accessible, more easily remedied: guilt. I realized I'd left Billy and Mason in the lurch in lots of different ways. Who was working the farm stands on Saturdays? Who was collecting eggs and produce from Mason's greenhouse while he worked two jobs to try to keep the farm afloat? Was the school project going to be completed before the kids arrived back in late August?

When I'd finished work the second Friday after I'd gotten back, I walked home slowly, fighting with myself. When I finally arrived at the glass doors of my building, glancing around nervously as I let myself inside, I gave in. With my door locked securely behind me, I called Amelia.

"Heather!" She sounded so happy to hear from me, and my heart soared inside my chest. "I can't believe you left without saying goodbye. Did you get my texts?"

"I'm so sorry. It's been really crazy since I've been back. Work is nuts."

"Yeah, Mason said they really needed you there. He's been a joy lately, by the way."

I swallowed hard. Even hearing Mason's name made my heart stutter. "Is everything okay?" I wanted to ask about him specifically but couldn't.

"Things are fine. The same, you know? Not much changes here."

"Yeah."

"Good to be back in the city, I bet?"

I took a breath. "Well, that's kind of why I'm calling."

## 26
## MASON

I had expected to be lonely and hurt when Heather left—I knew I'd let myself get in too deep, and I angrily cursed the whole situation now as I went through the motions of my days. What choice had I really had? Brigsy had dropped his frightened, gorgeous sister literally on my doorstep, and then she turned out to be intelligent and kind . . . And I didn't really feel like I'd taken advantage of the situation.

Things had just happened.

And now I really wished they hadn't. I kept turning around at home, about to say something, or share some ridiculous part of my day, only to remember it was just me and Rascal.

The way I wanted it.

The way I used to think I wanted it, at least.

But I missed her. And I knew letting her inside my heart was a mistake, that it was only temporary and that she would leave eventually. And the more nights I spent holding her, burying myself in her soft comfort, feeling her body so close to mine, the more certain I was that it would hurt when she left.

But I hadn't expected this.

The joy had been sapped from within me, and I hadn't been an especially joyful guy in the first place. Still, there was work to do, and though I sometimes felt like I was just going through the motions, I had commitments to keep, people depending on me.

School started this week, and I still hadn't managed to finish up the greenhouse. The construction was mostly done—I just needed to tweak a few things. But there was nothing growing inside, and now that kids were back in school, the lessons my sister had been so excited about—tending, caring for, and harvesting produce while learning about the greenhouse itself—they were going to miss some of the impact if the kids walked into an empty earthen structure covered with plastic.

So I dedicated an entire Friday to getting it planted, brought seedlings I'd started at home, and dumped the soil and additives in piles in the back of the truck.

It was hard, sweaty work, especially with the sun beating down on me and the complete lack of breeze. I was hot and tired, and when I glanced toward the parking lot to see a gorgeous blonde with miles of tanned legs approaching in shorts and a T-shirt and wearing work gloves and a bright smile, I thought I might be having a heat stroke.

"Hey," Heather said, stepping near as I continued to stare, trying to decide if she was some kind of mirage.

I turned and picked up the water bottle I'd left on the ground and took a long swig before swinging back around to make sure she was actually there. She was.

"What are you doing here?" I asked, realizing too late that my tone was angry, accusatory, and totally at odds with the happiness I felt at seeing her.

Her smile faded. "Look, I know I don't really belong here, but I made commitments to you, to help you get this set up and to secure your produce sales through the winter. I left before I'd finished those things, and I think that's why I felt so unsettled when I was back."

I shook my head, confused. Why would Heather be bothered by these things in the midst of her busy days in the city? Unless that was just a reason to get back, and maybe there was something else drawing her here. The idea sparked the flame of hope inside me back to life.

"So you're back to help me?" I couldn't help imagining us back in my house at the end of the day, falling into my bed, sharing long warm nights together again.

"Yes," she said. "Your sister said I could stay with her for a couple weeks while I tie up the loose ends I left here."

My hope dissipated. She wasn't staying with me. "Okay," I said, trying to keep the disappointment from my voice.

"So how can I help?" she asked, rolling her weight back and forth between her heels and toes, making her bounce a bit in a way I told myself was not adorable.

"Right now, I'm just carrying loads of dirt over from the truck," I said, pointing back to the still full bed of my vehicle. "Pretty exciting."

"Got another shovel?" she asked, looking around.

I did, and I handed it to her, and then we pushed the wheelbarrow over to the truck bed, and I jumped inside and began shoveling topsoil down into the big bucket while I tried to sort through the warring feelings inside me. I couldn't even figure out if I was glad she was back, since she clearly hadn't come back for me. Heather climbed up and was about to join me when we noticed Principal Franz crossing the grass toward us.

"This is really coming along, Mason. Hello, Heather."

"Hi, Principal Franz," Heather said, her light, bubbly voice making my heart twist uncomfortably inside me. I tried for a pleasant expression. Words were beyond me at the moment, with Heather standing so close, up in the truck bed.

"The kids are really excited about helping out in the greenhouse this year," she said, smiling widely. "It's going to be a great addition to our curriculum." The principal turned her sharp gaze on Heather. "I don't suppose you've thought any more about just chucking it all and moving out here, getting your Vermont certificate." She laughed, but it was clear there was an element of seriousness in her question.

Heather crouched and then jumped down from the bed of the truck, stepping near the principal. "You still haven't found anyone?"

"We have a long-term sub for the classroom I told you about," she said. "But we'll need someone permanent soon. I don't suppose you know anyone?"

Heather frowned, shifting her weight. "I wish I did," she said. "I wish I could do it, honestly."

My heart jumped. Might she actually stay?

"But I'm just here to wrap a few things up." She laughed lightly, but the sound was forced, unnatural.

"I wish I could give you a reason to stay, but I can't exactly tempt you with the incredible pay." The principal shrugged. "Benefits are good though, and I can offer a lot of fresh air. Good people."

"Thanks," Heather said. "I'll keep my ears open and let you know if I hear of anyone."

The principal gave her a sharp nod, accepting this. "Thanks for helping here," she said, then turned her gaze to me. "Mason."

I lifted a hand and then returned my attention to my shovel, trying to shut down my circling thoughts.

We worked through the morning, kids coming out in groups to play on the nearby blacktop and a few wandering over now and then to ask questions or just watch as Heather and I carried shovelfuls of topsoil and compost inside the greenhouse, spreading it on both sides of the center aisle.

That afternoon, my sister appeared, smiling broadly. "He really put you to work, huh?"

Heather laughed. "It's fine. It's why I came back."

I stood near to listen—Heather and I hadn't been talking at all as we worked, and I loved the sound of her voice, even if she wasn't talking to me. I was beginning to realize how much I wanted her to stay, how much she meant to me. And I thought maybe I could even tell her, ask her to consider staying, try to explain how we might give it a try. The pain of the last couple weeks was more than I wanted to experience again, and maybe I was the one causing it.

My heart lifted as I thought about what I might say, how I might ask her to consider trying something real. With me.

"My class is in media right now," my sister was saying. "So I have a few minutes free, and I hoped you might give me your opinion on a couple lesson plans I'm thinking about."

"Definitely," Heather said brightly. "You can spare me for a couple minutes, right?"

I looked up, meeting her eyes. "Sure," I said, the words coming more easily—as if I'd finally gotten myself over some kind of mental roadblock internally. I'd talk to her. Maybe tonight if I could find a chance. But if she was staying a couple weeks, I had time to think about what I really needed to say.

I watched as my sister led Heather in the side door of the long, low school building, and something inside me settled. I went back to work, feeling lighter and happier than I had since Heather had left. But as I continued focusing on my work, a niggling feeling began to grow in my gut. I ignored it at first, assuming it was just lingering doubt—I was about to take a major chance, after all. And that wasn't something I did often. But what I'd thought was nervousness kept pinging, and after a little while I realized what it was, why that particular ping felt so uncomfortable and unfamiliar.

It was my intuitive alarm, the one I'd relied on to keep me alive when I was in the military. And it was screaming at me to listen, telling me something was wrong.

I raised my head and stepped away from the greenhouse, scanning the area around me, my senses leaping to focus and my body beginning to tense. There was danger. I could feel it, but I didn't know where it was coming from, where I needed to defend.

And then I saw the smoke, and an alarm began to blare loudly, ringing like a Klaxon call across the field to where I stood as every single cell inside my body leapt into panic and chaos. The smoke was coming from an open window on the far end of the school. Where my sister's classroom was. Where Heather had just gone.

My body reacted almost before my mind had processed what was happening, and as I sprinted toward the door through which my sister and Heather had disappeared, images flickered through my mind even as I tried to push them away.

I saw my home engulfed in flames, the destruction glowing bright against the darkness of the night. I saw the charred, darkened trunks of fig trees. I saw my sister's face, smeared with tears and soot, her hair clinging to her face even as she clung to me. And I saw myself, standing helplessly in the road as everything I'd ever known went up in flames, and I did nothing.

Just as I reached the door, my heart in my throat and my breath coming in ragged desperate gasps, Amelia emerged, leading a line of children behind her. She was calling out commands to them, telling them to stay calm, to stay in line, and they filed out toward the blacktop, joining other classrooms lining up there.

As the students exited, I bolted inside, desperate to find Heather. I nearly collided with her, leading another group of kids down a long tiled hallway.

"Let's get outside," she was calling back to the small group. "Remember how you do this for drills. This is exactly why you practice, and I know you're great at this." Her voice was calm and clear, despite the smoke hanging over our heads and building in the narrow corridor. My heart was in my throat, my body frozen.

Heather's eyes met mine, a quizzical expression there. "Let's go outside, okay?" She said, placing a hand on my elbow to turn me and get me walking out the door with the students.

As the little group of kids joined their schoolmates on the blacktop, Heather frowned at me. "Most people evacuate when a fire alarm goes off, Mason. Why were you going in?"

"To find you," I said, my voice louder than intended.

Her eyes softened, and she squeezed my arm. "I'm fine. But I need to help Amelia make sure she's got everyone." She turned and moved to where my sister stood, both of them looking calm and collected, even as the entire school emptied and joined them on the hard black pavement, even as the blare of a siren screamed into the close, hot air, mixing with the frightened cries of the children.

The teachers and administrators counted kids, consulting clipboards and tablets, as firemen leapt from the truck and entered the building behind us.

I felt useless, standing at the edge of the pavement, watching as children and adults clustered together, hugged one another in their fear. It felt like a movie playing out before me, and I was as powerless to act here as I would have been if it had been a film.

Eventually, the fire chief, a little red-haired woman who introduced herself to Principal Franz as "Horrigan," came out and had some quiet words with the administrators. Then she turned and talked to the gathered group before her.

"You all know that electricity can be dangerous, right?" she asked the kids.

"Like lightning!" one little voice called out.

"Or the bathtub," someone else added, and it took me a minute to figure out where they were going with that.

"Right," Horrigan said, clasping her hands in front of her. "And sometimes the wires that bring electricity from there"—she pointed at the power poles marching in a line next to the school —"into the walls of buildings can start fires. If they're put in wrong, or sometimes if they've been damaged."

"So this was wires?" a student asked, sounding worried.

"In this case, we think the wires were in a new coffee maker the school had just installed in the teachers' lounge," she said. "That's where this one started, and luckily there was not a lot of damage done—at least not to any of your classrooms. But school will probably be closed for a little while so we can clean up, and your teachers will have to eat lunch somewhere else for a while."

The adrenaline was seeping out of me, leaving my limbs heavy and my senses dulled, and as I stood useless, watching this scene, a sprout of panic jumped to life inside me. I'd almost lost them. To a fire, of all things. Fear bloomed large and terrifying inside me.

A few students and teachers chuckled at the fire chief's joke, and Principal Franz thanked her and addressed the group, telling them that they'd stay outside for the rest of the afternoon, going in class by class to collect their things after the chief assured them that the smoke had cleared and everything was safe.

Amelia moved to my side as the chief and principal walked together back toward the fire truck and other vehicles gathered in the parking lot. "Hey," she said, looking up at me as her arm slipped around my waist. "You okay?"

I sucked in a shuddery breath and realized suddenly how very not okay I actually was. I was drenched in sweat, and my chest felt tight, my skin too small. My arms pulled my little sister close, the same images I'd seen earlier running on repeat through my mind. This had been too much. Too close.

"Mason." She pulled back slightly and stared up at me. "It's okay. Everyone is okay."

I heard the words, but there was too much going on in my mind to respond as my eyes swept back and forth between Heather and my sister. Both here, both whole.

This was what I was afraid of. Exactly this. Loving someone and having them ripped away by a random event I couldn't control. What if the day had ended differently? What if I'd stood here again, watching a building burn with people I loved inside?

I could not do that again. I could never survive it again.

"I'm fine," I told my sister, trying to contain the edge of terror lining my voice.

"You don't seem fine," she whispered, hugging me tightly.

"I'm okay," I said. But I wasn't. And I didn't know how to be.

I pulled my sister's arms from my body and turned. "Gonna head home." I tossed my shovel inside the greenhouse, moved to close the tailgate on the truck, and then drove straight home, where I took the bottle of whiskey and a glass out to the back deck, hoping to drown the dark thoughts, the red terror inside me.

Rascal looked at me quizzically but settled by my side all the same. I stayed there, drinking, wishing for darkness, for calm, for nothing.

Instead, my mind raced through pointless cycles of panic, and my breath was coming too fast. I felt sick and afraid, and more alone than I could remember ever feeling before. Except right after it happened.

The feelings I'd had as a kid—terror, fear, loneliness, hopelessness—they circled and swooped around me, diving in to scrape me with talons that left my mind ragged, my soul drained.

Somewhere, rationally, I knew I was having a panic attack—or multiple panic attacks—but in the moment, I felt like there was a good chance I was dying. And that I would die alone, which was probably for the best.

If I could pull myself through this night, through the fear and pain that plagued me, I would make myself remember that.

Alone was good. Alone was safe.

## 27

# HEATHER

The entire school stood out on the blacktop under the blazing sun, watching smoke pour from one side of the building we'd just left. And that was where I came back to myself, realized exactly what had just happened in a holistic way. Prior to that moment, I'd been acting on instinct, adrenaline fueling my calm assertiveness as I'd shepherded kids down the hallway, organized quiet and orderly lines of terrified and confused children, and taken them outside to safety.

I had done what anyone would have done, but it might not have meant as much to anyone else afterward. I'd been saved my whole life. My father saved me from drowning as a toddler, and my brother had taken it upon himself to save me from that day forward, whether I needed it or not.

But today, I'd moved with purpose and intent in the face of a very real danger. And I'd saved myself. And helped all these kids to safety.

I watched the students and adults around me, hugging one another—some of them laughing with relief, and I felt a sense of confidence seep in around the edges of all the insecurity I'd been carrying for so long without knowing it.

I was just about to move toward my friends, to check in with

Mason especially, because he looked stunned and upset, when the fire chief addressed the group.

And even though her words calmed the children still upset by what had happened, and she reassured us all that this could have been much, much worse, I could think of nothing except moving to Mason, wrapping my arms around him and burying my head in the strength of his chest. Because along with the realization of my own capability, I'd realized that the fear that always held me back was holding me away from him too. I'd left because I'd been afraid—afraid that if we tried, it would give him the chance to hurt me.

But I knew it was worth the chance now. I knew I was strong enough to try and that I'd never forgive myself if I didn't.

Plus, a letter had arrived at Amelia's from the Vermont Land Trust. I had good news to share with Mason. Maybe I'd even get a chance to save him a little bit, I thought with pride.

I turned back to where he and Amelia stood as the fire chief finished, but he was walking rapidly away, heading for his truck. His posture was stiff and mechanical, and my heart swelled with worry and concern.

"Amelia, are you guys okay?"

She shook her head at me, tears standing in her eyes. "I'm fine," she said. "I mean, fire is not my favorite thing . . ." She trailed off, attempting a light chuckle. "But I'm worried about my brother."

Mason's truck left the parking lot, and my heart sank a little, knowing how hard it must be to relive the dark memories of his youth, wanting to be next to him, to help in any way I could.

"Should I go after him?"

Amelia looked around at the milling groups of kids, the firemen entering and leaving the building. "I'm guessing we could actually use you here until the kids all get home safe." Cars were already speeding into the parking lot, parents essentially abandoning them along the edges of the school's field as they ran toward the gathered group of kids outside. "There are going to be a lot of parents with questions. News travels fast here."

"Right." My heart sank a little at the thought of Mason on his own, battling whatever demons the fire might have brought to life in him. But Amelia was right—I was needed here.

For the next several hours, I helped explain the situation to worried parents, walked kids into classrooms to get their belongings, and gave my statement to the investigators for the official record. By the time I was able to leave, the sun was getting low in the west, and I was exhausted.

It didn't matter though. I needed to see Mason. I needed to make sure he was all right and tell him about the conservation funds he was being offered for the farm.

My mood lifted as I drove down the curved, tree-lined country roads out to Mason's farm. This place—a place I'd never thought of before two months ago—had nestled into my heart, my soul. I wanted to stay here, to live here. I wanted to make a life here.

Mason's truck was parked in front of his house, and I was glad to see it, since I'd wondered if he might have gone over to the farm.

I stepped out of my rental car, taking the envelope from the Land Trust with me, and was just closing the door when Rascal appeared from around the side of the house. He paused, then galloped in my direction, skidding to a stop on the soft earth at my feet just before crashing into me.

"Hey, buddy," I crooned, sinking my hands into his soft fur. I was surprised how much I'd missed this furry brown dog. I squatted down and rubbed him for a few minutes, expecting Mason to emerge from the house. But he didn't.

When I stood again, Rascal whined softly, which was unusual, and then trotted back to the side of the house from which he'd come. He waited there, and when I headed for the front door, he barked once. In all the time I'd known him, Rascal had never barked. It struck a low chord of worry in my gut, and I turned to face the dog. "What's going on, Rascal?"

He disappeared around the side of the house, and on instinct, I followed him, a knot of fear lodging in my stomach.

Mason was on the back deck, his body slouched low in one of the big Adirondack chairs and his hands covering his face. He wasn't moving, except for his chest, which was rising and falling quickly. The bottle of Half Cat whiskey and a glass sat at his feet.

He didn't move as I stepped up onto the deck.

Something was very wrong.

"Mason?"

Mason's hands dropped from his eyes, and his posture stiffened as he sat up. He didn't answer me but turned to look at me through glassy eyes, his face creased with worry.

I wanted to run to him, to take him in my arms, to comfort him. But while he looked distressed, there was a warning in his face too. He looked wary, and I had to push down a hint of misplaced fear within myself to take a step toward him. "Are you all right?"

"No." The word was flat, dull. And after it escaped his lips, he turned away from me again, dropping his elbows on his knees and his head hanging down.

"Hey," I said, moving closer. I placed one hand between his shoulders. The muscles beneath my hand quivered and tensed. "Hey, it's okay," I said, sensing that Mason was in the midst of something I might not have the ability to handle. I'd seen panic attacks before and wondered if this might be the aftermath of that. I'd had one, and it had left me sweaty and confused.

I lowered myself in front of him, the letter forgotten in my purse, which I dropped to the deck. I slid to my knees, letting my hands fall onto Mason's thighs so I could look up at his face. And the expression there shredded my heart into pieces. Fear, remorse, guilt. I thought Mason was in the midst of them all, and there was a desperation in his eyes that made me react without really thinking.

"Hey," I crooned, as I would to the dog, to a child. "Hey, it's okay." I slid nearer, reaching up and wrapping my arms around his shoulders, rising to move between his legs.

A sound came from him, somewhere between a groan and a grunt of pain, and then his arms went around my waist, and he held me there tightly, pressing his face into my stomach. For a few minutes, his back shook, and his breath continued coming in those fast gasps. I didn't know what to do, so I stood, holding him, telling him everything would be okay.

I let my hands stroke the broad planes of his back, play with the short hair at the back of his neck, doing my best to transmit comfort through my touch, through the gentle stream of words coming from my mouth. My heart was shredding into dust inside me, seeing him like this and not knowing how to help.

After a bit, the shaking stopped, but Mason's grasp on my body tightened, and he held me slightly away from himself, tilting his head to look up at me, standing between his thighs as he sat.

I expected him to speak—there was confusion and crisis in his eyes, and I knew he needed to talk, that we needed to talk. But he didn't speak. Instead, his hands moved to the waistband of my jeans, and within seconds he was pressing my pants down my legs, dragging my underwear with them.

Desire ignited in me, but it was an unfamiliar version of what I had felt for Mason before. This feeling was born of the sudden confidence I'd found in myself during the fire today, and the worry and pain I felt for Mason over the same event. I needed to help him, to save him, but I didn't know how, and if somehow feeling my skin against his might help him, then I'd do it.

I stepped back and pulled my T-shirt off over my head, and Mason rose just enough to pull his own pants from his narrow hips, revealing a thick erection that jutted up. He reached for me then, and I let him pull me in, wordlessly, his eyes tracking every inch of my skin as my knees found their way to each side of his hips.

His hands controlled our motion, bracing me as I lowered

myself onto him, gasping at the slow, delicious intrusion of his flesh moving inside me. I hadn't come here for this today, not at all, but I found I needed it. I'd missed him, had missed this.

Mason's strong arms lifted and lowered me, the muscles of his neck and chest straining with the effort as he stared into my eyes, demons dancing there in the midnight depths. My hands caressed the sides of his face, his neck, traced lines across the hard expanse of his chest, looking for the thing that would make him okay again, that might ease the pain he felt.

I could feel my body coiling, every muscle tightening in response to Mason's thrusts, and the look on his face changed, the pain and fear sliding away to make room for something else, something just as wild and desperate, but something I could help release. I gripped him tighter, my hips beginning to take over his rhythm as I pressed my knees into the hard seat of the chair, looking for more friction, more contact.

We weren't silent, but we didn't speak as we each sought our release on Mason's back deck under the tall pines surrounding his little piece of property. And when the world erupted into bright, glittering shards of light and then cascaded in swirls around me, I heard myself cry out at the same time as I heard Mason's guttural groan. His arms became steel around me as he thrust up into me, and when he stopped, his face was buried in my chest, his body pressed so tightly to mine I could barely breathe.

I didn't complain though. This was what I'd dreamed of those long weeks back in DC. This was what I wanted. To be here, with Mason. I knew it now, and I was ready to tell him, to find a way to stay here, in this life.

Just as I opened my mouth to speak, Mason's arms released me. His hands lifted me from his body and pushed me away, setting me back on my feet.

"I'm sorry," he whispered, not looking at me.

Every thought in my mind, every image I'd been entertaining of the two of us together, here, crashed to the ground around me. "What?"

"You should go." He wouldn't look at me, just uttered the words in a low, painful monotone.

"Mason," I said, desperate for him to look at me again. I touched one strong forearm, longing for the connection we'd had just seconds ago. "No, I . . . Listen, we can get dressed, I'll make dinner. Let's talk, okay?"

He didn't answer me, and suddenly I felt very, very naked. I began scooping up my clothes and carried them inside, through the familiar cottage where I'd realized who I really was, what I really wanted. But as I cleaned up and pulled my clothes back on, the reality of Mason's words sunk in. *You should go.*

I gazed into the mirror, pushing a few waves back off my forehead and swiping at the mascara that had smudged beneath my eyes.

"Mason?" I said, stepping back onto the deck. He'd put his pants back on, but maintained that hard, desperate gaze out into the woods. Rascal whined at his side, having crept back up to the deck now that the humans had their clothes on again. "Mason, we should talk. About what happened today, about everything. I have news, I—"

"Just go, Heather," Mason said softly, getting to his feet and facing me. Those dark eyes burned into mine. "Just go. You're safe now, you don't need me anymore. Go back to DC and live your life."

"No, I—that's what I wanted to talk about, I—"

He cut me off, swinging around and picking up the whiskey bottle, muttering. As he swayed slightly, I realized he was probably very drunk, though it hadn't affected his ability to melt me into a puddle a few minutes before. "Please go away," he said, his voice a whisper.

I couldn't talk to him like this. Not if he was drunk. "I'll go," I said, feeling like it was the wrong thing to do. "But maybe I should just be here? Just in case—"

He didn't answer me, just headed into the house, slamming the door behind him.

And the sound of that door was like a death knell. I understood then. He'd walked away from me. From us. He didn't even care enough to tell me why.

I stared at the door for a few minutes, Rascal at my side.

This wasn't right. It didn't feel right, and I couldn't accept that this was it. Not when Mason was drunk. Not after everything that had happened today—or the way he'd made love to me just now.

I'd come back tomorrow, tell him about the Land Trust funding, and we'd talk.

"I'll be back, boy," I told Rascal, petting him a few times before heading to my car and driving myself to Amelia's house.

# 28

## MASON

I didn't sleep. Not exactly.

I was drunk enough to fade off into a haze of self-loathing as I collapsed onto the couch after coming in from the back deck. I awoke to pure darkness, the sound of Rascal's cries pulling me from my stupor.

As I stumbled to the back door, letting in my poor dog whose doleful eyes were too kind even to accuse me of forgetting him in my own misery, my mind flashed back to Heather's face. To the hurt and surprise there when I'd ordered her to go.

What she couldn't see was that it was better for both of us that way. I was certain, though, that in the light of day, she'd understand.

I fed the dog and forced myself into a long, hot shower before drinking a huge glass of water and then climbing into bed. I'd washed the sheets after Heather had left weeks ago, but I had held onto one pillow where she'd lain her head while she'd stayed with me. And I put my own head on it now, my senses filling with the faint scent of her shampoo, her face wash.

After a few minutes, though, I had to push the pillow away from me. The scent of her, those traces I'd clung to, they didn't bring me comfort now. Instead, they stoked the sparks of fear and worry smoldering inside my gut. I needed to let her go. If I didn't do it now, I'd be forced into it later, through some act I had no control over. This, at least, would be my choice. This pain I was feeling now was nothing in comparison to what I'd be feeling if she'd been ripped away from me by that fire today. That would have been out of my control, completely outside the possibility for me to choose. Like my parents.

I knew what that kind of pain was, and I would do anything to protect myself from ever feeling it again.

Maybe that made me damaged, unlovable, incomplete. But it also kept me safe.

The night ebbed and pulsed around me, and I endured scattered flashbacks—our farmhouse burning, smoke billowing from the school, my sister standing beside me both times . . . Heather's calm presence near me on the blacktop. Fire engines, flames, crying children. Heather's face above me as I held onto her desperately on my deck.

Morning came, and I milked the goats, barely speaking to Billy.

"You look like goat shit," he commented, and that was the extent of our pre-dawn exchange for the day.

"Rough night?" Roderick asked when I arrived for my shift at the Busy Bean.

I might have responded. I tried.

"A grunt!" He stepped in front of me and gave me a level look. "Mason Rye, did you just answer me with a grunt?"

"Sorry," I muttered.

He looked at me for a long moment and then took a step back. "I'm not going to get into your business," he said. "But if you want to talk, you know where to find me."

"Thanks." I realized as I turned back to the counter that Roderick was probably the closest thing to a friend I actually had. My solitary life ensured I didn't have anyone to talk to when I needed it.

Roderick stayed in the kitchen during most of my shift, and I went through the motions, trying to take comfort in the efficiency of the coffee shop, the routine of it all, but it wasn't very effective.

Zara came in to relieve me and close, and she spent a few minutes bustling around the tables out front before coming behind the counter where I was essentially hiding, trying to look busy scrubbing an already gleaming coffee pot.

"You write that one?" She stepped close and pointed to my newest scribbled quote. It wasn't very uplifting, even I could admit.

"Yeah."

She read it out loud. "'The only thing standing between you and happiness is reality.'" Her keen eyes turned to study me. "What's wrong, Mason?"

"Nothing," I lied. "Just felt like maybe we needed to offer a new perspective. Can't be butterflies and unicorns all the time."

"Are you ever butterflies and unicorns?"

"Not really."

"You do seem darker today than usual though. Need an ear?"

I did. "No."

"Is it that cute blond girl? Amelia's friend?"

"Heather."

"Heather," she confirmed, tying on her apron. "Right."

"No."

She nodded to herself, tidying up the pastries in the glass case. "Okay then. Seems like you're good."

"There was a fire at the school yesterday," I blurted.

She straightened up and turned to look at me. "Everyone's okay though? I would have heard."

"Everyone's okay." How could I explain how not okay I had been since the fire? What a near miss it felt like? "Just a reminder how fast things change, that's all."

She squinted at me, a tiny half smile lifting one side of her mouth. "Or a reminder how precious our lives are, how much we should treasure what we've got."

I blew out a frustrated breath. "Sure. Or that."

"You're determined to be dark today."

"Or just being a realist." I took off my apron, ready to head for the door.

"Hey." Zara stepped in front of me. "I don't know what's going on with you. I knew you were the intense, moody type when we hired you, and you're a good worker. But this gloomy dark shit? Take it somewhere else, okay? The world is exactly as shitty as you think it is, Mason. If you need to talk to someone, I'm here. And I'm a good listener. But this is my business, and I need you to move away from the murderous glare you're giving everyone right now and find your way back to just plain intense, okay? We don't need you scaring the crap out of our customers."

I dropped my head and took a deep breath. "Yeah. Sorry." I needed to get myself together.

When I got home, she was there. I saw her car first, the little rental Toyota parked out next to the Karmann Ghia I still hadn't been able to bring myself to return to the barn at Uncle Billy's.

But I could feel her there too. The air was different, the molecules aligned differently. There was no sound, but I could feel the way the place settled around her presence, made space for her. Where there was a tight silence when I was here alone, squeezing me in close, pressing up against me, now there was a looseness to the very air. It made no sense, and I shook my shoulders out as I walked through the house, peered through the back windows to see her sitting on my deck, petting Rascal.

My heart lifted involuntarily at the sight of the fading sun sifting through her hair, the way my dog leaned into her, sensing her innate goodness.

Yeah, buddy, I thought. I love her too.

But as soon as the thought was formed, I squelched it. No good could come of that kind of thinking. She was like a bright flash of light that would disappear, whether I shut my eyes tight or watched—and either way, I'd mourn its absence. I couldn't love her. Because I couldn't keep her, couldn't hold her. Life was built that way. I admired those brave enough to love, knowing they'd most likely suffer loss. But I'd been through it already, and maybe we each had only so much we could take.

"Hey," I said, stepping out the back door, gratified when Rascal came to tuck his head beneath my palm. His constancy made me feel less lost.

"Hi," she said. She didn't stand but turned to face me as she sat on the chair where I'd taken her the night before, burying my fear and terror inside her, seeking comfort where I had no right to look for it. She held a long white envelope between her palms, her hands resting atop her bare knees. She was wearing a dress, which was something new, something I longed to explore and investigate. But I wouldn't. I needed to let her go.

I knew it was my turn to speak, but I couldn't find the right words, and as confusion swirled inside my dark gut, she stood.

"So, I wanted to talk to you," she said, and I could tell she was nervous. I hated myself for making her feel that way, and yet I stood silent, letting her suffer.

"I, uh . . ." She trailed off, dropping my gaze, staring at the wide wooden planks of my deck for a long moment. "Mason," she looked back up, her gaze naked, vulnerable. "Are you okay? After yesterday, I mean. I'm worried."

"I'm fine."

"It's just . . . I can only imagine. Having your sister there . . . another fire."

"Right." I didn't meet her eyes. I did not want to talk about this.

She let out a sigh, and her shoulders dropped. "Why are you acting like this?" Her voice broke.

I glanced up and found that I wasn't strong enough to hold her gaze. "It's better this way."

"What is better this way?" she asked. "Who is it better for? You? Because you seem miserable. Or is this supposed to be better for me? Because you know what? I am miserable. I hate seeing you like this, not being able to touch you, to talk to you."

I was doing the right thing. The smart thing. I just needed to keep telling myself that.

"I came back here to talk to you," she said, her voice almost a whisper. "Because I thought . . ." She laughed, and I hated that it sounded like she was laughing at herself. "I stupidly thought there was something here. Between us. I thought we were good together, and that maybe I'd find a way to stay here. To be here. With you."

My heart leapt at her words even as I forced myself to stand still, to hold my hands at my sides, to keep my eyes from finding hers. It didn't matter. It would still end the same way. In pain. In heartache.

"I thought maybe I loved you, Mason," she whispered. "And I thought maybe you loved me too."

I did love her. I wanted to tell her then, and I raised my eyes to meet hers, the words on my tongue, but she turned away from me, and I watched one fat tear splatter against the deck at her feet.

She sniffed audibly, and then surprised me by stepping close. "Now I see that it would never have worked anyway. Here. I'll just let you read this since it's clear you won't let me get the words out." She shoved the envelope at me, and I instinctively raised my hand to take it, pressing it against my chest as she turned on her heel and fled.

For a second, I stared at the paper I held. What did she need to say that she had written into a letter? She'd already told me maybe she loved me. My heart twisted up inside my chest as I heard the words again.

But I hadn't let her finish. Maybe she'd been going to explain why it would never work, why someone as incapable of humor and fun as me could never really make her happy, something I already knew. Maybe the letter was just her way of telling me what she couldn't say to my face, what she thought might hurt too much for both of us. I gripped the paper tightly, and then let my hand fall to my side. I couldn't read it now.

I listened as her car started up in front of my house, and then heard the sound of the engine fading as she drove away. From me. From the life we might have had. From all the things I'd said no to.

Mindlessly, I put the envelope on the counter inside as I brought the bottle of Half Cat back out to the deck and sat down.

It was better this way.

So why did it hurt so much?

## 29

# HEATHER

I drove back to Amelia's house, tears streaming down my face the whole way as sobs pushed their way up from somewhere deep inside of me.

She wasn't there when I returned home, and the windows of the tiy house were dark. Amelia lived in town—not far from the green, the main park in the heart of the small village. Her house was one street back from those that lined the green, on a quiet street with big arching tree branches shading picturesque yards and kids riding bikes in the afternoons.

I parked in the driveway and let myself inside with the key she had given me, lifting a hand to wave to Mrs. Grace in her window next door, and then dropped my keys on the little entry table and made my way in the dark to the bedroom at the back of the house that was mine. For now.

The bed gave beneath me, a vague comfort in the face of the pain that was pulsing through me at my own stupidity. For a moment, I just sat, staring into the darkness, considering all that I'd done to land myself in this situation.

I'd thought I would come back here, that Mason and I might find a way to be together. I thought he'd see that I didn't want to be in Washington DC, that I wanted to be here, that I could stay and be happy—make him happy.

And that was what I didn't understand. Why wouldn't he let me near now? I knew he was closed off and distant. He'd been that way when we met. But things had changed, hadn't they? He'd opened up. We'd shared intimate, close moments, shared thoughts, hopes, dreams. I thought I'd really known him.

It was painful now to reflect on those quiet nights curled up in his arms as we lay in his bed. Remembering that he had talked to me, confided in me, trusted me—it was torture now thinking about the way that trust had been withdrawn suddenly. And why?

I was in a ball on top of my comforter when Amelia came through the front door.

"Hey, Heather! You here? I see your car, but there are no lights on. Are you just . . ." Her voice trailed off as she walked through the house, approaching my room. She'd switched on the hallway light, and she could certainly see me now as she stood in my doorway. ". . . sitting in the dark?"

I didn't answer immediately—she could see pretty clearly that I was a disaster, so I worked at trying to muffle the sobs wracking my body and attempted to sit up.

Amelia moved to sit next to me. "Hey," she said, crooning the way I'd done with Mason the day before, after the fire. "Hey." Her weight depressed the mattress, and her hand landed on my back, soft, comforting. "What's going on? What's wrong?"

I made myself sit up now, sniffing and still not quite able to look at her. "I'm an idiot," I said, hoping that might cover everything.

"No, you're not. Tell me what's happened."

I snuffled some more, tried to think about where to begin, what exactly to say to explain that I'd thought her brother was someone else, that I'd been naïve and ridiculous, that I'd thought there was something there that had never existed at all. Just as I sucked in another shuddering breath, preparing to talk, she stood, taking my hand.

"This will be easier with wine," she said. "I picked up a couple of amazing bottles at the store. They just got them in from this winery in Virginia."

"Okay," I managed, letting her lead me into the living room. She'd dropped her bags on the couch, and I helped her pick them up and carry them to the little farmhouse kitchen at the back of the house. It was all white cabinets and butcher block counters and had a huge window overlooking the green backyard.

"The winery is called Whistlepig," she laughed, clearly feeling the need to carry the conversation for now, since I was essentially catatonic. "But the woman who makes the wine was at Speakeasy when I was there visiting my friend Melissa, and I got to taste these. They're incredible."

She moved around the kitchen as I sat at the end of the long counter, where a wider part was cut into a circle so stools could be pulled around it. Amelia opened a bottle of wine, poured two glasses, and then opened a couple of plastic boxes, setting them in the middle of the round. The smell of cheese and bacon and French fries wafted through the room.

"Here you go. This ought to help." She put a glass in front of me, took one for herself, and then pulled up the stool next to me as she pushed a plate across with a fork on it for me. "You have alcohol and carbs. And a sympathetic ear. Tell me what idiotic thing my brother has done."

That surprised me a bit. I guess I'd confirmed for Amelia there might be something between her brother and me, but we'd never discussed details. "No, it's not about him." I couldn't talk about Mason to his sister. It felt like a betrayal.

"Of course it is. I saw the way he reacted yesterday to the fire. I meant to get out and check on him today, but I talked to Billy, and he said Mason was in a shitty mood, but that he seemed okay otherwise."

"I don't know if he's okay, really," I ventured. "But I don't really know him that well."

"Oh please." Amelia took a long sip of the burgundy wine. When she set it down again, she sighed. "I think you know him better than anyone at this point."

"It doesn't matter," I said, the words barely audible.

Amelia didn't say anything, but studied me for a long moment as I looked back at her through watery eyes. She was beautiful in a girl-next-door kind of way. She had the same dark eyes Mason did, intelligent and intense. But hers sparked with laughter and fun more often than not, and her easy smile was a marked contrast to her brother. She had chestnut hair—thick and unruly, and usually piled on top of her head. A few tendrils hung around her face now as she considered me.

She sighed, took another drink, ate a fry, and then leaned back in her stool, crossing her legs.

"So my brother," she began. "Is an enormous pain in the ass."

I chuckled at the matter-of-fact way she said this.

"But his heart is tender, and he guards it because he thinks it's the only way someone with a heart so soft can survive."

I didn't like thinking of Mason having to guard his heart. My own pulsed in response.

"You know what happened to Mason when he was a kid. What happened to us. But he was older. And he felt responsible, like he had to choose between me and my parents." She shook her head and took another drink. "And it doesn't matter what you tell him, that's a guilt he'll fight for the rest of his life, I think."

Amelia looked into my eyes. "But I was there, remember. And even though I was a kid, I know there was nothing he could have done. The house was engulfed by the time we got to the road and turned back around to look. They were already gone." Her dark eyes shone, and she drew a long breath, maybe steadying herself.

"I'm so sorry, Amelia," I said, feeling a little calmer now. I took a sip of my own wine.

"I'm not telling you that to bring up past hurts. I want you to know the way my brother holds himself responsible for everyone he loves. Did you know he hasn't been in a real relationship since he got back from the Marine Corps? Maybe not ever, not really."

That was still hard to fathom. "He said that."

"There have been dates. I mean, look at him, right?"

I laughed, the effort loosening some of the tightness and pain in my chest.

"But he said something to me once that I'll never forget."

I found myself leaning in.

"He said, 'I've got enough at stake just keeping an eye on you, Amelia.' I'd asked him why he didn't date anyone seriously. That was his answer. He thinks he's responsible for me, that if anything happens to me, it will be his fault."

I thought about that. "I understand him looking out for you, but—"

"I've thought about it a lot, asked him about it. And here's what I've figured out. He's pretty sure he won't be able to handle losing someone else he loves. He thinks that ferociously guarding me is taking care of me, but it's actually super selfish. He's guarding his own heart because he doesn't think he could deal with it if he lost me."

"That's not really selfish," I said, thinking about the way Kevin looked out for me. "My brother is kind of the same way."

"But in this case, it is. Putting all his effort into 'protecting' me and putting up those walls around his heart to make sure he doesn't accidentally connect with anyone else is something I think he does because he's afraid. Inside, he's still that confused kid who watched his parents die in a fire. He thinks that if he never loves anyone else, he won't risk feeling that kind of pain again."

Poor Mason—it made sense. I'd pretty much understood this about him, but hearing his sister articulate it made it feel that much more reasonable. "But he'll never feel anything else either."

"Right," she said, finishing her wine and reaching for the bottle. "But it's too late."

"What do you mean?" I ate a fry, feeling a little better.

"He's already in love with you. So now he has to deal with that."

My heart surged even as I shook my head. "I don't think that's true."

"Oh, it is." She sounded so sure, so confident.

"Well, it doesn't matter. He won't let me near him. He practically ran me off his property today when I went out to try to talk to him."

Amelia sighed, a sad smile pulling one side of her full lips up. "He's a moron. And I think that fire at the school really threw him."

"It wasn't that big of a fire," I said, not really thinking about the fire, but instead hearing Amelia's words over and over about Mason protecting her, protecting himself.

"Even a spark would be enough to set him off. Fire is one thing he really cannot handle. It was like his two greatest fears converged, right? Fire and losing you and me."

"It's nice that you think that," I said. "But I think I may have overinflated his feelings for me, seen something that wasn't there. He was just being nice—what choice did he have? He was basically forced to host me at his place. Maybe it was just a convenience, getting intimate." It was like I was trying this idea on, but I knew it didn't fit.

"He doesn't operate that way."

I sighed. Analyzing Mason with his sister was a little bit helpful, at least it gave me some insight, but it really didn't solve anything.

"Are you going to stay?" Amelia asked. "At school yesterday, you said you might talk to Principal Franz."

I had thought about talking to the principal again. When I'd been inside with Amelia, I found myself second-guessing the words I'd said when I'd stood next to Mason in the back of his truck and she'd put me on the spot. But now, staying here didn't seem wise.

"I don't think so. I just came back to finish up helping with the greenhouse, to fulfill the promises I made. I guess there's no real reason to stay. I mean, I live in Washington."

Amelia made a face.

"What?"

"Maybe you and Mason belong together then."

*If only.*

"Neither one of you will acknowledge what's so freaking obvious to everyone else." She stood and took a last long drink from her glass. "Most people wait their whole lives to find someone they can love, and you're both just going to walk away." She put her glass down. "For those of us who are still painfully single, it's an affront."

Amelia turned and walked out of the kitchen, and I could hear her bedroom door shut and the tub begin to run in her bathroom. Guilt combined with my sadness. I was sorry for making her feel bad.

I finished my wine, rinsed the dishes, and put the food into the fridge, and then got ready for bed. Amelia had given me a lot to think about.

---

The next day dawned bright and hot, and I woke early, missing Mason, the goats, and the strange routine I'd begun to establish when I'd lived and worked on a little Vermont goat farm.

It felt like a dream now, all of it. Even the fear that had plagued me, that had driven me to Vermont in the first place, felt distant and almost imagined.

My phone rang as I was making coffee, and I was surprised anyone would be calling me so early. I jumped to answer, hoping it would be my brother—I hadn't gotten to talk to him at all since he'd left me in Vermont, and I felt I needed to let him know that things were okay, that I was safe.

But it wasn't Kevin calling.

"Heather? This is Principal Franz. Colebury Elementary School."

"Good morning, Principal Franz." Surprise swept through me.

"I'm sorry to bother you so early, but I hoped you might be open to an opportunity. We discussed it a bit, so I wondered if the bug I planted in your ear might make you more apt to consider saying yes."

My stomach leapt, but I kept my voice steady. "What do you mean?"

"The sub we found for the opening has had a family emergency out of state. He won't be returning when the school reopens next week, unfortunately. Which puts me in a position I hate—I'm desperate."

"Oh no." Confusion swirled within me.

"But I thought of you. You said you were back for a little while at least. Is there any chance I could convince you to stay a bit longer? Even as a trial? Take over the fifth-grade class as a sub, and if you think it's a good fit here, you could pursue your Vermont certification while you teach?"

I wasn't sure how to answer. I felt as if I'd just decided to give up, to go back to DC and start again. "I don't know, I—"

"I need to fill this spot before the kids come back next Monday," she said. "And I'm not sure where else to look. At this rate, I'll be teaching myself. But I do understand if you can't do it."

"Principal Franz, I hadn't planned to stay," I said, my head spinning.

"Understood. Well, thank you for—"

"But I could maybe stay temporarily. Until you find someone who can take it?" The words flew out of me, though I didn't know I was going to say them. A strange contentment followed the words.

"That would be a huge relief," she said. "You're sure?"

"Yes," I said, suddenly certain. "I'll stay until you can find a replacement."

"Thank you. If you can come in tomorrow, I'll have some paperwork from the district."

"Okay, sure."

I hung up, feeling a little blindsided. It was at that moment that Amelia emerged, bleary-eyed and tousle-haired.

"What's up?" she asked, making a straight line for the coffee pot.

"I'm going to sub temporarily starting next week when the school reopens."

"Yeah, you are!" Amelia cried, turning from the coffee pot to hug me. "That's awesome."

"Is it okay if I stay with you here a little longer?" I was cautiously excited. This was the first thing that had felt right in so long.

"Of course," she said.

"I'll pay rent," I told her.

"Are you still paying rent in DC?"

"Well, yeah."

She laughed. "When you see what you're getting paid here, you'll hate yourself for offering. Don't worry about it for now. I covered the house myself before. I don't need your rent."

I shook my head. "That doesn't feel right."

"Pay me by figuring things out with Mason."

I wasn't sure that was something I could do. "Thanks, Amelia."

When Amelia headed off to school, I called my office in DC.

"You're staying," Morgan said before I'd even gotten a hello out.

"I . . . I mean, yeah. Is that okay? I know we had the meeting to plan. I left you hanging again."

"Heather," he said, and I could hear by the tone of my voice that this was my friend speaking, not my boss. "Your paycheck is on the way to the address you gave me. We're a business, and here in DC, we will not have trouble finding employees, though I assure you they won't compare to you. Consider this a leave of absence. Your job is always here for you if you decide to come back."

"It feels wrong, to just . . . leave."

"Does it really feel wrong? You don't owe us anything. What's in your heart?"

"They want me to teach. Be in the classroom again." I felt the smile in my words.

"I think you'll be great." Morgan sounded genuinely happy for me, and the tension in my chest loosened. "Will there be any goat farmers in the picture?"

I sighed. "I don't know." I honestly didn't.

"I hope so," he said. "Don't be a stranger."

"I'll miss you," I told him.

"Oh, don't you worry. We're already planning a trip up to visit."

I laughed. "I hope so."

When I hung up, a little bubble of excitement inflated inside me despite the pain and confusion I felt over Mason.

At least I had something to do, somewhere to be needed. And I was excited at the idea of returning to the classroom. Even if it was only temporary.

# MASON

The next week passed slowly, and the only thing I managed to be grateful for was the hectic pace of my day-to-day life. I went to the farmers' market alone, and while I sold most of what I'd brought, it was nothing compared to the days I'd been there with Heather at my side. People wandered to the booth and then quickly turned away once they got a glimpse of the grumpy guy sitting behind the table.

"Your murder face is back," Amelia told me when she popped into the Busy Bean during my shift the following Thursday evening.

"Your irritating personality has never left, I see," I snapped, feeling immediately remorseful.

Audrey stiffened beside me, turning to cast her wide-eyed gaze my way.

"Nice, Mason," Amelia said, unfazed by my dark mood. She was familiar enough with it after all these years. "So my brother's back to spreading sunshine and joy all around the café, I see," she said to Audrey.

Audrey glanced at me, as if uncertain where to come down on this sibling scuffle. "He's been a little . . . intense," she hedged.

"This you, Mase?" Amelia pointed to what I'd written the

previous day when Roderick had asked if I had a quote to chalk on one of the beams where he'd erased one he said he wasn't feeling anymore. I'd written, "Love is a construction invented by people afraid to be alone."

"That's him," Audrey confirmed, her voice not completely happy. I got the sense she was regretting hiring me now and wondered if she and Zara had chatted about it. Unfortunately, the minimum payment on one of the loans that was dogging the farm was coming due this week, and I'd been picking up extra shifts, so she was getting a bigger dose of me than usual. I couldn't afford to lose the job—it was the tiny hit of extra income keeping me afloat. This and the restaurant supply deals Heather had set up.

"Oh my god, Mason," Amelia said in a hushed voice, picking up the coffee I'd just put on the counter in front of her. "What are you doing? You know Heather is still here, right? All you have to do is give her a reason to stay, and she'll pack up her stuff in DC and come here permanently. We need her at school. And god knows you need her."

"I don't need her," I said, and something inside my chest kicked up a protest. I winced. "This is better for everyone. I'm not built for relationships."

"Keep telling yourself that," my sister said, rolling her eyes. "You're such an idiot."

On that kind note, my sister took her coffee and headed for the door. "Bye, Audrey," she called. "Don't put up with too much from that one."

Audrey sighed. "I'm going to go get some of the cookie dough ready for tomorrow," she said. "Can you catch the last few customers without scaring anyone away permanently?"

"Yeah." I had to say yes. In reality, I doubted I was capable of anything beyond mere civility. Everything inside me felt heavy, dark. I knew it would pass, that it would get better with time, but the hours between now and then looked long and empty and cold.

When I arrived home that night, I let Rascal out and then

walked around to the greenhouse. It was warm and humid inside the small dug-in structure, and the interior was a riot of color and scent. Tomatoes were exploding from their vines, oranges and lemons hung heavy on the branches of their trees. And my fig trees were green and healthy, too, the first crop of teardrops starting to swell and color. I stepped nearer to the brown turkey fig at the end of the center aisle, pushing aside the huge leaves to inspect the fruit ripening on its branches.

My eye landed on one perfect fig, swollen and heavy, the skin a dark purple-brown color touched with striations of green. As I lifted the fruit against my palm, not pulling it from the branch yet, my mind raced backward to the hot summer days I'd spent in my father's grove in California's Central Valley. I could almost feel myself standing there beneath the arches of the fig branches, hung with fruit that looked just like this one, filling the air with the same honey-sugar scent. The difference was the lightness I felt inside when I cast myself back there—a little kid, clueless and happy because he didn't know any better.

I plucked the fig, almost reverently, remembering the way my mother's slim fingers had pulled them from the branches, how she'd licked the tip of her thumb when a dot of milky sap stood there as she held the fig out to me.

The single fruit sat heavy and warm in the palm of my hand, and I knew it was just a fig, just a product of sun and heat and water. It was science, nothing magic or special.

And yet.

It felt like the past and present intertwined in a single moment, a solitary puzzle piece meant to finally, finally, let me take a step back there and somehow finish something that had felt undone for most of my life.

I sat on the edge of the deck, one of August's long evenings illuminating the sky overhead with vestiges of the dropping sun. Rascal sat at my side, quietly, as if he understood the gravity of the moment, the importance of the strange small thing I held in my palm.

"It's a fig," I told him, my voice sounding distant, foreign. "My mother loved these," I went on, needing to talk, needing to explain, maybe to myself. "I didn't know if I'd be able to grow them. But there are more in the greenhouse." I thought of my mother's face, smeared by the years I'd spent trying desperately to remember her features, faded now like a photograph that had been handled too much.

"You can peel them," I told my dog, repeating words I'd heard my mother say. "Or you can eat them just like this. The skin can be bitter, but the inside is the sweetest, most incredible thing you'll ever feel on your tongue."

Rascal looked intrigued, and under his gentle gaze, I peeled one part of the skin away, pulling the stem carefully downward and revealing the pithy white beneath the skin. I let the skin fall from my fingers to the deck and sank my teeth into the fruit, taking half of it into my mouth and closing my eyes as the sugar filled my senses. It was like going home again, for a single brief second.

But then, I was just a sad man sitting on a deck, eating a piece of fruit. Alone.

I'd been impossible this week, I knew. Amelia and Billy had both told me so. Even my dog seemed less inclined to spend time with me, and he wandered away from me now, dropping into a pile in front of the back door.

I finished eating the fig, wishing I could recapture that feeling I'd had when I'd lived with my parents. What had it been exactly? What had been so different there?

My eyes slid shut, and I thought about it, but I didn't really need to search for an answer. I had been loved. But more importantly, I had been too young to know that loving people back put your heart at risk. And I'd enjoyed the blind certainty that only children have, that the people I loved would always be with me, that love would be enough. That I was safe.

I'd protected my heart, hadn't I? By keeping myself solitary and secluded, I'd made sure not to fall into love's trap again—or that had been the plan. I had no choice but to love my sister, my uncle—but I did have a choice about letting anyone else in too close, and it was a choice I'd made deliberately. And still . . . it hurt.

Inside the house, I washed my hands and then stood in front of the refrigerator, intending to pull a beer from within it, but I found myself staring at the long white envelope I'd stuck there instead. I'd spent a decent amount of time considering it the last few nights.

I wanted to open it, to read whatever words Heather had intended for me. But I couldn't bring myself to do it. I had a feeling she'd put in there something she hadn't been brave enough to say. And whether it was her explanation of why I wasn't worthy of her love or her suggestion that I was, either thing would be too much for me to handle.

Taking the edge of the envelope, I snatched it from the refrigerator, sending the magnet skittering to the floor and making Rascal jump from where he'd curled up in his bed. I walked to the sink and pulled the lighter down from the little shelf next to the curtain, flicking it to life.

The flame glowed orange as I held it to the corner of the envelope, and I watched as the flickering heat touched the paper, slowly smoking and then catching.

I snapped the lighter shut and dropped the paper into the empty sink, the flame turning to singe as the corner met the damp surface. I couldn't read it, but I couldn't destroy it either. Maybe one day I'd be strong enough to handle the words Heather needed to say to me.

But I didn't think it would be anytime soon.

## MASON

After another long night staring at the ceiling, I dragged myself to the farm to help my uncle milk. What had felt novel and even fun when Heather had joined us now felt like dogged routine again, slow and tedious and necessary.

Billy coughed several times while I was there that morning, bending in half once, caught in the throes of a fit of hacking.

"You all right?" I asked him, worry making me tense.

"Just old," he grumbled, straightening up again.

He was old, and at his age, he should probably not be dragging himself from bed before dawn to manhandle goats.

"Sounds like more than old. Let's make an appointment to go see Doc Harris, okay?"

Billy waved the idea off. "Nah."

"I'll make the appointment later. For now, you get out of here. I'll come check on you when I'm done here."

"I'm fine," he said, but the words ended in another coughing fit. When he recovered, he wiped his mouth with his flannel sleeve and glared at me. "Fine," he said, rising and shuffling slowly out of the milking parlor. I pushed down the fear clawing at me.

I could handle milking alone. It was easier with two people, but it wasn't something I needed Billy doing, especially not if he was getting sick. It felt right to have to do it alone anyway. Hadn't this been exactly what I wanted? To be alone?

When I returned to my house around ten, I was surprised to see a car sitting in the driveway, a large, luxury SUV that belonged to no one I knew in town. I parked my truck next to it and hopped out, moving to the driver's side window to see a man reclined in the seat, evidently asleep.

As I rapped on the window to wake him, I realized who it was.

Kevin Brigham shot up to sitting, his mirrored aviator shades covering the eyes that matched his sister's, and a wide smile taking his face as he stared back at me.

I stepped back, and the door swung open, Brigsy hopping out.

"What's up, brother?" he asked me. "You look like shit."

"Thanks a lot." I stepped close, gave my old friend a quick hug. "Glad to see you in one piece."

He smiled again and looked around. "Heather here? Wanted to surprise her."

She would be surprised, all right. "No," I said. "She's, uh, staying with my sister now."

He pulled the shades from his eyes but didn't comment on that.

"Come in for a bit?" I asked him. "You hungry? I haven't had breakfast."

"I could eat," he said, following me into the house.

Kevin talked as I made eggs, bacon, and coffee for us both, describing what he could about his most recent time overseas. I knew enough to understand that there was more he wasn't telling me because he couldn't, but it was enough to see him back safe, smiling again.

As we finished up our meal, he put down his coffee cup and narrowed his gaze at me. "So what's going on with my sister? You just get tired of her? She can be a lot."

"No," I said, maybe too quickly. "She's great. She's really . . ." I trailed off, unable to find the right words. "She's great," I said again.

I could feel Kevin's shrewd eyes on me, so I kept my gaze in my mug. "She just thought it would be better to be with Amelia," I said.

"Because why?" Kevin asked. "What happened, man?" His voice was sharp. Not hostile, exactly, but I knew Kevin was every bit as protective of his little sister as I was of mine, and he wouldn't be pleased to know what had gone on here, how I'd crossed a line.

"Just wanted someone to talk to probably. You know I haven't won any personality awards."

He sat back in his chair and crossed his arms. "You sleep with my little sister, man?" His tone was neutral.

I took a deep breath. I was not going to lie to my best friend, but I didn't think he'd like the truth. "Things got complicated," I told him. "But she was always safe, and things have calmed down in DC now. She decided to stay longer, she just didn't want to stay here."

Kevin didn't say anything for a long minute, watching me. He picked up his mug, found it empty, and crossed the kitchen to refill it. After taking a sip, he turned back around to face me and put his mug on the counter beside him.

"You're clearly miserable. You say her name like it's a prayer you're offering some god somewhere." He stared at me, that narrow-eyed gaze pinning me in place. "You love my little sister."

"Brigsy, I—"

"That's fantastic."

"What? No, I—"

"But she's not here, so clearly you fucked it up."

It was my turn to stare.

"Oh, you thought I'd be pissed."

"Yeah, pretty much."

"I am." He picked up his coffee cup again and strode back to where I sat, looking down at me. "Mason, you're the best guy I know. Solid, sure, totally reliable. It's why I brought her here. And I definitely wasn't playing matchmaker—that's not my style. But if the two of you found some common ground, some reason to be together . . ." He shook his head, a wry smile on his lips. "That'd be great."

He sat back down across from me, and I met his blue-eyed gaze. "I fucked it up."

I realized that now. I had. I'd wanted to protect myself, protect us both. And I'd failed.

"So fix it," he suggested.

"I don't think it's that easy."

Kevin didn't say anything else, and we finished our coffee in silence. Finally, he stood, taking his plate to the sink. "Well, I guess I'd better go see her. Can you give me directions?"

"Yeah." I told him how to get to Amelia's and watched him back out.

I wondered what Heather would tell him, what he'd say to her.

But it didn't matter, not really. I was pretty sure it was already much too late.

---

I spent the day tending the goats and mending the fence line around the eastern paddock, checked on my sleeping uncle, and when night fell, I realized I couldn't stay in my silent house alone for one more minute. I drove to town, parked at the Gin Mill, and found a seat at the bar.

A drink was probably not what I needed, but it turned out that knowing what I needed was not something I was good at. Or admitting what I needed. Or maybe it was just actually going after what I needed that I sucked at.

"What can I get you?" Alec Rossi stood before me, smiling, a bar rag clutched in one hand as he swiped at the counter next to me.

"Shipley Cider on tap?" I asked.

"Good choice," he said, his head ducking once as he turned to pull my cider. He would say that. He and May Shipley had been together a while. Her brother Griffin made the cider.

"Thanks," I said, wrapping my hand around the cool glass as he set it before me.

"You doing okay, Mason?" I hadn't been totally sure Alec recognized me—I'd been in school with him, but we'd never really been friends.

"Yeah, good." I looked around, hoping to keep the focus anywhere but how I was doing. "Business good?"

"Can't complain," Alec said. "Give a shout if you need anything, okay?" He shot me a smile and moved down to help a woman who'd just come in.

I let the relative noise of the bar sift through the air around me as I nursed the sweet, tangy cider in my hand, and I tried not to think about what Kevin might be saying to his sister at this very moment.

"Praying to the gods of alcohol, Mason?" A familiar voice pulled my attention to the left, and I realized I'd been hanging my head over my glass—I probably did look like a man repenting for something.

"Billy," I said, swiveling to take in my uncle, who was wearing a clean shirt, had his grey beard trimmed close, and had obviously combed his hair with water, judging by the way the dark silver strands clumped together in rows and clung to each other as they left his part and curled between his ears. "You're all dressed up." For a man who wore overalls ninety percent of the time, the jeans and sneakers my uncle wore equated to formalwear.

"Gotta get out now and then, hit the town."

I raised an eyebrow at him. "You feeling better then?"

He shrugged. "Laid in bed all day feeling sorry for myself. Couldn't do it for another minute. I'm fine. Just old, like I told you."

I wasn't really buying it, and seeing him now reminded me to make him a doctor appointment the next day. But I wasn't going to harass him since he did seem better. "You come here a lot?"

"Now and then, like I said." He nodded at Alec, who pulled a beer and set it in front of him.

"Mr. Rye, how are you, sir?"

Clearly Uncle Billy did come here often. He sipped the stout that had been placed in front of him and smiled at Alec. "Can't really complain, Alec," he said. "Except my nephew is crappy company lately, so I had to come here to find some entertainment. And now, here he is." Billy shot a look over his shoulder at me.

"I can scoot down," I told him, nodding at the empty stools to my right.

"Nah." Billy took another long sip of his beer, leaving a little foam along the ends of his mustache.

"Well, if this one bothers you, sir, you let me know." Alec grinned at me and moved away.

"Seriously, if I'm cramping your style, I can find another place to sit," I told my uncle, wondering if Billy came here to meet women.

He turned on his seat and looked at me, the clear eyes more focused than they'd been a moment ago. "Glad you're here, actually."

I didn't know quite how to respond, so I just lifted my glass and touched it to his, and for a few minutes, we drank, side by side, in companionable silence. With my uncle next to me, my thoughts felt slightly less tragic and painful, and that made me think a little bit too. Having someone you loved near, even when things were awful, made awful feel a little bit more tolerable. I knew it was true, and yet I'd spent my whole life pushing people away—I wasn't sure I could change the habit now.

"You just about done?" Billy asked after a while, and I looked at my half-full glass.

"Not really in it for speed tonight," I told him.

"Not with your beer, you idiot."

That got my attention. I turned to face him fully. "What?"

He coughed then, and the worry spiked in me again. Billy had smoked a lot when I'd been a kid. It had always seemed like he'd gotten away with the habit, quitting when I was in the military and seeming no worse for the wear. But this cough had me concerned.

He wiped the back of his hand across his mouth. "You nearly done feeling sorry for yourself, I mean. Acting like a fool and refusing to appreciate what's right in front of you?"

I sighed. "I doubt it. It's a habit."

He shook his head. "It's lazy, that's what it is."

I narrowed my eyes at him. "I work more than anyone I know. Lazy is not in my nature."

"Tell me about Heather. How'd you leave things?"

I frowned. "She left."

"She's still here." He took a long, slow sip of his beer. "Staying with your sister. Saw her this afternoon."

"You said you were in bed all day."

"I had a few things to take care of," he said, his tone defensive now.

"How is she?" I hated that I was asking, but it was out before I could stop the words.

"She's cute and funny, and she's gorgeous, and for whatever reason, she loves you even though you're a moron."

He might as well have stabbed me with the toothpick laying on the bar top next to him. I felt a sudden sharp jab in my chest. "I already ruined everything there," I told him, willing to take the blame.

"Then fix it."

I sighed, dropping my head over my cider. Why did everyone seem to think this would be easy? "It isn't that simple." The idea of going to Heather, of asking her to give me another chance after I'd pushed her away and told her to leave . . . Well, I doubted she was waiting around for me to apologize. "She's going back to DC anyway."

"She might not," Billy said, and I glanced at him sideways.

"She's teaching at the school with your sister for a while." He broke into a coughing fit again as I considered that news.

Was Heather planning to stay here?

"Shouldn't make a damn bit of difference," Billy said. "Whether she's here or there. Not if you love her."

That was the problem. "I don't want to love her."

"Got a choice?"

I was so tired of fighting the way I felt, of letting the fear inside me dictate how I approached everything in the world. But I didn't know how to stop. "I don't know how to do it," I admitted. "What if I love her—what if we're together—and then something happens?"

"Something will happen." Billy took another long drink. "That's the nature of life."

My heart twisted inside me again. He didn't understand what I meant. I was about to try to explain what I was afraid of when he started speaking again.

"What do you think about dogs, Mason?"

I paused. "I like dogs."

"You think Rascal's gonna be around forever?"

I thought about my little brown dog, about his quiet presence in my life, his big loving eyes. It hurt to imagine him dying, but I knew it was inevitable, though hopefully a long ways off. He was only six. "Of course not."

"But you love him?"

I let out an exasperated sigh. "Yeah, I mean. Of course. What's your point?"

"You let yourself love him, even though you know he's most likely going to die in your lifetime. That will be hard, don't you think?"

I squeezed my eyes shut. "Yeah, that will be hard."

"You love me, Mason?"

"That's a ridiculous question." I was starting to regret my outing this evening.

"I know you do. But guess what? I'm old. I'm sick."

"You're sick?" I put my cider down and looked at him. "Why didn't you say something? I knew you weren't feeling well this morning. You should be in bed."

He blew out a frustrated breath and frowned at me. "Wouldn't make a damn bit of difference, and I'm not spending my time in bed until I have to. But you're missing the point. I'm not sticking around, Mason. And your sister? What about her?"

My heart froze inside my chest. "Is Amelia sick?"

"No, son. She's human." His face cleared as he looked into my eyes, and for a moment, I saw the man he'd been all those years ago, when we'd first come to live in Vermont. The understanding gaze, the kind smile. "We're all just human, and our lives are like a drop of rain tracing down a window. We follow a path, we get diverted, we regroup and continue, and eventually, the run ends."

I squeezed my eyes shut, surprised at the pricking sensation behind my lids. I couldn't remember the last time I had cried, but something about Billy's description was pulling at me, twisting up my emotions and making me feel less steady than I had in years.

"You can't plan everything. You can't protect everyone. But the nature of life is in its very unpredictability, son. And if you embrace the wonder of it, the uncertainty, you have a real chance for joy." He looked at me for a long moment, then continued as I struggled to swallow down the lump in my throat. "Heather is a beautiful and vibrant person. And she loves you. You can choose to protect yourself and live the rest of your life trying to control the path you follow, trying to avoid pain and fear. Or you can embrace the opportunity you have to find happiness."

My lungs felt like they were being pressed through a pair of rollers, tight and painful, and I struggled to take a deep breath. I knew he was right, but I was afraid. And fear had guided me for so long, I wasn't sure I could escape it.

"Your aunt was the love of my life," he said. "And I knew when I married her that she was sick."

My aunt had died of cancer, and it had been a long, slow death that spanned years. She'd managed it well, but the last year of her life—when I'd been away on deployment—had been hard, Amelia had said.

"I didn't know that," I said.

"And if I lived by your guidance, I would have run far away when I found out she was sick," he went on. "I would have protected myself from the knowledge that I was going to lose her one day."

He was right.

"But it wouldn't have mattered. It would have been worse. I would have let her die, loving her still, but never having had the chance to be with her, to make her laugh, to see her smile."

I dropped my gaze to the amber liquid in my glass, the pale foam at the edges of the cider, the tiny bubbles popping, one by one.

We finished our beers in silence, and after I paid Alec, I turned to Uncle Billy. "Drive you home?"

He shook his head. "I'm not dead yet."

I watched Billy pull out of the parking lot in his truck, and when he was on the road, I pulled out behind him. We parted ways at the cottage, where I pulled into my driveway, my dark, empty house sitting silent as ever as I switched off the engine.

Inside, I hugged Rascal tight and thought about what Billy had said.

I needed to find the strength to face the fear that had governed my life for as long as I could remember. I would choose love over fear, I promised myself. I would choose Heather.

# 32

## HEATHER

Having a few days without kids in my new classroom gave me the time I needed to do two things. One, I was able to organize the physical space the way I wanted it, arranging desks into small work groups and keeping the center area clear. I moved the large teacher's desk into a spot at the side of the room—I was not the kind of teacher who needed my own big desk at the head of the class. When I'd been in the classroom before, I'd rarely sat except to work directly with the students.

I brought in a few comfortable bean bag chairs and small upholstered chairs, and a rug, creating a group area that felt a little bit like a game room or a living room—things I'd been able to pick up at a thrift shop in Burlington with Amelia's help.

Lesson plans and textbooks were scoured and modified, based on my quick read of district and state standards. Fifth grade was a big responsibility—these kids needed to be ready for middle school, but you also had to remember that fifth-graders were still kids, only ten and eleven years old for the most part. School needed to be fun, encouraging, and accepting too.

The other thing I did with my prep time was work to get my own head on right. That was more challenging. I lived and worked with Mason's sister. And while Amelia was gracious enough not to mention my moping or the fact that I spent a lot of time distractedly staring out the window as I tried to grapple with my emotions, it was hard. I'd fallen for Mason. It should have been a wonderful thing—I wasn't sure I'd ever really loved anyone before, not like this, and not for the right reasons. But he'd sent me away, banished me from his life.

And you couldn't love a person who wouldn't let you.

I walked through my days with a bone-aching sadness, not just for myself and the happiness I thought I might experience if the Mason I'd seen glimpses of actually existed and was part of my life, but I felt sadness for Mason himself. Would he never let anyone close enough to share the loads he carried, to tell him he was doing a good job, to remind him that what happened when he was a kid hadn't been his fault?

When I thought of him, pushing himself relentlessly through his days, trying to save the farm, I wanted to rush back to his side. To help if he'd let me—but I knew he would not. At the very least, I told myself, I'd made the connection with the Vermont Land Trust for him, and he had the offer letter they'd sent. If he sold the development rights, it would pay off the debt, and he could focus on building the business, maybe even leave the Busy Bean.

All of this was rolling around in my head as I stood at the side of my classroom, staring out the window toward the walipini I'd helped Mason build and the parking lot beyond. A big white SUV had just pulled in and parked, a Range Rover like the one my brother had rented when he'd first dragged me up here, kicking and screaming.

I watched as the big car's running lights switched off, wondering idly who would be driving such a nice car here—certainly not a teacher, and I'd seen the principal's little minivan. There were no parents around this week, so when I watched a set of long jean-clad legs hop down, connected to a broad torso and a very familiar blond head, my heart lifted. Kevin!

I turned and jogged out of my room to the side door of the school, which was just down the hall from my classroom. The door squealed as I burst through it, and I ran toward my brother, across the grass. "Kevin!" I cried, leaping into his arms.

He laughed as he caught me, those strong, familiar arms wrapping me up in a bear hug, just like he'd done when I was little. "Hey, sis." His voice rumbled through his chest, and I felt it settle me, just as it always had. I missed my big brother when he was gone, and the worry I always tried to stifle about the nature of his job was a constant companion.

Kevin released me and set me back on my feet, removing his sunglasses and hanging them on the collar of his black T-shirt. "Teaching again, huh?"

I lifted a shoulder, glancing at the school and then back to my brother. "Only temporarily. I'm figuring a few things out before I go back to DC for good."

He nodded, his eyes telling me he wasn't buying it.

"How'd you know I was here?" I asked, walking him toward the front doors of the school.

He grinned at me. "I'm smart."

I rolled my eyes.

"It's a small town, Heather. I talked to Mason, he sent me to his sister's, and her neighbor told me you were both here after giving me the third degree about why I wanted to find you."

"Mrs. Grace," I said, smiling. The old woman who lived next door to Amelia sat in front of her window all day, and if anyone knew the comings and goings of the people of Colebury, it was her.

"A fine woman," Kevin said. "We are invited for tea tomorrow."

I sighed. She was a fine woman. But I'd been to tea with Amelia, and it was an hours-long affair with watery tea and tiny tuna sandwiches made from Wonder bread and cut into shapes with an assortment of cookie cutters.

I walked my brother to my temporary classroom, and he settled himself into a tiny chair, leaning back and dropping his hands behind his head. It was a ridiculous sight, his long legs stretching out before him as he made the chair look like it belonged in a doll's house.

"So when do you want to talk about what's going on with you and Mason?" he asked, the grin still in place.

"I don't," I told him, shooting him a fiery look. "Especially not with you."

"I might be upset, though," he said, his voice far from upset. "My little sister and my best friend? I trusted you both to behave like adults."

"We did," I bit out, busying myself with stacks of construction paper that had already been organized.

"So do I need to beat the shit out of him?" Kevin asked, his face darkening. "You don't seem happy. What did he do?"

I turned to face Kevin, the fight whooshing from my lungs with a sigh. Sinking onto a desktop, I said, "He didn't do anything. He won't. That's the entire issue."

"I don't get it."

"Neither does he."

"Come on, Heather. I'm gonna need a little more."

I crossed my arms, not sure how much I wanted to tell him. "I fell in love with your stupid grumpy friend, okay? And he knows it. And I'm pretty sure he feels the same way, but he won't let himself, so it's completely pointless."

"What do you mean, he won't let himself?"

"You know the guy. He's too devoted to being an angry, stoic jerk to actually let himself be happy."

"Sounds about right," Kevin mused.

I stared at him for a long moment. As much I wanted him to fix this situation somehow, mostly because Kevin tried to fix everything that was wrong in my life and I was used to it, I knew he couldn't. And his inability to fix this made me irrationally angry—maybe because I couldn't fix it either. But I needed somewhere to put all these emotions. I'd been holding so much inside I felt like I might burst. I had no idea how Mason survived this way, burying everything he felt.

"You know, it's all your fault," I said, my voice low as I convinced myself of this new line of argument.

"Oh yeah?" Kevin looked amused, and that irritated me even more.

"Yeah. You dragged me up here, completely against my will, and forced me to stay with him. He didn't want me there, I didn't want to be there, and it's pretty much all your fault."

"So you guys went ahead and slept together to get back at me then?"

"Maybe." It was so far from the truth it was hard not to smile at the idea.

"Well, you really got me," he said, the stupid grin still playing on his lips. My brother was infuriating.

I rolled my eyes and blew out a breath. "You're so smug, you know that? It drives me crazy."

"Good thing I'm hardly ever around then," he said. "What time are you . . ." Kevin trailed off, his gaze sliding to the side to stare at something just over my shoulder.

I turned to see what had caught his attention and found Amelia standing in the doorway. "Hey," I said.

"Hi," she said slowly, her eyes moving from Kevin to me, a question dancing there as her smile grew.

"Amelia, this is my brother, Kevin. I was just telling him how completely annoying he is." I stood and gestured toward my annoying brother. "Kevin, this is Amelia, Mason's sister. She's been nice enough to let me stay with her for a while. She teaches here."

Amelia took a step forward, her focus trained on Kevin like he was the most interesting thing she'd ever seen. He stood, looking equally enthralled. Suddenly, I felt like a third wheel.

"This is the inimitable Kevin Brigham?" Amelia asked, her voice filled with a mixture of awe and fun. "I've heard a lot about you."

"All of it true," Kevin quipped. "I mean, if it was good stuff, at least. Don't listen to Heather." He glanced at me, but his eyes were on Amelia again a second later.

"Let's see," she said, her weight shifting to one foot as her voice turned playful. "You can lift a car with one hand, saved an entire Syrian village from certain destruction, and no one can beat you at poker."

"Oh, that's all true," he said, his grin widening.

"It's nice to finally meet you," Amelia said. "I've heard a lot about you from my brother—he thinks the world of you."

"That makes one," I muttered.

Kevin shot me a look, and Amelia turned as if just remembering why she'd come in.

"Hey," she said. "I'm going to head over to visit Billy. Mason said he's not feeling great, and I just want to make sure he's okay. I'll be back for dinner, I think."

"Can I take you ladies out?" My brother was trying to be debonair, but I wasn't going to turn down dinner.

"Sure," I said, raising my eyebrows at Amelia.

"I'm game," she said, grinning at my brother.

I hoped I wasn't going to regret introducing them.

Amelia left, and Kevin helped me finish up in the classroom, then followed me back to the house to leave a car. We were watching television and relaxing when my phone rang, and Amelia's name flashed across my screen.

My brother caught the name and listened to my end of the conversation with a comical interest. "Tell her I say hi," he mouthed, only half-joking.

But it wasn't going to be that kind of conversation.

"Hey, Heather." Amelia's voice was sober. "I'm at the hospital in Burlington with my uncle. I don't think I'm going to make dinner tonight. Can you apologize to your brother for me?"

"Of course. Is everything okay? Is something wrong with Billy?" My stomach clenched in fear.

"I don't know," she said, and I could hear the worry in her voice. "He wasn't doing well when I got to his place, had a high fever and was coughing so much he could barely talk. I convinced him to let me bring him in, so they're running some tests, but they've already said they're probably going to admit him."

I didn't even want to think about how Mason might be handling this, but I asked anyway. "Is Mason there?"

"On his way," she said.

"Can I do anything?"

"No. I'll let you know how he is, okay? I'll probably be home really late."

"Yeah, of course." My heart ached for Amelia and Mason. I hoped Billy would be okay—I didn't even want to think about how losing him would affect Mason and his sister. I hung up and turned back to my brother, who thankfully had dropped the comic act.

"Everything okay?"

"Not really," I said.

We did go to dinner, but it was a quiet meal at the diner instead of what might have been a laughter-filled evening at Speakeasy with Amelia. We ate, and then I made up the couch for my brother, sending Amelia a text to warn her that he was crashed out on her couch. She texted back that she wouldn't be home tonight anyway.

As darkness and silence crept through the little house, I lay in bed and thought about Mason, about how he must be handling the potential of losing Billy. I wanted to go to him, to reach out. But I wasn't sure he'd let me. My heart actually ached inside my chest as I finally fell asleep.

## 33

## MASON

Amelia called me from the hospital, and even before I answered the phone, I could feel the news inside me. Bad.

"Hey," I said, my voice wary even to my own ears.

"Mase," Amelia said softly. "Can you meet us at the hospital in Burlington? I'm here with Billy."

"I knew something was wrong. He was coughing like mad and talking about dying, and—" Anger and fear danced inside me.

"We can talk about all that," she interrupted. "Just come here, okay?" My little sister's voice broke on the last word, and my protective instincts took over.

"I'm on my way."

"We're in the ER. I'll call you if they move us. They're going to admit him."

"Got it."

I drove to Burlington in the Karmann Ghia, though I couldn't explain even to myself why I hadn't just jumped into my truck like always. Or I could, actually, but I didn't want to look too closely at something that was just a basic want. I wanted Heather. And this car still held some traces of her in its upholstery, its very air. I could feel her here, and I wrapped those lingering traces around me and took comfort in them.

"How is he?" I asked when I found my sister in a quiet waiting room, her arms wrapped around herself as she sat. Billy had been admitted, and they had asked her to wait out here.

"They're running some more tests," she said, looking up at me and then rising to her feet to step into my arms.

I held her for a long moment, neither of us saying anything, and I tried not to think about how I'd held my little sister before on another night, on that dark road, the house burning before our eyes. Were we losing someone else now? My heart was clenching painfully in my chest.

"Have they told you anything?" I asked as she released me, keeping my hand in hers as she guided me back to sit down.

"They're pretty sure he has pneumonia," she said, pressing her palm to one eye and then the other and sniffing. "But they're worried it might be something more since his white blood cell count is really high. When they asked him how long he's been feeling bad, he said months, Mason. He's been hiding this from us for months."

The hurt and pain in her voice matched what I felt inside. I took a deep breath and let it out with a shuddery exhale. Despite my instincts—to run, to hide, to keep myself behind a wall so no one could make me feel what I felt now—I forced myself to be here instead. I was going to face this situation, just as I'd vowed to face the other emotionally complicated situations in my life.

"We'll just wait to hear what the doctors have to say," I told her. "And we'll go from there."

She nodded. "Either way, at least we'll get a little more time, you know? To say . . . what we need to say."

Neither of us needed to add the rest. *The time we never got with Mom and Dad. To say goodbye.*

We sat in the waiting room for a couple hours because they'd given Billy something to help him sleep. The night beyond the hospital was smeared with a thick darkness that matched the fear and worry inside me. Time stretched and contracted as I sat, my arm around my sister's shoulder, and thought about the last years of my life and how I'd spent them. Wasted them, in some ways.

In the small hours of the morning, I asked my sister for help to stop wasting the time I had with the people I loved. She agreed, and despite the morose stillness of the environment around us and the worry eating at our souls, we smiled and laughed together, as she helped me plan a way to show Heather that I was done being afraid, that I wanted to be with her, no matter what might come our way.

"Mr. and Miss Rye?" A doctor stepped through the hallway door and approached us, her hair gathered to one side in a bright red ponytail that flowed over her shoulder. "I'm Doctor Trager. I've just come from your uncle's room."

Amelia and I stood and went to greet the doctor.

"He's doing quite well," she went on. "We've got him on some fluids, which is already helping with the dehydration, and that's helping that persistent cough. He was able to get some sleep." Her eyes were kind as she looked between my sister and me, and she smiled lightly as she went on. "He has a pretty impressive pneumonia, and his white count is high, but the infection would explain that. We are worried about a potential mass that is visible in the scans of his lungs, but with the pneumonia in there, the radiologist can't be certain what we're seeing."

"Cancer?" I asked, hating the word as it came out of my mouth.

"That's the concern, yes, especially given your uncle's history as a smoker. But we won't be able to make any kind of definitive diagnosis until the pneumonia clears up so we can get a better view."

Amelia blew out a slow breath next to me. "How long do you think that will be?"

"He's on some strong antibiotics now, and we'll keep him for a few days to make sure he's on the right track. Once we release him, we'll follow up in two weeks for another scan, and hopefully the radiologist will be able to give him the all clear then."

"And if not?" Amelia asked.

The doctor smiled kindly and looked between us. "Let's cross that bridge if we need to," she said. "For now, he'd like to see you both. Just a quick visit though, okay? You can come back tomorrow and stay longer."

We agreed and followed her down a long hall to a room where Billy lay in a wide hospital bed, his body covered by a blue blanket that made the outline beneath appear so small and frail that my heart pinched inside me.

"Looks like you're gonna be milking on your own for a while," he said, his eyes opening at the sound of us crossing the floor.

"That's no problem," I told him. "You focus on getting better." I thought about how quiet it would be at the farm without him there. I wanted it to be temporary. I needed more time with him.

He smiled and looked between us. Amelia was sniffling, and I didn't need to look at her to know tears were running down her face.

"None of that," Billy said, reaching a hand to her. "I'm not dead yet."

Amelia's shoulders shook as he said that, and she stepped up to take his hand, leaning forward to give him a light hug. "Don't say that."

"You kids know better than anyone that we don't get long in this life," Billy said, his voice beginning to fray and weaken. "So do the best with it you can." He nodded over my sister's head, his bright eyes catching mine.

"I'm going to try," I told him, dropping a hand on his shoulder and another on my sister's back. I stood there for a long moment, just breathing and feeling all the things I'd worked so many years to push away. Love swelled inside me for these two people—my family—and I let myself feel it, examine it. It was soft and huge and overwhelming, and it had a long thin edge of fear attached to it, like a razor. It was that sharp edge that I'd run from for so many years, not understanding that it was part of the package, but that the rest of it was so much more than that single line of pain. And while the pain cut deep, the love was so much more lasting.

"I love you guys," I managed to say, realizing it might have been the first time I'd ever actually told them.

Billy's frail hand clamped over mine, and my sister turned to bury her face in my shoulder. And for a long time, I just stood there, loving the family I had and honoring the family I'd lost and the one I hoped to make in the future.

"Go home, you two," Billy said finally. "I'm an old man, and I need to sleep."

"Of course," Amelia said, wiping at her eyes and straightening her shirt. "You sleep well. We'll be back tomorrow."

Billy's eyes were already drifting shut as we reached the door, and I followed my sister out to the parking lot, where her face crumpled again.

"What if we lose him, Mason? What if it's cancer?"

I pulled my sister close and held her in the night air for a long time. "We'll figure it out," I told her. "We'll handle it."

"I'm so glad you're here," she whispered.

---

We left Amelia's car there, and I drove her to my place and put her in the guest bed at the end of the hall. She confirmed that Brigsy was still with Heather, so I didn't think she'd mind, and I didn't want my sister driving home so tired.

The morning came abruptly after such a long night, but at least the goats were happy to see me. The kids lifted their little heads as I strode down the center aisle, and they roused themselves quickly, standing to shaky legs and then starting to dance in little circles, bleating up a racket.

Milking went quickly, or maybe it took a long time, but since my mind was in other places, I didn't notice.

Amelia and I had breakfast and then went back to the hospital, where Billy already looked better, color returning to his cheeks and his sense of humor firmly intact.

I watched Amelia climb into her car as we departed, and she promised that she would be ready that Friday, though I wasn't sure I could possibly wait that long. We needed the time to plan my surprise, and I wanted to let Heather get situated in her new position before intruding on her time—but those four days stretched ahead of me like a wide sea, and I was desperate to jump in and start swimming across. I'd do whatever I needed to do to get to Heather.

I spent the rest of the week bringing half of my citrus and fig trees to the school greenhouse and working with the classes there to teach them to tend and harvest the produce. Heather's class wasn't slated to visit me there until the following week, which was good, because I didn't think I'd be able to speak around her until I'd said the things I needed to say to her.

## 34

# HEATHER

My first week back in the classroom was crazy. There was so much I'd forgotten about spending the day with kids, so much more energy that had to be expended than I'd remembered. You were there to teach, but with twenty-five little developing personalities surrounding you all day, looking for reassurance and testing limits, you were never quite off guard.

"But it's good, right?" My brother asked, lounging on Amelia's couch at the end of my third day. He hadn't told me yet of his plans, only that he had a bit of time and he wanted to spend it with me. Amelia didn't seem to mind having him taking up space in her little house—her eyes went round every time he was near, and I worried a bit that her crush would be painful when he finally disappeared into the ether yet again. Kevin was not a good guy to fall in love with—he never stayed in one place longer than a few weeks. But it was nice to see them interested in one another.

At least someone should be happy.

By Friday, I was looking forward to the weekend in a way I hadn't in years. I felt fulfilled, exhausted, and miserable all at once, and I needed some time and space to get my head together.

I'd been informed Wednesday that Friday would be a special

school picnic day, but when I'd asked about preparations, Amelia had waved my questions away.

"Your class knows what to do," she'd told me, and I wondered what she meant. It must have been something pre-arranged with the previous sub. The fifth and third grades were part of a reading buddy program, so all my students had spent an afternoon in Amelia's room, listening to their third-grade buddies read to them, while I'd talked with Principal Franz about requirements for certification in Vermont. And since then, I had noticed some strange little giggles and smiles among my class, an atmosphere I didn't quite understand weaving between them, especially on Friday morning.

"I'll take your kids outside," Amelia announced to me when I saw her during our specials period, when her class was at PE and mine was in the media center. We each poured a cup of coffee, eying the new machine a bit suspiciously, and went to sit for a moment at the round table in the center of the lounge.

"Why do I feel like there's something going on?" I asked her.

"Because you're paranoid and weird," she suggested.

"Nice."

She lifted a shoulder in a half shrug and grinned at me. "Have them ready at eleven," she said and then rose and left the lounge.

I stared out the window at the parking lot where Mason's truck sat once again. He'd been in the greenhouse all week, teaching the younger kids about growing food and tending produce. My own class wasn't going to visit him there until the following week, and I was still trying to figure out how I could be somewhere else during that hour. I knew nothing would ever come of my persistent longing for Mason Rye, but I couldn't seem to make it stop. And knowing he was right there—so close and so untouchable—it was a special kind of torture. I knew I'd have to go back to Washington DC soon, not because I didn't want to stay here, just because I didn't think I'd survive being this near to him for the rest of my life and not being able to have him.

At ten-fifty, I led my class from the media room to our classroom to drop off their books and pick up their lunches, and then Amelia's classroom filed into the hallway, and my class combined with hers.

"Don't look out the windows," Anna told me, giggling. She was one of the students who had seemed unnaturally giddy all week, and now my suspicions ramped up.

"Why not?" I asked.

"Just let it be a surprise," suggested Eaton, one of the quieter boys I taught.

"All right," I laughed. "I'll see you guys in a little while."

"Eleven forty-five," Anna said loudly, shaking a finger at me.

"Right." I exchanged a wide-eyed smile with Amelia and watched as the kids filed out the side door. Back in my room, I watched them head out to the field next to the walipini and sighed, wondering if Mason would be there while we had the picnic.

He was there now, greeting the kids with a wide smile on his face, his dark hair shining in the sun. He looked a little more dressed up than he usually was, in a pair of dark jeans and a crisp button-down shirt. It was not his usual digging in the dirt attire, that was for sure.

The kids were busy running to his truck and back, carrying baskets and boxes, spreading blankets, and leaping around in a frenzy. Some of the kids were dashing to the soccer fields across the blacktop, picking flowers and returning with big handfuls, which they handed to Amelia, who was sitting on the blankets with her back to me, busy doing something.

When they weren't working, kids were jumping around Mason's feet, a few of them tugging on his hands and even climbing up his big body. He grinned through it all, complying with piggyback rides and spinning around, and my heart hurt, watching him. He looked so happy, and I hated that my mind began wondering what kind of daddy he would make—he was so good with kids.

But so bad with himself.

I sighed. I couldn't change him. He was who he was. And maybe I was just doomed to be in love forever with someone who wasn't willing to take a chance on loving me back.

"Miss Brigham?" A little voice came from the doorway, and I turned to find Eaton there, waiting.

I swiped at my face, realizing too late that I'd been crying again, as my heart twisted at thoughts of Mason Rye. "Yep!" I said brightly, trying to cover my emotion.

"Are you ready?" he asked, ducking his little blond head and blinking at me.

"Sure," I said, taking a deep breath to try to prepare myself to be near the man I had just been watching through the window, the man I'd always want with a desire so ferocious it frightened me.

"I won't tell them you were peeking," Eaton assured me, taking my hand and leading me from the room.

"Thanks," I said.

Eaton led me across the field and directed me to sit in the center of one of the blankets.

I was surprised to see Kevin there, next to Amelia. He raised a hand in greeting, but before I could question his presence, I was seated, and whatever strange program was underway began.

Once I was settled, one of the kids pulled Mason from the greenhouse, and he stood next to its door, looking at me with a strange expression on his face. My heart thumped in my chest at the eye contact, and I felt my skin heat. Amelia had a small group of kids sitting around her, and now one of them rose, running toward me, arms full of flowers.

"These are for you," the little girl said, a huge grin on her face as all the other children stepped nearer to hear.

I felt like I had broken the mood, that my presence had shifted the carefree nature of the picnic, and suddenly it had become something else altogether. Something serious.

The little girl pushed the huge bouquet of wildflowers into my arms. The flowers were tied with a yellow ribbon, and they were bright and summery and perfect, and for some reason, I found myself close to tears again. "Thank you," I managed, and the little girl ran back to Amelia's side.

"And this is for you too," John, one of the boys in my class, said, presenting me with a plate of goat cheese and figs with a little dollop of honey on one side.

"Wow, thanks," I said, knowing exactly where the cheese and fruit had come from.

This was sweet, but my heart couldn't take many more direct reminders of Mason Rye. I squeezed my eyes shut and steeled myself, knowing with certainty now that I would need to leave Vermont sooner rather than later. This place was so entirely representative of this man—I'd never escape these feelings without escaping the place.

Mason was smiling almost shyly, still standing off to one side of all the kids near the greenhouse.

Soon, there was a smorgasbord of food all around me, and the kids had begun to wander again, cartwheeling on the lawn and running around the greenhouse laughing and calling to each other. Some sat down to eat, tasting the variety of things that had come from the greenhouse, while others opened their own bagged lunches. I was just beginning to relax when Mason crossed the blankets and stood in front of me, gazing down with that questioning smile on his lips.

I dropped my eyes to my lap. I found it almost impossible to be this close to him.

"Can I sit with you?" he asked.

No good could come of any more time spent with Mason, but I couldn't say no. I wanted him too much, even if I could only have a few fleeting moments of his attention. "Sure," I said, trying not to look at him.

"Are you enjoying the picnic?" he asked.

I nodded, not wanting to engage, not sure I could do it without crying again. "It's amazing," I said.

"Heather," he said softly, and my heart crumbled into pieces.

I looked up at him, meeting those dark eyes that I'd once thought might hold my future, and felt everything inside me reach for him. "What?" My voice broke on the word, the pain I felt leaching around it.

"Can we talk for a second?"

God, I wanted to say yes. I wanted him to talk with me, to be with me. "Mason," I said, my voice betraying the exhaustion I felt inside. "What would be the point?"

He didn't wait for my answer. Instead, he folded his long legs beneath him and sat at my side on the blanket. I squeezed my eyes shut for a long second, desperately trying not to notice the comforting heat of him next to me, the familiar scent of his shaving cream and soap, the way my body immediately aligned every cell to his location, as if he were my true north.

"I hoped you might let me talk to you for a couple minutes," he said, his voice quiet, careful, but also brooking no argument. Whatever it was Mason Rye had come here to say, clearly he was going to say it.

All around us, there was sunshine and the joyful sounds of happy kids, running and leaping on the grass, eating good food and enjoying a gorgeous, late-summer Friday outside. But my whole body was rigid as I tried to hold myself together. I took a deep breath and turned slightly to face the man I'd fallen in love with. And when I let my gaze meet his, my resolve shattered.

Those familiar dark eyes were soft, shining with emotion. "I've been an idiot," he said, and I laughed—mostly because there was so much emotion swirling inside me I had to release it somehow.

He smiled in return, watching me with an uncertain smile on his face, lifting those full lips slightly. He took a deep breath and began again. "I've been afraid."

That got my attention. Suddenly, I wasn't paying attention to the swirl of emotion within me. I was entirely attuned to whatever it was Mason was trying to tell me, and even as I tried to douse it, a tiny lick of hope was springing back to life, glowing inside me. What was he saying?

"My whole life, really," he went on, shaking his head and rubbing the side of his stubbled jaw with one big hand. "My whole life, I've told myself that I would never allow anything to hurt me the way I'd been hurt when my parents died. I decided that if I never loved anyone—besides those people I had no choice about, Amelia and Billy and my aunt—then I could never feel that way again."

I felt a strangled sob climb my throat, and I swallowed hard. Thinking of Mason as a scared kid, feeling so alone and frightened as he'd watched his parents wiped from his life, tore at my heart. Thinking of any kid having to experience that hurt. I couldn't imagine actually living it.

"I thought if I just guarded myself, kept myself apart from the world, then I could just live a quiet life, and it would be enough." His eyes found mine again, and he leaned in slightly, his voice dropping to a pained whisper. "But it's not."

"It's not?" I heard myself ask.

"Not even close."

I let out the breath I'd been holding and tried to steel myself. "Mason," I said, my voice weak and tired. "I don't know what you're trying to say to me, but it's really hard for me to be around you now, knowing . . ." I couldn't bear to tell him again how I felt, only to know it wouldn't be returned. I dropped my gaze to my lap. "I can't do this."

"That's what I need to tell you," he said, sounding slightly exasperated. "None of it will ever be enough," he said. And then, in a low, serious tone, he added the words that brought my eyes to his once more. "Not without you."

I stared at him, unwilling to allow myself to believe what I thought he might be saying.

"Heather, I love you. I didn't want to, and god knows I tried to stop it when I realized it was happening." He paused and took a deep breath, his eyes never leaving mine. "I'm not going to be afraid anymore. Because each day that I live with that fear is a day I can't be with you."

I couldn't answer, couldn't trust his words or the way my heart was leaping in response. I stared at him, mute.

"I would rather get one amazing, incredible day with you than live sixty more years alone, never experiencing the way I feel when I'm around you." He reached out slowly and tentatively touched my hand where it lay on my crossed legs.

I wrapped my fingers around his, needing him to say more, to say it again, to reassure me that I wasn't just imagining these words, hearing what I desperately wanted to hear. He lifted my hand toward him and held it between his own, looking down as if to examine my fingers against his darker skin.

"I love you, Heather." He said the words in a clear, strong voice that couldn't be mistaken.

Our gazes met as my heart unlocked itself inside my chest, all the messy, bright feelings I had for this man spilling out of it like a flood of colorful paint bringing every color back to the world that had turned gray when I'd left him.

"I love you, and I want the chance to be with you. To live my life—or as many days as we get—by your side, hearing your laugh that makes me think of wind chimes, seeing your smile, feeling your skin." He shook his head as if he couldn't believe the words he was saying. "I love you, and it scares the shit out of me to say it, but I don't care. I love you." He said the last words quietly, and they lay there in the warm air between us as Mason held my hand in his own.

I leaned forward, needing to touch him, to reassure myself that he was solid, that this was truly happening. I traced a hand along the rough side of his face, marveling as his eyes dropped shut for an instant as he leaned into the touch.

"I love you too," I said, pleased that my voice was still there, still strong, despite the way everything around us felt like some kind of fantasy.

His eyes opened and met my own as a big smile pulled his mouth wide—and the sight of a happy Mason sent my insides shivering. He was gorgeous. But the smile dropped almost as soon as it had appeared, and he dropped my hand, a frown taking its familiar place on his lips as he reached for something in his pocket.

"Good," he said, dropping the envelope I'd left him between us, one corner of it singed. "Then I don't need to read this."

I stared at the unopened envelope, not understanding. "Why not?"

His eyebrows lowered beneath a furrowed forehead as he looked up at me again. "The last thing I want to read is whatever words you wrote after I hurt your feelings. I know I was wrong. I know it was stupid. And I promise to read any and all letters you write to me in the future, but I don't want to read this one because I'm not sure I can take it."

Understanding dawned, and I struggled not to laugh. "Mason, that's not a letter from me."

He frowned deeper. "It's not?"

"No, it's not."

"What is it?"

"Maybe you should open it."

He cast a suspicious glance at me, as if maybe I was trying to trick him, but then he lifted the envelope and opened it, unfolding the letter from the Vermont Land Trust and reading it slowly. As his eyes reached the bottom of the letter, the wide smile returned. "This is for real?"

I nodded.

"Holy crap, Heather, you did it." His voice was reverent, disbelieving.

"We did it," I corrected. "They buy the development rights to your land, which gives you the capital to pay off debt and expand."

"But we still own the farm."

I nodded. The arrangement was a way for the organization to help preserve Vermont's open spaces and farmland, to prevent overdevelopment.

"This will pay off the debt and then some."

"I hope so."

"Heather . . ." He looked back up at me with tears shining in his eyes.

The man I loved took a deep breath, clearly steeling himself against whatever emotion was running through him at the realization that now maybe he could work less and live more, enjoy the beautiful land where he lived instead of struggling every day to keep it.

I waited for whatever Mason was going to say, but no words followed. Instead, he shoved the paper into his pocket again as he took my hand and pulled us both to standing. And then, he looked deep into my eyes, sending a full-body shiver through me, and slid his arms around my waist, pulling me gently against him.

"I love you," he whispered, and then his lips met mine, and I let my eyes shut and allowed myself to feel every single thing I'd been trying to deny since Mason had pushed me away. That kiss was one of the single defining moments of my life as I felt the world right itself and my future click into place.

Mason's lips were soft against mine, his tongue teasing lightly against my own lips in a promise of what would come later, when we weren't standing in an elementary school playground surrounded by children.

"They're kissing!" I heard one of the little girls near us call, and soon there were hoots and hollers from all around us.

"Get a room!" My brother's voice boomed, and that did it. I pulled away from Mason, wiping at my eyes and smiling so widely it almost hurt.

We linked hands and turned to see everyone grinning around us, the warm sun beating down on us as children laughed and played. My brother and Amelia both rose and came to hug us, and it felt like we were all standing together on the threshold of a brand new world.

## MASON

"You sure you're all set?" I asked my uncle, tucking the blanket around his legs in his brown leather recliner in front of the second *Star Wars* movie. He'd vowed that if he had weeks of doing nothing ahead of him, he was going to watch every single movie he'd wanted to see in the past ten years but had been too busy to watch. He was a week in and had been through the *Back to the Future* series and *Die Hard,* and now we were moving to *Star Wars.*

"Go handle the goats, Mason. Darth Vader and I have some quiet time together scheduled." Uncle Billy was looking better, the color back in his face and the worrisome cough mostly quiet. We had another week before he would go back for the second scan, but so far we had every reason to believe he was fine.

"Your lunch is in the refrigerator," Heather said, coming to my side and then moving past me to give Uncle Billy a kiss on the cheek. "I'll check on you when I'm done at school."

"You guys are worse than my parents were," the old man grumbled, but I knew he liked all the attention, and my heart hurt when I thought about how many years I'd let him spend all his time over here in the big farmhouse alone, mostly because I was afraid to get too close.

"Have you thought any more about my suggestion?" I

asked him.

Billy made a show of pausing the movie and turning to look at me. "You just want the bigger house."

I'd offered to renovate the farmhouse and build him a first-floor bedroom that would be easier for him as he got older. I'd also suggested that maybe I might move in here and use the cottage as a rental property or a guesthouse. I wanted to spend as much time with my uncle as I could.

"I'll think about it," he said. "I've gotten used to my space."

"I guess we know where Mason gets it from," Heather said, poking a finger into my ribs. I slung an arm around her and pulled her in tight to my side, burying my face in the curls atop her head for one long breath. She always smelled like sunshine.

"Okay," I agreed, knowing Billy would come around. "I'm headed over to the Bean."

"And I'd better get to school," Heather said, turning to kiss me quickly.

"Get on with both of you," Billy muttered, but he didn't protest when I bent down to hug him before heading for the door.

"Call me if you need anything," I told him.

Billy had complained that we'd all babied him since he'd gotten released from the hospital, but I knew he didn't mean it. He might be a man who liked his quiet and privacy, but I was the best person to attest that even a loner needed some affection now and then. And I wasn't about to let one more person leave my life without having spent every quality moment with him that I could.

Outside, Heather paused to kiss me one more time, and I let myself feel the way my heart actually lifted in my chest when she was close.

"You telling them today?" she asked, stepping back and smiling up at me from the circle of my arms.

I nodded. "I'll stay as long as they need me, but it doesn't make sense to race back and forth between the Busy Bean and the farm now." The money for the development rights hadn't come through yet, but knowing that we were heading for salvation instead of ruin made it easier to let go of the second job and use that time to improve the farm and be with my family.

"See you later," she said, and I smiled as the little blue Karmann Ghia motored down the lane, the woman I loved at the wheel and part of my heart with her.

---

I tied on my apron, part of me wishing I could stay at the Busy Bean forever. Despite the fact it was a second job and served a very specific purpose, I would miss the place. I liked the steady efficiency of work behind the counter, the regularity of the customers, and the rewards of helping people enjoy their days just a little bit more.

"Who wrote that?" Zara asked, stepping out of the kitchen and scanning my latest quote over the window.

It read, "Keep your face always toward the sunshine, and the shadows will fall behind you."

"I did. It's Walt Whitman."

"It's certainly not Mason Rye," she said, turning to me with one eyebrow arched.

"Maybe it is, actually," I said, smiling at her.

She glanced around uncertainly. "I'm not sure how to handle this new version of you. It makes me feel a little off-balance."

"Sorry for that," I said.

She laughed. "It's good. How's Heather?"

Even the sound of her name made me smile. "She's great. She's talking to the principal about finishing up the requirements to get licensed here in Vermont so she can stay at the school."

"And stay with you," Zara added.

"Hopefully," I said, my heart lifting.

"You gonna make it official soon?" she asked.

"What, like propose?" I couldn't really pretend I hadn't thought about it.

"Yeah." Zara leaned down, rearranging the Danishes in the display case next to her as I moved to help a customer.

When we had another moment, I turned back to my boss. "Maybe. But not quite yet, I think. I just want to enjoy this moment for a bit."

She nodded, as if she understood exactly what I meant.

"Hey, Zara?" I ventured, less happy about what I had to say next. "I actually need to talk to you. I don't want to let you and Audrey down, so I'll stay as long as you need me, but—"

"It's happening again," Zara moaned, lifting her hands to her dark head. "This is like the coffee curse, I swear. Lonely people come in here, and once they get their hands on our magical Astra machine and start serving up this delicious coffee, they go off and fall in love and leave us." She shook her head, but a little smile played at the corners of her mouth.

"Well, yeah," I said, pushing my hands into my pockets. "I'm sorry. I don't want to leave you hanging."

"It's fine, it's totally fine," she said, her voice stringy with stress. "You'll stick around until we find someone else?"

"I can do that," I promised.

"Okay, Mason. That's good. We can probably at least cut your shifts a bit if you need more time around the house. To spend with Heather. You know, like, in bed." She wiggled her eyebrows suggestively, and I frowned severely at her, making the smile drop from her face. "Yikes, okay. You can still do murder face, I see."

"When necessary," I agreed.

My shift that afternoon felt like it flew by, and I actually made conversation here and there with customers who stopped in. It was strange—I knew something inside me had changed, but suddenly everything outside of me looked a little different too. People seemed friendlier, the sun seemed just a little sunnier.

I went home that night to find Heather's car in the driveway but no sign of her or Rascal in the house. I stepped out on the back deck and heard her laughter ringing through the trees at the back of my property. I headed off toward the sound and found her standing in the chicken coop, Rascal watching intently from just outside.

"Mason!" She exclaimed, turning that bright, beautiful smile on me.

"Hey," I said, feeling almost shy under the weight of her beauty. I squatted down to scratch Rascal a few times, and he leaned into my thigh as I stood up again.

"Watch this. Tully learned a new trick."

"Wonderful." I loved Heather, but my chickens did not need to know any tricks. They just needed to lay eggs.

Heather made her arms into a wide circle, which she held about two feet off the ground just in front of a little ramp I'd constructed to help the girls get up into the coop. Heather had moved it and was using it for some kind of launch for her new trick.

"Okay, Tully, ready?" The chicken actually seemed to pay attention to this question, and the little brown bird waddled over to the bottom of the ramp. "Ready, set, go!" Heather called, and Tully's little feet picked up speed as she accelerated up the ramp and then launched herself through the circle of Heather's arms, flapping as she landed on the other side.

Heather turned to me with a grin. "Ta-da!"

Rascal yipped appreciatively.

"Should I clap?" I asked her, but my smile gave me away. If Heather wanted to teach my chickens tricks, then I was happy for her to do so. As long as my girl was happy, I was happy.

She did a little curtsy and then pushed the ramp back into place, letting herself out of the coop a moment later to wrap her arms around me and plant a kiss on my lips that shot heat through the rest of me. "I missed you," she whispered. She tucked her nose into the collar of my T-shirt, pressing herself against me. "You smell like coffee," she said, her breath tickling my neck.

"I'll go inside and shower," I said, beginning to step away.

"No, I like it," she said, turning a soft smile up toward me.

I inclined my head, catching her mouth with mine again, and

felt a low rumble escape my chest as her tongue teased a line along my upper lip.

"Can I show you how much I missed you?" she asked, her voice barely a whisper as her hand slipped over my jeans to cup me through the fabric.

"Fuck yes," I managed, my mind already reeling ahead, imagining her beneath me again. We'd spent a good amount of time in bed—and on the couch, and against the wall—since Heather had come back to stay with me a week earlier. I couldn't get enough, and the second she looked at me a certain way, my entire body caught fire. When she touched me? All bets were off.

I scooped her up and carried her toward the back deck, preparing to take her inside.

"Here," she said, pointing at the lounge chairs positioned on the wide plank deck.

I looked around. It wasn't like anyone would see us back here. "You sure?"

She nodded, and I deposited her gently on the cushioned chair. Her hand went immediately to my waistband, and she made quick work of unfastening my jeans and pushing them down my hips, along with my boxer briefs.

"Take these off," she commanded, and I complied, never taking my eyes from her flushed face. "One leg here, one here." She pointed to either side of the chair, so I was effectively straddling her as she leaned against the upright back. "Closer," she said, and I stepped closer, my erect penis just inches from her face.

Rascal seemed to grasp what was about to happen, and he politely barked once and then trotted around the side of the house to give us some privacy.

Heather's soft hands cupped my balls and she guided me toward her perfect lips. I gripped the back of the chair over her head, every rational thought leaving my head as her mouth took me in. All I could think about was the hot, wet motion of her mouth, the way her hands followed her lips along my length, the sexy little noises she made as she took me deep.

I tried to let her direct the action, but as the tingling tightness grew at the base of my spine and my legs threatened to dissolve, I began thrusting, striving to control my movements.

Heather made encouraging noises that spiked my desire as everything inside me gathered into a tense swirl of need. I opened my eyes and stared down between my hands at where my hard, thick cock was sliding between her perfect, pink lips. Her cheeks were flushed, and her eyes were shut as she focused, and the sight of her holding me, taking me, was so erotic, my orgasm caught me almost off guard.

"Heather," I managed, my voice a ragged breath. "I can't..."

She slipped one hand over my ass, holding me to her, and I let go with a groan and a shudder, wondering in some distant part of my brain if I'd ever actually been that turned on before. My legs shook, and I feared my grip might shatter the back of the wooden lounger.

After a moment, I disentangled myself and lowered to a seated position, facing her between her legs. "Holy shit," I said, rubbing my jaw with one hand.

"Good?" she asked, smiling with something like pride.

Her lips were swollen and red, her eyes wet, and she had never looked so fucking sexy. I leaned forward and kissed her again, wrapping her tightly in my arms.

"How did I get so lucky?" I asked the universe.

"So it was good?" She laughed.

"Fuck, it was amazing. But I'm not talking about that." I sighed, still holding her close and trying to gather my thoughts. "It's you. It's everything." I pressed my forehead to hers. "I've never been happier. I thought I didn't need this in my life, that I was fine without it. But now I understand—even one day with you is better than a lifetime alone. I want to treasure every single second we get together."

"I do too," she said. "I love you, Mason."

"I love you too."

## 36

# HEATHER

Over the course of the next few weeks, I slowly moved my life officially from Washington to Vermont. Thought it felt quick, I moved in with Mason—but not to the little cottage where I'd first known him. We moved into the farmhouse, where Billy was recuperating from his illness.

We set up a bedroom upstairs, and I marveled at the dramatic change my life had undergone in one summer.

"You don't miss city life, huh?" Billy quizzed me over dinner one night. Mason sat at my side, and Amelia and Kevin sat across the table from us. Kevin had been lingering in Vermont, never exactly clear about his plans. For now, he was staying at the cottage, and any questions about the future were returned with jokes or non-answers. Something was up, but I wasn't sure how to go about figuring out what it was. Knowing my brother, he'd be gone again soon. Kevin took care of himself, and the Marine Corps took care of him too.

"Not really," I said, smiling at Mason. "I guess I miss having everything I want within a cab ride, you know? But I have everything I need right here."

"You must miss the action, though," Amelia said, sounding wistful. "The energy?"

"Don't overrate action," Kevin said, then went back to eating like a man who hadn't seen food in weeks.

I wasn't sure what to make of that but let it go. "I do a little, but the action that was going on right before I came here was pretty terrifying. I never realized that I was always on guard there, always looking out for myself. Here, I can actually relax. I just feel happier, calmer. More me."

Mason kissed my cheek.

"And when do you take the test for certification?" Amelia asked me again. I'd answered the question several times, but it was beginning to seem like proximity to my brother caused Amelia to forget everything I told her.

"Not until spring," I said. "But Principal Franz is happy to have me stay on as a long-term sub through the rest of the year. We should know by the end of summer if I can have my own class next year."

Mason was smiling beside me, and I grinned at him, my heart lifting every time I caught a glimpse of this sunnier, happier version of Mason Rye. The intense, grumpy farmer was hot, that was sure, but this Mason was even better. He held me close at night, spoke his heart whenever we were alone, and stood by my side to support me the rest of the time.

"Farmers' market this weekend?" I asked him now.

"Yup. Kevin and Amelia are going to do the Montpelier market though. We'll go to Burlington." Mason had been taking my suggestions about expanding the presence and outreach efforts of Garden Goat Farms, and he was working on plans to build a bigger walipini on the main farm property. Soon Garden Goat would be one of Vermont's premier suppliers of semi-exotic produce and gourmet cheese. We were even experimenting with a combination goat and cow's milk cheese that was incredible, buying the milk from a nearby farm that Mason knew was struggling just as he had been when he'd had cows.

"Kevin at a farmers' market," I mused, watching my brother intently.

He didn't raise his eyes, and I wasn't even sure he knew I was talking to him.

"It's a far cry from toting a rifle through the desert, I would guess," I said. "When do you have to go back?" I asked again, wondering if the presence of other people would get me a real answer.

He met my eyes then, and there was something in his gaze I'd never seen before—something broken, shattered. He shook his head lightly. "I don't know yet."

I was pretty sure military leave didn't work that way, but I wasn't going to question Kevin. There was something wrong, I was sure of it now, but my brother wasn't exactly the forthcoming type. He saved people—that was what he did.

But what if he needed saving?

That night I mentioned my concerns to Mason.

"Kevin's the toughest guy I know. Whatever it is, he's handling it."

I shook my head lightly, sitting up in our bed, waiting for him to shut off the light and come join me. "I don't know. There's something off. And when do special ops Marines ever get weeks on end to just hang around in Vermont?"

Mason sat down and took my hands in his, his dark, gentle eyes watching our fingers intertwine. "I think you're probably right," he said. "And you know your brother better than anyone. But I know him pretty well." His eyes lifted to mine. "And he's the kind of guy who will handle things on his own if he can. He'll come to us if he needs help."

A tiny spark of fear jumped to life inside me. My brother had always saved me. I didn't like the idea that he might need saving —I had no idea how to even begin.

"Don't worry," Mason said. "I'll keep an eye on him."

"Okay," I breathed, and Mason stood and shut off the light, sliding into bed beside me and pulling me close to him.

"I love you, Heather."

"I love you too," I said, and my heart swelled with the truth of it. I loved Mason, and I loved the life I'd found, and was building, with him in Vermont. A warm certainty I'd never experienced suffused my limbs, and I let myself drift to sleep in the safe circle of Mason Rye's strong arms.

## 37

# MASON

*Thanksgiving*

There were three Thanksgivings that would always stand out in my mind. The first was the last one I remember with my parents in our house amid the sprawling fig groves on the floor of the valley in California. Mom had cried that year because the oven hadn't worked properly and the turkey hadn't cooked. She'd complained that Thanksgiving was ruined, but Dad had made a run to some fast-food chicken place, and we'd ended up with fried chicken and mashed potatoes and been every bit as happy. It was always just us anyway—no one else around to impress—and I remember a look my parents shared as we ate, a look of complete trust or understanding. I was too young to have the tools to decipher the meaning of the look, but it was something that I knew meant that no matter what, they were in it together.

The second Thanksgiving I couldn't forget was the first one we spent in Vermont, when my aunt and uncle did their very best to make us feel welcome and loved, and my sister and I huddled together at the other side of the table, wishing with all our hearts we could just have fried chicken with our parents instead. There hadn't felt like much to be thankful for that year, but I was four-teen and angry at the world. No amount of perfectly cooked turkey would have fixed that.

And this Thanksgiving.

This would be another one that would always linger at the top of my memories. The year I stopped being afraid of losing the people I loved and finally lived my life fully. The first year I spent the holiday with Heather by my side.

"Love what you've done with the place," Kevin drawled as he carried a dish of sweet potatoes through the front rooms, which were hung with plastic as the renovation proceeded to make a master suite on the main level.

"It's a new style," I quipped. "Nouveau plastique."

Kevin stopped in the center of the hallway, swiveling to face me with the dish in his hands and his eyebrows high. "Mason Rye. Did you just make a corny joke?"

I had. I'd been doing it more and more lately. I grinned at my old friend and gestured for him to continue to the kitchen, where Amelia, Heather, and Billy were all laughing around the little round table where they sat having a pre-dinner drink. Rascal sat in the corner, his nose on his paws, big eyes watching us all.

"They haven't shipped you out yet?" Billy asked Kevin, rising to give him a hug. "Mason never seemed to get more than a week or two off when he was active duty."

"Then he was doing it wrong," Kevin joked, but as soon as he'd said it, his eyes swung to me, daring me to contradict him.

Something was wrong. Heather had been right about that. Kevin had left Vermont at the end of the summer but had reap-peared at the end of October and had been in town since, staying at the cottage and keeping to himself as much as Heather would let him. We were both concerned, but tonight, Kevin made a show of wearing a wide smile and joking with Billy whenever the old man allowed it. Amelia continued staring at him like he was the best thing she'd ever seen, and I couldn't tell from the way he acted whether there was anything actually happening there.

"Not that Kevin would tell me," Heather had said when I'd asked. "But Amelia probably would, and she hasn't said a thing."

I'd let it go, but a big part of me wanted my sister to find the kind of happiness I'd found with Heather, to experience a love so consuming that you'd take one day of that over the rest of your life if you had to make a choice.

Maybe Kevin wasn't the right guy for her though. Not if he was keeping secrets. And I was sure he was.

"Let's have a toast," Billy called, raising his beer high from where he sat. He looked healthy now, having recovered from his pneumonia, and his scans had thankfully been clear. But the incident had scared us all, made us aware of his age and his mortality. He still helped with milking, but only in the afternoons, and he had taken to working the farmers' markets with Heather in my place. Evidently his cheerful demeanor was better for attracting customers than my surly intensity.

"This is the first year in a long time that it feels like a real holiday," Billy said, looking around the room at us all. "And a lot of that has to do with this blond beauty right here." He winked at Heather, and I pulled her closer to my side. "She showed up here and fixed all the things that had been broken for a long time."

No one disagreed, but I was thankful Billy didn't expand on that thought.

We all sipped our drinks, and then Heather stepped away from me and lifted her own glass. "Well, I'd like to make a toast too," she said, her smile lighting the room and my heart. "To all of you. I finally feel like I've found the place I belong, and I couldn't be happier than I am right now. I've got a family I adore, a man I love with everything I am, and this incredible place to enjoy it all. Thank you, all of you."

"Cheers!" Amelia said, grinning widely.

"Thanks for having me," Kevin said, his smile thin, like a mask that was beginning to dissolve. "It's been a bit of a rough year on my end, and it's nice to have a place to land." He gave a sharp nod of his head, and I sensed that was as much as we were going to get out of him. I lifted my mouth to drink, but then he turned toward me and spoke again. "How long you think you need to wait, Rye?"

I lowered the glass I'd been holding to my lips.

"Wait? For what?"

"To propose to my little sister. Make her an honest woman?" He chuckled at this last question, and I felt Heather stiffen at my side.

"Kevin!" she hissed.

It was inappropriate, bordering on rude—but it wasn't wrong. There was no reason to wait. I didn't need to marry her to know I'd spend the rest of my life trying to make her smile, but I loved the idea of celebrating our love with a wedding—a ceremony to officially mark the incredible thing we shared.

I put down my drink, setting it on the little table with my eyes on Heather. She was watching me uncertainly, and I realized I was wearing a wide smile as I sank to one knee before her.

"No, you don't have to," she whispered, but I ignored her, taking her hands in my own. Rascal seemed to sense that something was happening, and he got to his feet, padding over to sit at my side and stare up at Heather with adoring eyes.

"Oh my god!" my sister whispered.

"I do want to marry you, Heather," I said, loudly enough for them all to hear. "But not to make an honest woman of you."

Heather's eyes were shining and wide as she stared down at me, a half smile playing on her gorgeous lips.

"I want to marry you because I can't imagine spending a single day of my future without you by my side. I want to marry you because you are the person who taught me how to love, how to really live, and how to appreciate every second you get with the people you care about. And I care more about you than I ever thought possible. You are my light and my air, my summer and my fall. In a short time, you've become my whole world, and I want to share the rest of my life with you. If you'll have me.

"Heather Brigham, will you marry me?"

Heather was nodding slowly now, tears standing in her eyes.

"Don't leave the man hanging, sis," Kevin said quietly.

"Yes," she said softly. "Yes, I'll marry you."

I was about to get to my feet, but Heather was already dropping to her knees before me, wrapping her arms tightly around my neck. She buried her face under my chin, and I wrapped my arms around her.

"I love you, Mason," she said, her voice thick with emotion.

"I love you too," I told her, the rest of the room fading to a blur as I held the woman I loved in my arms.

Heather pulled back a bit, and I leaned down to kiss her tenderly. I heard Rascal whine his approval at our side, and the sound made Heather chuckle.

Billy, Amelia, and Kevin cheered and slapped us on the backs. As we stood, my heart fell. I shouldn't have done it like that, I realized. Heather deserved a complete proposal, a real engagement, and I didn't have a ring.

I held her soft hand in mine and looked down at the slim fingers laying in my own. "I'm so sorry," I said softly. "I didn't plan that, so I don't have a—"

Amelia stepped to my side, almost forcing herself between us, and lifted her hands to her chest, struggling to pull a ring from her finger. "Here," she said quietly. "It was Mom's."

I stared at the little ring my sister laid gently in my palm, remembering it gleaming in the overhead kitchen lights of our house as my mother had placed a glass of milk in front of me at the table, recalling the way the metal band had felt against my forehead when she'd placed her hand there to check me for fever. For a moment, I couldn't speak because emotion clogged my throat as I looked at the simple diamond ring in my hand.

I lifted my eyes to my sister's, wanting to make sure this was really something she wanted, and what I found there was love, acceptance, and joy. She nodded her head. "Go on."

I looked at my fiancée again. "May I?" I asked her, and she lifted her left hand toward me. I watched as the ring slipped down the length of her slim finger, feeling a circle click shut inside me as it found its new home, gleaming there on Heather's hand.

"It's amazing," she said, glancing between my sister and me. "Thank you."

I kissed her again then, not caring if the kiss was a little over the top for your run-of-the-mill Thanksgiving display of affection. This was not a run-of-the-mill Thanksgiving. It was the one I would remember over all others, the Thanksgiving when the woman I loved agreed to become my wife.

THE
END

# ACKNOWLEDGMENTS

This book was a production! Every book is, but for some reason this one was especially. So there are a few people I need to say thank you to, for helping me out as it evolved!

First, thanks to Sarina Bowen and the always patient Jane Haertel for allowing me to come play in the world of True North. I've been a reader and a fan for a long time, and it felt a little like playing pretend to get to write a story in one of my favorite places to read about.

Thanks also, to my friend and the other half of my brain, Kelly Lambert. She keeps me sane during all things writing related, and I honestly don't know how I ever wrote stories before she was in my life!

Dawn Alexander gets a big kissy face for being an amazing developmental editor. She has talked me off multiple ledges and is always there to point out that someone cannot possibly go through that door because they went through it three paragraphs ago or to remind me that most participants in sex scenes should have only two hands.

Thanks to Jessica Snyder for making sure all my nitty gritty details were in the right places, with commas and correct spelling!

And finally, thanks to my awesome and super fun reader group, Delancey's Fancies. They're my happy place, and I will always be grateful for such an uplifting and optimistic community of readers and friends.